RANDOM HOUSE
CHILDREN'S BOOKS
A DIVISION OF PENGUIN RANDOM HOUSE LLC

Title: The Extraordinary Journeys of Clockwork Charlie:
                    The Kidnap Plot
Author: Dave Butler
Imprint: Alfred A. Knopf Books for Young Readers
Publication Date: June 14, 2016
ISBN: 978-0-553-51295-3
Price: $16.99 U.S./$21.99 CAN.
GLB ISBN: 978-0-553-51296-0
GLB Price: $19.99 U.S./$25.99 CAN.
Ebook ISBN: 978-0-553-51297-7
Pages: 304
Ages: 8–12

Please send any review or mention of this book to:
Random House Children's Books Publicity Department
1745 Broadway, Mail Drop 9-1
New York, NY 10019

rhkidspublicity@penguinrandomhouse.com

THE KIDNAP PLOT

THE EXTRAORDINARY JOURNEYS OF
CLOCKWORK CHARLIE
THE KIDNAP PLOT

DAVE BUTLER

ALFRED A. KNOPF
NEW YORK

DEDICATION TK

THE KIDNAP PLOT

Bucerius regenerans (common names: troll, hulder, jotun)——The trolls of Great Britain are one of the elder folk most frequently encountered in human society. Male trolls are recognizable for their size (averaging over seven feet in height, with large, heavy torsos) and for the bull-like features of their large heads, in particular their long horns and their bovine ears.

——excerpted from Reginald St. John Smythson, *Almanack of the Elder Folk and Arcana of Britain and Northern Ireland*, 2nd ed., "Troll"

"**C**harlie Pondicherry ain't got no mum!"

Charlie cringed. There would be a rock. There was always a rock.

"What are you talking about, Skip? Charlie Pondicherry ain't even got a dad! Charlie Pondicherry's a toenail fungus; that's why he's always got that goop smeared on him!"

Skip, Mickey, and Bruiser followed Charlie down the Gullet. Charlie was sure the three boys had just waited in the alley for him to come out. Charlie's shoulders slumped.

He hunched down lower over the basket of dirty laundry he was carrying. Sooner or later, there would be a rock.

"A fungus . . . ha-ha! A fungus!"

Whack!

That was the rock. It hit Charlie between the shoulders. He stumbled, but kept his feet.

He wanted to turn and stand like a ship's captain, letting the pirates have it with both pistols . . . but he'd soil the laundry. Plus, they outnumbered him three to one, and any captain knew those weren't great odds. Charlie gritted his teeth and hoped they'd give up.

The steam clouds that surrounded Lucky Wu's Earth Dragon Laundry were just ahead. Behind him he heard the sucking sound of the other boys' feet in the mud.

"Where you going, fungus? Get him, Bruiser!"

Bruiser grabbed Charlie by his jacket and shoved him against the brick wall. Charlie gripped tight with both hands and managed not to drop any of the laundry.

"You got any brass, fungus?" Mickey sneered. Mickey had ears like jug handles and teeth too big for his head. He spat when he talked.

Charlie glared at the bigger boy. "Do I *ever* have any money?" Charlie's bap—his *dad,* the other boys would have said, but Charlie's father was from the Punjab, in India, and insisted Charlie call him Bap—never gave him money.

"What you think we are, stupid or sumfing?" Skip shouted. Skip had a loose lower lip that flapped down and almost covered his chin. Also, Skip smelled terrible.

"Stupid or sumfing!" Bruiser echoed, and he laughed. Bruiser was a big boy, with man-sized knuckles.

"Going to Fathead Wu's again, yeah?" Mickey spat. "What, you ain't got a bit of brass to pay old Fathead?"

"Are you an idiot?" Charlie snapped. He was shaking, but he might as well speak his mind; whatever he said, he was going to get punched. "I *always* go to Wu's. And I *never* have any money." Charlie wished he were bigger. He'd pound Mickey and his friends flat. Maybe then Bap would let him out of the shop more. "Clock off!"

"How many times we gotta teach you this lesson?" Skip jeered.

Bruiser pressed Charlie against the wall with one hand and balled up his other fist. His big hand hung in the air like a wrecker's ball.

Charlie laughed. "You're slow learners, I guess." He smirked to distract them from his hands while he shifted his grip on the basket and made a fist inside one of his bap's shirts. He was Captain Charlie Pondicherry, priming his pistols.

Bruiser didn't know when the joke was on him. "Slow learners, ha!"

Mickey looked at Bruiser, irritated.

Charlie threw the basket of dirty laundry at Bruiser's face.

"Huh?" Bruiser shouted, and swung his fist—

Charlie ducked—

and pow! Bruiser's fist plowed right into the top of Mickey's head.

"Ow!" Mickey staggered back.

Charlie hurled his fistful of shirt at Skip's face and turned to run, but the shirt missed and Skip knocked Charlie down.

Charlie hit the mud in a rain of dirty laundry.

What was he thinking? He couldn't *really* run away and

leave the laundry. He couldn't really fight, either. There were three of them and one of him, and they were bigger. Best to just take a quick beating and not drag it out.

Charlie wasn't aboard a sailing ship in search of treasure, and he was no adventurer.

"Hit him, Broo!" Mickey showered Charlie with spittle.

Bruiser dropped to one knee and punched Charlie in the stomach.

It hurt. Charlie jerked his knees up to protect himself.

"Ow." Bruiser shook his hand.

"What's the matter, Bruiser?" Skip giggled. "Charlie Pondi-cherry too hard for you? He hurt your precious hand?"

"Hurt my hand, huh, yeah . . ." Bruiser chuckled slowly.

Mickey stepped deliberately on two shirts and a pair of Charlie's trousers, squashing them all into the filth with the heel of his square-toed shoe.

Charlie stayed down, grinding his teeth. His stomach hurt. Overhead, hundreds of yards above the rooftops framing the Gullet, he saw an airship drift slowly past. The craft had a hull like an oceangoing ship's, copper-bottomed, and it hung from beneath three oblong balloons. Steam puffed from a funnel at the back. The airship's motion was calm and graceful, and Charlie desperately wanted to be on it.

Or on the saddled neck of a vengeful dragon, blasting his tormentors with fire.

"Yeah, well, Charlie, it's been fun," Mickey said. "We got other customers to see, so we have to leave you now."

"Fun, ha-ha!"

Skip kicked Charlie in the shoulder. The kick hurt less than the punch, because the sole of Skip's boot hung loose and flapped just like his lip. Still, it knocked Charlie over. Charlie sighed, shook his head, and stared holes into their backs until the three boys disappeared down the Gullet.

Then Charlie climbed to his feet.

He spat mud out and gathered up the laundry. Only a few pieces had escaped getting trampled. And the pair of Charlie's trousers Mickey had trodden upon looked as if they'd been worn by a pig wrestler at a Sunday fair. Charlie had read about pig wrestlers, and about Sunday fairs.

Lucky Wu was not going to be happy.

Charlie moved quickly, worried he was running out of time. He heaped all the clothes back into the basket and trudged into the steam. The clouds jetted out of the mouths of brass dragon heads poking out of the front of the shop. Standing in the dragons' breath was a little like taking a bath, so Charlie lingered and wiped mud off his face. What with the white creams his bap put on his skin, the black mud, and the steam washing both off in rivulets, he knew he must look a sorry mess.

Finally Charlie pushed in through Lucky Wu's door, out of one cloud of steam and into another.

Hyoo-hyoo-hyoo-whee-up, hyoo-hyoo-hyoo-whee-up! chirped the little brass sparrows perching over the door. There were three of them, fixed on tiny pins, so they were forever flying in a circle around their brass nest, beaks open. Charlie smiled at the birds. They didn't move; they didn't do anything but sing when the door opened so that Wu would know he had customers. Still, Charlie's bap had made the sparrows, so they were Charlie's friends.

Not really, of course. Really, they were just a bit of clockwork.

"You stupid inbred sack of meat!"

Charlie flinched.

Lucky Wu rushed around his own counter in a clatter of wooden sandal soles and tore the basket from Charlie's hands. He threw the Pondicherrys' laundry to the floor and peered closely at the wicker.

The long braid that bounced along Wu's back from under his skullcap was jet-black. He wore white shirtsleeves, a green silk waistcoat, and a black skirt. Stitched around the edges of Wu's waistcoat were rows of gold characters Charlie couldn't read. Once, when he'd been brave enough to ask, Wu had told him that the characters were a spell that detected liars and thieves. He'd then stared at Charlie so hard that Charlie had backed out of the laundry without another word. He hadn't known whether Wu was serious about the spell, but he was pretty sure that the laundry owner had called him a liar.

"I'm not a sack of meat."

"Filthy motherless son of a goat!" Wu howled. He waved his arms, and his braid danced through the air, stabbing like a scorpion's tail. "This is *my* basket!"

He shoved the wicker into Charlie's face, and Charlie's shoulders slumped. He hadn't given a thought to the basket. It was filthy too.

Still, he didn't like being yelled at. "It's just a basket." He tried not to look at Wu, and instead let his eyes wander over the machinery behind the counter. Crunching forward three inches at a time as the gears inside the equipment shifted tooth by tooth, a parade of frock coats, trousers, and hats wound in an S-shaped curve around the back of the shop. Behind the clothing Charlie saw clamshell-shaped presses, many-armed stretchers, and enormous irons. Steam piped from the machinery as if from a dozen teakettles.

"You barbarian dog!" Wu shouted. "You stinking, flea-bitten monkey's armpit!" He towered over Charlie. "You *slug!*"

"What's wrong, Fathead? Accidentally put too much starch in your dress again?" Charlie meant his words as a defiant shout, but he muttered them at his own feet instead.

Wu didn't notice. The laundry owner thrashed the air in front of him with a finger. "You want to roll around in the mud like animals, I don't care! I'm not even *surprised!* But you leave my basket alone!"

"Yeah, okay." Charlie backed away. "Sorry."

Hyoo-hyoo-hyoo-whee-up, hyoo-hyoo-hyoo-whee-up! sang the brass sparrows.

"I have two shirt presses that need to be calibrated! If I have to clean your filth off my own baskets, at least my machines should all work perfectly! You tell your father—" Wu was still shouting when the door shut behind Charlie.

Charlie sighed.

A shadow loomed up in the steam. Huge boots swung toward Charlie.

Charlie flung himself out of the way—

thud! Right into the brick wall of the alley.

Charlie fell onto his back in the mud. "Ow!"

The big shadow rushed over Charlie so fast that all he saw were horns and a long coat. Charlie smelled a strong animal stink, and then something whizzed through the air unseen above his head. Shaitans, Charlie thought. He was being stalked by shaitans, who would kill him and take his place in the shop and his bap would never know the difference, because shaitans were shape-changers. Or maybe it was djinns or ifrits, or alfar, though none of those things were supposed to smell like beasts.

Didn't the *Almanack* say that trolls smelled like cows?

Charlie peeled himself out of the mud and limped toward home.

Emerging from the cloud of steam, he stopped. Just down the alley he saw Pondicherry's Clockwork Invention & Repair, and over the door the flexing piston arm that served as its signboard. For Bap's customers who didn't know how to read, the piston arm meant CLOCKWORK MACHINES BUILT AND FIXED HERE.

Ducking to pass underneath the piston was a very big man.

Charlie felt a shiver of excitement—the big man might be a troll. A hulder. He was tempted to run back to the shop and get a closer look, but a better thought stopped him.

The big man *might* be a troll, but he *must* be a customer.

His bap would be distracted, at least for a few minutes.

Charlie turned and sprinted back into the steam cloud. He

burst out the other side and raced to the mouth of the Gullet. There Charlie pressed himself against the wall and poked his head out into Irongrate Lane.

This was the absolute boundary of his life.

Charlie knew Irongrate Lane was in the neighborhood of Whitechapel, and Whitechapel was in the city of London, but he didn't have any good idea of the shape or size of either. Bap didn't keep any maps of the city in the house, and Charlie wasn't allowed to leave the Gullet. He very rarely snuck to the mouth of the alley for a peek, and he had absolutely never set foot beyond it.

He'd been knocked down by Mickey, Skip, and Bruiser, browbeaten by Fathead Wu, and run over by a passing hulder. He wanted an adventure and a victory, and with Bap distracted by a customer, this was his chance.

He stepped into Irongrate Lane.

The lane throbbed with life. Charlie saw a bookshop, an ironmonger, a pharmacist, the place of business of some sort of wizard (the signboard showed a human palm covered with astronomical symbols and an all-seeing eye), and other buildings he couldn't identify. A costermonger walked behind his shining cart of fruits and vegetables, shouting prices as the cart itself generated cubes of ice and dropped them one at a time among the vegetables to keep them cool. People flowed in and out of the shops and rattled down the cobbles of the street on their two-wheeled, pedal-powered velocipedes and on horses. Charlie saw passengers riding in rickshaws, too— small, two-wheeled wagons, each pulled by a running person instead of an animal. A four-wheeled steam-carriage puffed majestically past, carrying on its high platform three ladies in crinoline dresses spangled with clouds of ribbon. No animals pulled it; a driver sat on a bench high in front, behind a steering wheel and two long gear handles. Two zebras clopped nonchalantly along; their riders wore dark blue uniforms with short blue capes and lots of shiny buttons, and looked around at everything as if they were in charge.

Charlie stuck his hands into his pockets. This was no big deal for any other boy; it should be no big deal for him. He took a few steps, trying not to step in any horse manure, and whistled a scrawny note or two. He walked slowly and looked at a big pile of apples on the costermonger's cart. He wasn't hungry—he wasn't the sort of boy who ever really *got* hungry—he was just trying to do whatever it was people did on Irongrate Lane.

"Hello," said a voice in an accent Charlie didn't know.

Charlie looked up from the apples. The speaker was a tall man, with long arms and legs and long black hair and a thin mustache on his upper lip. He was dressed all in black, including a black cloak that fell from his shoulders to his ankles.

The cloak was pinned at the man's throat with a brooch shaped like a gearwheel.

"Hello," Charlie whispered.

The man squinted at him. "Is this the way to the shop of Mr. Rajesh Pondicherry?" he asked, and pointed over Charlie's shoulder, down the Gullet. He had a funny lisp to the way he spoke, and when he said *th,* it almost sounded like z.

Charlie swallowed hard. If the customer told his bap he had been out on Irongrate Lane, Charlie might get in trouble. Besides, there was something creepy about the man. His accent wasn't the problem; it was the way he stared at Charlie. He was too intense, too interested. On the other hand, Charlie couldn't turn a customer away. "What if it is?" he asked.

"Clockwork Invention and Repair?" The stranger tried again, gargling his *r*'s. He leaned down, putting his face very close to Charlie's. Charlie smelled onion and old butter.

The stranger reached out to touch Charlie's face—

Charlie turned and ran.

Great Britain's trolls are governed by their own legal code. Laws are set and cases are judged at a gathering of a community's adult trolls, called the *Thing*. Lawspeakers are trolls who are permitted to argue cases and laws at the Thing, enforce laws by raising the hue and cry, and perform such ministerial tasks as solemnizing marriages.

—Smythson, *Almanack*, "Troll"

oo-whoo, too-whoo! The brass owl mounted over the door betrayed Charlie's creeping entrance. Charlie's bap had built the owl, too, and because it was one of the first things a customer might see when he walked inside the shop, Bap had taken extra care to make it impressive. The feathers were individually sculpted, and when the owl sang to announce the door opening, it opened its beak and eyes and spread its wings out once before settling back onto its brass branch.

Bap's customer was a troll. Two yellow tusks jutted above a thick, scabby lower lip, and eyebrows hung over his face like furry shop-window awnings. Charlie had never seen a troll outside the pages of Smythson's *Almanack of the Elder Folk and Arcana of Britain and Northern Ireland*. It was the *Almanack*, too, that told him trolls were also called hulders and jotuns.

And here one was. He had nearly run Charlie down in the alley and now he sat in the reception room of his father's shop. The troll's long matted hair and bull-like ears and horns were surprisingly close to the white plaster and dark oak beams of the ceiling, even though he was sitting. He must be eight feet tall, Charlie guessed. The troll examined a piece of Charlie's father's work. Charlie tried to ignore the thick animal stink that filled the room. So that was what cows smelled like.

"Very clever indeed!" the troll bellowed.

Charlie circled around and sat by his father, out of the hulder's reach and just under the big portrait of Queen Victoria. She was dressed in the portrait as the Empress of India (the Punjab was in India), and she dripped with jewels, including the famous Koh-i-noor diamond. She frowned at Charlie.

Bap patted Charlie on his knee and pinched him. It wasn't a hard pinch, just hard enough that Charlie knew that his bap knew that Charlie had been gone too long. Charlie sagged on his stool.

"Clever? It is *perfect*," Mr. Pondicherry said in his birdlike chirp. He patted Charlie on the knee again to show his pleasure, and that he had forgiven Charlie. "Everything I make is perfect, thought that might not always be obvious at first." He picked up his little round-bowled pipe from the table, sucked on the clay stem, and exhaled a puff of sweet-scented smoke.

"Not sure I can work with a monocle, though," the hulder added. "I read a lot of papers, and I really need both my eyes." He held a single round eyepiece up over his right eye.

The lens was bound in gear-toothed brass and had inside it other, smaller rings. Charlie's father had shown him the night before that by rotating the outer ring, the inner rings could be made to move, and the various lenses of the eyepiece could be moved into position or out of the way. This let the wearer control how much the eyepiece magnified.

"The second lens is nearly completed," Mr. Pondicherry told his customer. "Do not worry; a complete set of Pondicherry's Close-Reading Spectacles will be ready tomorrow morning when we open." He smiled. "Patent pending."

"You should test this one first on an actual document, Mr. Grumblesson." This new voice was high-pitched and silvery, like a breeze through tiny bells, and suddenly Charlie realized that the troll had a companion. He hadn't noticed her, because he'd been staring at the troll. She was half the height of Charlie, who was not a very large boy, and she had green butterfly-like wings. She was a pixie, sometimes also called a fairy—Charlie knew about pixies from the *Almanack* too—and her clothing was boyish and old-fashioned. She wore hose and buckled shoes and a very simple waistcoat and a tricorn hat, as if she belonged in the year 1787 instead of 1887. Poking out beneath the hat, her hair was blond and curly. The pixie rummaged in a satchel at her waist and came out with a letter, which she unfolded and handed to the hulder.

"Thank you, Miss de Minimis." Mr. Grumblesson twisted the brass ring around the eyepiece with his thumb and squinted through the lens. The sheet of paper had seemed enormous in the pixie's hands, but it looked like a calling card in the hulder's. "The party of the first part, ha!" he roared. "You're right, Mr. Pondicherry, it *is* perfect!"

"Aye, and just in time, too," added the pixie. "Can you send your lad round with it tomorrow morning?"

"I'll go," Charlie offered.

Charlie's father shook his head and set aside his pipe. "Oh, no, I'm afraid that will be impossible," he said. "I may perhaps bring it to you myself, a little later in the day. Yes, I can close the shop down at noon and bring the spectacles. Your office is in Tumblewain Close, yes?"

The pixie arched a little eyebrow. "How old is the boy, then? He's not tall, but I'll not hold that against a fellow. I took him for twelve or thirteen."

"Come on, Bap," Charlie pleaded.

Mr. Pondicherry nodded. He looked impatient. "Yes, but I shall be the one to deliver the Close-Reading Spectacles."

"The boy'll not take up his father's trade, then? He doesn't work about the shop?" Miss de Minimis asked with a grin. "Every youngster should follow in his parents' footsteps. 'Tis the natural thing."

Mr. Grumblesson chuckled.

Charlie's father patted his leg again. Charlie gritted his teeth. The pat reminded Charlie that his bap was in charge. "Charlie is sensitive to the sunlight. Besides, he's far too clever a boy to spend his life playing with gears and valves like his old bap."

The hulder looked at Charlie through the one lens, his right eye gigantic while his left glittered blue and small. "I'd send my fine-print clerk in the morning," he said, waving at Miss de Minimis, "only today is her last day. Tomorrow her grand tour ends and she goes home, which is why I need the spectacles. Day after tomorrow I sit the bar exam, so I *really* need them."

"Are you not already a solicitor, then?" Mr. Pondicherry asked.

Mr. Grumblesson shook his enormous head. "A law-speaker," he said. "That's a hulder lawyer. But there aren't enough of us around here to pay my bills, so I need to be able to get human clients." He sighed, a heavy sound like a wheezing engine. "And of course . . . mixed-folk families."

"I see," Mr. Pondicherry agreed.

"Look, Grim," the pixie said, "I'll come round for you in the morning anyway. One last little commission, and if you'll not have me as your clerk for a few final hours, then I'll do it for you as your friend."

"You're a fine young lady, Natalie de Minimis," Grim Grumblesson snorted, "and the Baroness de Minimis and Underthames are blessed to have you." He handed the eyepiece back to Charlie's father, who took it and wrapped it in soft cloth. "But I won't be using them before we take you back to your mother, in any case. Mr. Pondicherry, happy to see you tomorrow at noon."

The hulder picked up his headgear. It was an enormous top hat with holes cut neatly in the brim for his bull-like ears and more holes for the two long horns that sprouted from the top of his forehead. The troll stood—

crunch! And jammed both his horns into the ceiling.

"Loki's spats!" A chunk of plaster tumbled from the ceiling. It trailed white dust over the troll's hair and shoulder, and then he caught it in his hat.

"Sorry," Grim Grumblesson said. "I'll pay the damages, of course. Add it to my bill."

"Easy, Grim," the pixie said. "Just come straight down."

The hulder let his body sag, and his horns pulled down out of the ceiling. The craggy top of his head was dusted white, which made him look like a snow-covered mountain. He bowed, sheepishly set the bit of knocked-out plaster on the table, and turned to go. He stooped even farther to pass out the front door, the door owl *too-whoo*ing and spreading its wings.

Natalie de Minimis swept her own floppy black tricorn past her knees in a deep midair bow that was as old-fashioned as her clothing, then flitted out in the troll's wake.

"Charlie!" his father snapped the instant the door shut. Charlie hung his head. His father grabbed him by the shoulders.

Then Charlie's father hugged him.

"I was only in the alley, Bap," Charlie lied. "Taking the laundry to Wu."

"I worry, don't you understand?" His father looked him up and down. "And you're filthy! If it weren't so dangerous, I'd take you anywhere in the whole wide world. You're fragile, and the world isn't safe for a boy like you."

Charlie didn't think he was all *that* fragile—he'd been kicked and punched by bigger boys in the alley, and the ache was mostly gone already—but he didn't argue. "He has shirt presses that need to be calibrated," Charlie muttered.

"Promise me you'll stay inside and be safe," Mr. Pondicherry hissed. His eyes were intense, and when he demanded Charlie's promise, Charlie couldn't refuse.

"Yes, Bap," he said, "I promise. But it was only the alley." He slumped even lower on his stool.

His father hugged him again. "Come on," Mr. Pondicherry said. "We've got some chocolate biscuits; let's have a little tea."

Charlie changed his clothes and washed his hands and face. Then he poured the tea and arranged a packet of biscuits on a plate while his father made a few more adjustments to the second lens of the spectacles. The Pondicherry men were bachelors, so although Mr. Pondicherry did most of the cooking and Lucky Wu did all the laundry, Charlie tried to make himself useful about the shop. Now he arranged the tea, and tried to ignore a vague feeling of being trapped.

Charlie and his father sat down across the reception-room table from each other. Queen Victoria hung on the wall as the third point of the triangle, almost as if Her Majesty were having tea too. Almost as if Her Majesty were Charlie's mum.

Mr. Pondicherry poured. Charlie served half a biscuit to himself and three to his father.

"Have I told you the story of the little mermaid?" Mr. Pondicherry asked.

"I read it, Bap," Charlie said. "Hans Christian Andersen." He had read every book in the house, every page, more than once.

"A mermaid fell in love with a prince whom she had saved

from a terrible storm." Mr. Pondicherry looked at Queen Victoria, as if he were telling the story to *her*. Her Majesty looked fascinated. "She wanted to be with him, so she went to a sea witch and struck a bargain. The sea witch gave the mermaid legs. But walking on those enchanted legs felt like walking on sharp swords, and her feet bled all the time. And if she failed to get true love's kiss from her prince, and he married someone else, she would dissolve into sea foam."

"Also, the sea witch took her tongue."

"I see you remember the story."

Charlie nodded. He even liked the story, but he knew it well enough that his mind could wander a bit during the telling.

"So the little mermaid danced for her prince, though it made her feet bleed." Charlie's father gestured at Queen Victoria, as if she were the one dancing on bleeding feet. "And the prince loved her, but sadly, he loved another girl even more, a girl who wasn't mute. She was the princess of a neighboring kingdom, and the prince mistakenly thought *she* had saved him from the sea."

"He married the other girl," Charlie said, and then movement beyond the shop's window caught his eye. The window was filled with brass slats that could be rotated vertically so that they formed a solid wall at night. Right now they were horizontal so a customer could look in the window, and through the slats Charlie saw a man. Mr. Pondicherry's back was turned to the stranger; Charlie squinted to get a better look.

"That's right," Mr. Pondicherry agreed. "He married the other girl. And do you remember what happened next?"

The man outside leaned close into the window, and Charlie saw his sneering face clearly. It was the stranger Charlie had met in Irongrate Lane. Charlie shifted in his seat. The man didn't belong; he was up to no good. *Sinister* was the word to describe him, Charlie thought. *The Sinister Man.*

Should he say something to his bap?

"Yes," Charlie said. "The mermaid's sisters tried to convince her to murder the prince."

Charlie's father chuckled. "Yes, and she didn't do it. But that's not *the* part I meant."

Charlie couldn't be sure because of the shadows, but he thought the man outside was looking directly at him. "She threw herself in the sea," Charlie said slowly. "She jumped into the water and drowned." He looked up at the portrait of Queen Victoria. It was a trick of his imagination, he knew, but she looked afraid of drowning.

"Yes," Mr. Pondicherry agreed. "She threw herself upon the rocks of the sea and drowned. She wanted to see the great wide world . . . and it killed her without a second thought. She was a fragile and special person, and the world showed her no mercy."

The Sinister Man pulled away from the window and disappeared. Just before he vanished from view, just as Charlie's bap said the words *upon the rocks of the sea,* Charlie saw again the cogwheel at the man's throat. In his mind's eye he and Queen Victoria fell together onto the teeth of that wheel and were shattered into a thousand pieces.

Semihomo longidigitus (common names: kobold, trasgu, goblin, pukwudgie [North America])—The kobolds of Great Britain are to be distinguished from human beings principally by their diminutive stature. Kobolds are beardless and have slender fingers and steady nerves, which together make them expert craftspersons, especially in the field of fine machinery.

—Smythson, *Almanack,* "Kobold"

Charlie wanted to tell his bap about the Sinister Man. But he didn't know how he could say anything without either admitting that he had gone out to Irongrate Lane or lying about where he had seen the Sinister Man. He shook his head over and over as he cleared the table.

Just as Charlie finished washing up, the door owl announced two more customers. These were ordinary humans—boys, though bigger than Charlie.

Charlie followed his bap into the reception room.

"You will be Masters Micklemuch and Chattelsworthy," Mr. Pondicherry greeted his customers. "Welcome!"

"Sir Oliver Chattelsworthy," the first of the two boys said, with long, educated-sounding vowels and ghostly *r*'s. "Baronet."

He was freckled and ginger under a dented bowler hat. Both boys wore navy peacoats and striped trousers that might have been smart except that they were frayed at the cuffs and dark with filth. The one named Micklemuch had black grease smudges about the face and wore an oversized airman's leather cap with its chin straps flapping about his ears. Even the baronet, though his neck and cheeks were pink and clean, left a black smudge on the corner of the calling card that he handed to Mr. Pondicherry.

"You can stop it with the 'master' right there an' call me Bob," said the other, while Mr. Pondicherry examined the card. "An' if you've got to extinguish me from other Bobs, I'm 'Eaven-Bound." Bob's *th* sounded awfully close to his *f.*

"*Dis*tinguish, Bob," Chattelsworthy hissed.

"Yeah," Heaven-Bound Bob agreed. "'Eck, I thought that's what I said."

"Raj Pondicherry, and this is my son, Charlie." They all shook hands.

"Clockwork Pondicherry," Chattelsworthy said. "You're very nearly famous in Whitechapel."

"An' Clockwork Charlie, too." Bob winked at Charlie. "Not so famous, but 'andsome."

"Just Charlie," Charlie told him.

"You must be the aeronaut," Charlie's father said to Bob.

"Yeah," Bob admitted. "We talked with the kobold before. Clockswain, 'e said 'is name was."

Too-whoo!

"Goodness gracious, I did say that indeed," admitted Henry

Clockswain as he scuttled in through the front door, juggling brown paper parcels. "Raj, I believe I mentioned these lads to you. They're likely young gentlemen, and they've paid their deposit."

Mr. Clockswain was Rajesh Pondicherry's partner, but he was Charlie's size because he was a kobold. He was Charlie's size, pale, beardless, and balding. He smiled and blinked at Charlie as he came in. Then he pushed a stool up beside Charlie's and climbed onto it. After opening the parcels, he proceeded to carefully remove their contents.

"Look 'oo's 'ere, then," Bob said. "Mr. Cheerful 'imself."

"Who are you calling *likely*?" muttered the baronet.

The kobold looked up from his carefully arranged objects. "I only mean, er . . . *likely*. I mean you show promise."

"The 'eck, Ollie . . . Sir Oliver." The aeronaut, Bob, plucked at his companion's elbow. "No need to pick a fight right 'ere at the old auntie."

The baronet harrumphed.

"Auntie?" Charlie asked.

"Aunt Mabel, table," the aeronaut said, as if that were an explanation.

"Yes, you mentioned the gentlemen!" Charlie's father exclaimed, rubbing his hands together. "The Pondicherry Articulated Gyroscopes!" He looked down his round nose and over his thin spectacles at the two boys. "Patent pending. Not content with montgolfiers and zeppelins, gentlemen?"

"That isn't a very discreet question," the baronet objected.

Heaven-Bound Bob ignored his comrade and kept talking.

"'Ot-air balloons work well enough, but I reckon the old Greeks 'ad it right," he said. Charlie liked the rough and jolly accent of the boy in the aviator cap. "You wanna 'ave the freedom of a bird, you got to 'ave its wings."

Henry Clockswain had removed everything from the parcels and ordered it neatly on the table. He faced rows of small gears and valves, one spanner, two brass tubes, six plums, and a hard sausage, the results of his shopping expedition. He had also flattened the brown paper wrapper, piled it together and folded it once, and wound all the wrapping twine around the fingers of his left hand. Now he plucked stray bits of twine and paper from his jacket, clucking softly.

"But Icarus flew too close to the sun, and his wings melted," Charlie's father observed sagely. "Inventions of all sorts must be handled wisely, or disaster may follow."

Bob shrugged. "If I ain't got old Icarus beat for brains, which I reckon I 'ave, then I've got 'im beat for pluck." He poked his chin up. "I've got everybody beat for pluck."

Mr. Pondicherry smiled. "Come back tomorrow morning, gentlemen," he said, "first thing."

Bob grinned, and Charlie wished *he* knew how to fly.

The baronet smiled too, but more slowly, and looking only at Charlie's bap. "We'll pay the balance tomorrow, of course," he said. "Are you sure the gyroscopes will be ready in the morning? First thing?"

"Are you going be in the Jubilee aeronautical display?" Charlie asked. "The queen's progress flotilla from Waterloo and the London Eye to the palace? Isn't Her Majesty going to be followed by a procession of airships, to show the great advances that have been made during her reign?"

"I won't be in the flotilla officially," Bob said, and he grinned again. "But I will say that I am becoming very familiar with Waterloo Station."

"Oh dear." Henry Clockswain looked up from fussing with his twine. "That almost sounds as if you're up to mischief."

"It ain't mischief exactly." Bob's grin got even wider. "But the flotilla men are aeronauts, see? Practical chaps, 'oo care as you know 'ow to do something, an' not as you 'ave a university degree."

"Are you saying you're going to attempt to get the attention of Britain's aeronauts by . . . by joining the flotilla *uninvited*?" The kobold's eyebrows were raised in shock.

Bob winked. "When you ain't got many cards, mate, you play what you 'ave an' you bet big."

"And Mr. Ferris's Eye? Is it true that it's an enormous leisure wheel, right next to the station?" Charlie had read everything he could about the London Eye.

"It's true—built for the Jubilee itself. Starts with paying passengers at the very moment Queen Victoria departs from Waterloo Station, 'eaded for Buckingham Palace an' the garden party."

"Bap, let's go see it," Charlie urged his father.

"Harrumph," Mr. Pondicherry snorted.

"I don't know why they're even 'aving the party in the garden," Bob continued. "Don't you reckon Emperor Franz-Joseph and King Humberto and Prince Bismarck and all them others would like a go on the wheel? Seems like a waste of a trip, come all the way from Europe and not 'ave a spin on the Eye. 'Ave they got leisure wheels in . . . where is it Humberto comes from, again?"

"Italy," said his friend. "And it's *Umberto*."

"Right. You know your foreign lavatories better than I do."

"Dignitaries, Bob."

"But the Eye is for the people," Charlie said. "Not the lavatories."

Henry Clockswain chuckled. "Goodness gracious."

"I mean dignitaries," Charlie said. "I mean, maybe they'll ride the wheel later."

"Seems like rather a lot of to-do for an anniversary," Oliver Chattelsworthy said sourly.

"Yeah, it's a lot. An' when *you've* been queen of England fifty years, Sir Oliver, I'll see to it we throw you an even *bigger* party."

The boys shook hands with Mr. Pondicherry once more. Bob gleefully grasped hands with Mr. Clockswain, too, but Oliver Chattelsworthy just frowned and nodded. Then they tipped their hats and left. Charlie looked over their shoulders, trying to spot the long-faced, sneering Sinister Man. He didn't see anyone.

"That's it for me, then," Henry Clockswain said. He unwound twine from his fingers and wrapped it loosely around the folded brown paper. "I've put a couple of small pieces into my rucksack for this evening. Are you sure you can finish the spectacles and the gyroscopes both tonight?"

"Of course." Mr. Pondicherry smiled. "Stay and eat with us. I have some lamb."

"Oh, er . . . I've a bit of bread and cheese that will go bad if I don't eat it. But thank you, Raj." The kobold scooped up his rucksack, fiddling with its buckles for a moment before hoisting it onto his shoulder.

"Good evening, Mr. Clockswain," Charlie said. Henry Clockswain sometimes forgot to greet Charlie.

"Ah, yes, Charlie, thank you"—the kobold smiled back, blinking furiously—"and good night to you, too." He pulled the lever in the bottom left corner of the shop's front window; with a soft whirring the wide brass slats crossing the windows rotated into vertical position and shut tight. The kobold let himself out.

Then came the evening routine.

First Charlie read the *Almanack,* as well as Sir Walter Scott's *Among Jacobite Dwarfs*; Captain Burton's *Book of the Thousand Nights and a Night, Annotated and Illustrated Edition, Including Historical Bibliography on the Taxonomy of Djinns, Afreets, and Shaitans*; several of the shorter lyrics from Child's *Popular Ballads,* and even *Mrs. Beeton's Notes on Proper Management of the Modern Steam-Powered Household.* Meanwhile his bap continued to work, and the lamb stewed in rosemary, tomato, and red wine on a rack of steaming hot pipes in the corner of the workshop.

Then they ate, under the serious but loving smile of Queen Victoria. Charlie had only the smallest amount, a cup of the stewed lamb and half of one of Henry Clockswain's plums.

After dinner he lay on his cot in the corner of the workshop while his father smoked his pipe, rubbed Charlie's shoulders and back in a gentle circle, and told Charlie stories. Most of the tales were about what life was like in the Punjab. The Punjab was a magical place where the dowries of princesses beautiful beyond imagining were paid in rubies the size of your fist and the riflemen of the East India Company fought princes mounted on war elephants.

"Why did you ever come here?" Charlie asked. He had asked the question before. "How could you leave the elephants for . . . for *this*?"

"I came here," Mr. Pondicherry answered, with as much drama in his voice as he'd had the first time he'd answered the question, "because if I had not come here, I would not have been able to have my beautiful son."

Charlie sighed.

"I know, Bap," he said.

Then Charlie's father returned to work, on the second lens of the Close-Reading Spectacles and on the Articulated Gyroscopes. These were two linked series of spheres within spheres, each series bolted onto a seven-foot-long leather belt. All the spheres were studded with cranks and dials and well-oiled cogs so tiny that Charlie could barely see them. Not wanting to distract his father, Charlie went upstairs.

Charlie and his father worked, ate, and slept on the ground floor. Above the shop was the attic, a low-ceilinged room full of shelves. The attic held books, mannequins, tools, diagrams, spare mechanical parts, clothing, and outright junk. Where the ceiling sloped down on one side, the attic became a low crawl space over most of the shop. The crawl space was hidden behind a plaster wall and was accessible by squirming through a narrow crack in one corner.

Charlie reshelved the books he had been reading and lay on his belly. He wriggled forward to the wall above the street, where he planned to spend the next several hours looking out the window.

Charlie wished that Pondicherry's Clockwork Invention & Repair were located on a busy street, such as Cheapside or the Strand. Even better would have been a view of one of London's famous markets, Charing Cross or Covent Garden. Charlie would have liked to see more people, both in front of the shop and through its doors. Instead, during the day he watched his father's customers. At night he peeked out the attic window and watched the alley.

The Gullet did see traffic, all of it on foot because it was so narrow. Charlie saw mostly hats and shoulders, and he tried to guess what business each passerby could be up to. He assigned some of them to be secret agents of the Crown in pursuit of foreign villains, others mad inventors pacing frantically to stimulate their powers of creativity, and yet others carrying out missions of charity, distributing the wealth of a successful industrialist to the poor folk of East London.

Charlie's imagining was interrupted by the appearance of three persons. They marched through the dim, window-leaked light of the alley and stopped at the door of the shop. Two of them were obviously hulders, from their size and their huge, bull-like heads. Charlie began to feel nervous when he noticed that one of them carried a heavy ax.

He became even more nervous when he noticed that the third person, behind the hulders, was the dark-haired, sneering Sinister Man whom Charlie had seen earlier in the day on Irongrate Lane, and again through the shop window.

But Charlie Pondicherry was truly seized by panic when the hulder with the ax raised it over his shoulder and swung it down hard into the door.

Semihomo barbatus (common names: dwarf, dwerger)—
Male dwarfs are known for their long and often elaborately groomed beards, but their vanity manifests itself also in a love of colored silks, especially scarves, and gold jewelry. This fascination with gold adornment may have given rise to the traditional legends about dwarfish wealth. Since Britain's dwarfs are a wandering folk who generally dwell in small wagons, actual hoards of any size, at least in contemporary Britain, are improbable at best.

—Smythson, *Almanack*, "Dwarf"

Crack!

"Stay there!" Charlie's bap hissed. "And whatever happens, my boy, stay hidden!"

Charlie ran halfway down the stairs and hesitated.

"Go!" His father shooed him back up to the attic.

Charlie crept to the top of the steps and watched.

Mr. Pondicherry rushed to the back wall of the workshop, just within Charlie's sight. He threw open two tall wooden shutters to reveal a window that led into another alley—even smaller than the Gullet, and if it had a name, Charlie had never heard it—at the rear of the shop. Behind the shutters, the window was barred by a dense latticework of iron.

Crack!

Mr. Pondicherry grabbed a short brass rod at the side of the window. This was the emergency lever, which Charlie knew to pull in case of fire. Mr. Pondicherry threw his whole weight into yanking the rod down.

With a *sproing!* and a *k-k-k-krang!* the iron bars bounced out of the window and crashed to the ground. Charlie's father rushed three steps up the stairs to call to his son again.

"If I am gone, go to Wales! Go to a mountain called Cader Idris and find Caradog Pritchard. Tell him you're my son!" He smiled at Charlie, then frowned. "Now hide!"

Charlie froze.

Wales? His mind spun in circles. His father had never mentioned Wales before in Charlie's life. Charlie only knew that Wales existed, and that it was a country to the west of London, because he had read of it in books. Why Wales?

Crack!

Charlie scuttled into the crawl space. It was a tight horizontal gap into which neither Mr. Pondicherry nor the Sinister Man could have fit, let alone the trolls. There was no floor in the crawl space, only the tops of the oak beams that crossed the ceilings of the rooms below and the plaster between them. If he slipped off the beams, Charlie would fall through to the ground floor, so he moved carefully. He made his way to the part of the crawl space that lay over the shop's reception room.

A spray of brilliant light cracked the darkness, shooting up through two holes in the plaster, poked earlier that day by Grim Grumblesson. Charlie lay along the beam and pressed his eye to the nearest hole.

"Run, Charlie!" Mr. Pondicherry shouted into the work-room, backing away from it.

Crack!

The handle of the shop's front door and one of its big brass hinges gave way at the same moment. The door sagged into the room.

Too-who-ng-ng-ng! shrieked the door owl as it sprang from the wall.

Two hulders surged in. The first held an ax and the second a long rifle, and they stooped under the shop's ceiling. Charlie pulled his face back a couple of inches; if either of these hulders was as clumsy as Grim Grumblesson, he might lose an eye.

But he kept watching. Smoke blew up and around the hulder holding the ax. Charlie guessed the troll must be smoking, but his bap's pipe smoke was sweet and woody and comforting, and the smoke the hulder was blowing didn't smell like anything at all.

Mr. Pondicherry spun to face the trolls.

Men rushed into the reception room from the workshop beyond. They were big men with dirty woolen trousers, shirt-sleeves rolled up past the elbows, and faces unshaved. They held naked cutlasses in their hands, heavy swords, each with a basket of metal around the handle and only one sharpened edge. Pirate swords, Charlie thought.

When he saw the men, Charlie understood why his father had opened the shop's secret back exit but then hadn't used it to flee. These armed men had been waiting in the alley beyond.

Charlie's father was trapped, turning first one way and then the other between the two groups of rough-faced enemies. Behind the hulders, the Sinister Man now stepped into the reception room.

"You!" Mr. Pondicherry gasped.

The Sinister Man was silent.

"I have nothing to do with the Iron Cog anymore," Mr. Pondicherry said slowly. "And I have said nothing to anyone." His pronunciation was especially clear when he said *the Iron Cog.*

The Iron Cog—the three words rang heavy in Charlie's mind. Charlie had seen a cog at the throat of the Sinister Man. Was that the *Iron Cog*?

"How nice." The Sinister Man waved at some of the sword-wielding men. "You two, find the thing. You, the broadsheets. You, gather up everything in the shop that the good doctor is working on."

"I will yell and the police will come," Charlie's father threatened.

The men scattered to their assigned tasks. "Oh, yeah?" one of them laughed roughly. "'Ey, Captain . . . this citizen 'ere wants to make a complaint." He pulled a stack of large sheets of papers from inside his dirty shirt and set one on the reception table before disappearing into the workroom.

The captain was a heavy man with pouchy eyes. "I shall file a report. Shop broken into, shopkeeper abducted. Mind you, I don't think the police will do anything about this particular crime. Since, you know, we're the ones abducting you."

"You won't find my son," Mr. Pondicherry said.

"Your *son*, Dr. Singh?" The Sinister Man laughed harshly, and the captain chuckled.

"He's long gone." Mr. Pondicherry looked at the back window.

Heavy booted feet tromped up the stairs and kicked around in the attic. Charlie tried to lie still as he heard shelves toppled over and boxes smashed open. He mostly succeeded, though his hands shook.

"Nothing!" The men thumped back down the stairs. "It must 'ave gone out the back window an' we ain't seen it." They sounded like Heaven-Bound Bob, only cruel and hard.

The Sinister Man shrugged. "We have the doctor." Charlie wondered why the Sinister Man referred to his father as *the doctor* and *Dr. Singh*.

Below, the hulder with the ax grabbed Mr. Pondicherry. Charlie's bap struggled, but in vain, as the Sinister Man snapped an iron collar around his neck and locked it. Then he handed the end of the chain that hung from the collar to the second hulder.

Charlie gripped the beam he was resting on, so hard his fingers gouged out splinters. He wished he were bigger, or there were more of him, or he were armed. If only he had a pistol, he'd rush downstairs and free his father.

"Cowards," he muttered.

But he didn't have a pistol, and he was only a boy, who couldn't stand up to trolls and men with swords. And also, his bap had told him to hide. Charlie had brought this disaster on his bap by being disobedient—the Sinister Man had followed Charlie back from Irongrate Lane. He wouldn't make it worse by being disobedient again.

Charlie hid. He trembled as the Sinister Man and his henchmen led his father away. At the end of the line of armed trolls and thugs came two men carrying crates. In those crates Charlie saw his father's life—the Articulated Gyroscopes, the Close-Reading Spectacles, and everything else he was working on—carted away in two smallish heaps of jumbled brass and steel.

He knew he had no chance of fighting the men, but the sight of the crates pushed Charlie into action. If he couldn't rescue his father, at least he could follow the kidnappers. Maybe he could find an opportunity to free his father later.

Stretching carefully but quickly from beam to beam over the plaster, Charlie moved to the exit. He found it blocked by a fallen bookcase. No way was he strong enough, Charlie thought, to push the shelves out of the way by himself. He didn't even waste his time trying.

He was being left behind. Charlie rushed back over to Grim Grumblesson's horn holes in the plaster and looked down.

Two people were hard at work in the shop's reception room below him. They were short, and they occasionally looked up as they worked, so Charlie had a good view of them. They were dwarfs, also known, as the *Almanack* explained, as dwerger. Their long beards were braided in forks down their chests, and they dressed in wild colors, with puffy sleeves and striped pants and scarves wrapped around their heads. They wore gold rings on many fingers and in their ears.

They were fixing the door. They had already replaced both hinges and the destroyed planks and were now putting the final brass screws into the repaired lock. Charlie thought they must be friendly. He almost yelled to them through the ceiling—

but he caught himself.

It was the middle of the night. They must have come *with* the Sinister Man. Why would the Sinister Man have brought dwarfs with him to repair the door he shattered?

They were covering up the crime. If they cleaned up the mess and went away, no one would know that anything had happened.

Soon the dwarfs finished their work and left. They turned down the lights as they went, plunging the reception room into deep shadow.

Charlie lay on the beam and thought.

Someone had kidnapped his father. His father had expected it and had even prepared a secret escape route, but the kidnappers had known about the exit. Mr. Pondicherry had known his kidnappers, or at least he knew the Sinister Man, and they had talked about something called the Iron Cog. The Sinister Man wore a pin shaped like a cog. The kidnappers had tried to take Charlie, too. Finally they had taken all of Mr. Pondicherry's projects and cleaned up the mess they left behind them. Other than some papers, which they had left on purpose.

It made no sense.

And it was all Charlie's fault. The Sinister Man had seen Charlie on Irongrate Lane and had followed him home.

Charlie curled up into a ball.

He almost gave up, he almost just lay still and quit, but a tiny part inside him refused. The men who had kidnapped his bap would *want* him to give up. What would they *not* want him to do? Charlie asked himself. They would not want him to rescue his bap, so that was exactly what he should be doing.

But how?

He needed to see the papers. That meant that he needed to get out of the crawl space. But the one entrance was blocked.

He knew what he had to do.

Charlie stood up as straight as the low ceiling would let him and stepped off the beam. He placed both feet squarely between the holes left by the troll's horns. To his surprise, the plaster held.

So Charlie jumped, straight up and down, and collapsed in a cloud of plaster dust into a tangle of knees and elbows on the floor below.

The impact jarred him, but Charlie wasn't hurt. He stood up and began to dust himself clean. The shop was quiet and empty now. The invaders had replaced the workroom window bars and reclosed the escape door, too. Only the dust and plaster—silvery gray in the darkness—looked out of place, and the door owl, which hung upside down from the wall by a single screw, its eyes and beak open and its wings stuck in their extended position.

This was not the first time Charlie had been in the shop alone. But every other time his bap had gone out, Charlie had known he was coming back. Charlie had never thought about it before, but it was bearable to be alone because he knew his father was returning. Charlie could handle the fact that Lucky Wu hated him, because he knew his father loved him. It wasn't pleasant, but Charlie could stand to be punched and hit with rocks when he knew that Bap was on his team, that he and his father would have tea together and then dinner and then he would read while his father worked.

Now Charlie's father was gone, and Charlie had nothing.

He looked at Queen Victoria's portrait for comfort and got none. It might have been the deep shadows of her frame, but she looked sad too.

Loup-Garou (other names: loup-garou, werewolf, skin-walker, shape-changer, spriggan)—Properly speaking, there is no species *werewolf*, in Great Britain or elsewhere. That strain of magical talent, identified with the French nation, that produces shape-changers sometimes produces individuals whose particular talent is to transform themselves into wolf or wolflike form.

—Smythson, *Almanack*, "Loup-Garou"

Charlie stood in the workroom, staring at the closed shutters.

He was casting about to find one of the broadsheets the attackers had left behind when he heard a noise inside the chimney.

Slithering.

Charlie hid.

A wide and thin sheet of brass stood in the corner. His bap used it to punch out custom parts, and now Charlie threw himself behind the metal to hide. He pressed his eye to a hole the shape of a crescent moon. The workroom was only lit by low flames in the gas sconces on the walls and by pilot lights under the burners, so at first Charlie saw nothing.

Then he saw shifting inside the darkness of the chimney. And then a twitching on the shadowed floor in front of the fireplace.

Something moved, low and shapeless.

Charlie heard a soft *bamf!* Something smelled of rotten eggs.

A silhouette of a man stood up where the twitching had been, and brushed itself off with its hands.

Whump!

A black cloud billowed out of the fireplace, and a second man shape stumbled out of it. Both silhouettes coughed briefly and spat on the floor.

"Right," the first shadow said. Charlie recognized the voice but couldn't quite place it. Something about it sounded wrong. "Let's get it and get out."

The intruders rifled through the workroom, rummaging across worktables and benches and shelves on the walls.

"It ain't 'ere," one of them said after a minute. It sounded like one of the Sinister Man's strongmen. Had they forgotten something? Why would they come down the chimney when earlier they had used the door?

"You sure?" asked the other. "You sure you'd know what it looks like?"

"Yeah, I'm pretty diffident. It's got to look like the picture I drew."

"*Confident,* you mean."

"Yeah, that's what I said."

Heaven-Bound Bob and the baronet Oliver Chattelsworthy. Charlie almost stepped out, but caught himself. Why would his father's customers climb in through the chimney? And at night?

He stayed hidden.

Bob in his searching walked up to the big brass sheet. Oliver Chattelsworthy was right at his shoulder. "'Ere now," Bob said, "there's something behind this."

Bob dug an object from his peacoat pocket. He fumbled with it, and then Charlie heard the *scritch* and saw the flare of a match being struck. In the sudden light and through the punched-out moon, their eyes met.

"Get out!" Charlie shouted, and pushed the sheet forward.

The sheet toppled toward the boys, who both yelped. Chattelsworthy stumbled, but he caught the metal before it hit the floor.

"It's the boy!" Bob hissed to his companion. He gripped Charlie by his shirt with one hand. Charlie grabbed him back by the peacoat, and they dragged each other awkwardly into the middle of the room. "It's Clockwork Charlie!"

Chattelsworthy laid the sheet back against the wall with a clink. In the yellow wobble of the match's light Charlie saw him pull something small from his pocket. "Keep quiet!" the baronet whispered. He waved his object in Charlie's face.

It was a knife. All the waving blew out the match, and they were plunged into darkness again.

"Easy, Ollie," Bob said.

Charlie slapped at the weapon, but in the darkness he only hit a jacket.

"'Ey now, stop it!"

"Mum, you get it, mate?" Chattelsworthy hissed. "You don't wake up your dad, and we don't have to kill him." The baronet was no longer talking with his fancy vowels.

"Easy," Bob said again, and struck another match. Reluctantly the baronet put his knife back in his pocket. Bob smiled at Charlie. "It's all right; we ain't gonna 'urt you."

"Get out of here!" Charlie was stuck. He could fight, but it was two to one, and they were bigger and armed.

Chattelsworthy squinted at Charlie. "He looks *scared*, don't he?"

"Like you'd be if I stuck that thing in *your* face an' made threats."

"Sorry," Chattelsworthy said to Charlie, looking a little abashed. Then he screwed his face into an angry and violent expression. "But shut it, yeah?"

Charlie's bap always spoke in a calm voice with his customers, even when they were unhappy. Especially when they were unhappy. Charlie wasn't naturally calm in that way, but he tried. "I'm sorry to tell you that my bap—I mean, my *father* isn't here right now. May I help you?"

"For real your dad's not here?" the baronet asked.

Charlie nodded.

Bob hissed and dropped the second match as it burned down to his fingers. He let Charlie go and edged over to the wall, where he turned up the gas lights halfway.

"We don't want no trouble, see," Bob said. "We've just come for the things your dad's making for me."

"And we won't want a receipt, if you know what I mean," Chattelsworthy added with a swaggering step back.

"You mean you won't pay for the Articulated Gyroscopes," Charlie guessed. "You're going to steal them. You're not really a baronet, are you?"

"No, 'e ain't," Bob admitted. "An' yeah, we are."

"Hey!" Oliver Chattelsworthy cried.

Bob ignored him. "Sorry, mate," he said to Charlie, "I ain't got a choice. We only barely 'ad the brass to pay the deposit, an' a bit of street sweeping such as I am ain't going to get a second chance like the Jubilee. All those aeronautical men in one place, that won't 'appen again in my lifetime; I've got to strike while the iron is 'ot. Someone's bound to notice me, but not if I ain't there."

Bob seemed like a nice young man. Where Ollie seemed to want to look cruel and dangerous, Bob was almost apologetic about the fact that he planned to steal from Charlie's bap. Charlie needed help, and the only person he knew who might help was Henry Clockswain . . . only the kobold was fussy and easily surprised, and Charlie couldn't imagine him being very useful. Charlie needed allies who were bold and took risks.

Adventurers.

"Yes," Charlie agreed, "I understand. And I'll help you, if you help me in return."

Ollie looked suspicious; he put his hand back in the pocket with the knife.

"What kind of 'elp you need, then?" Bob asked.

"My father isn't here because he's been kidnapped," Charlie explained. "Half an hour ago."

A nasty little grin spread across Oliver Chattelsworthy's face. "That's bad luck, that is, mate. We'll just collect our Articulated Gyroscopes right now and get out of your way then, shall we?"

"You can't," Charlie said. "They took the gyroscopes, too."

Bob and Oliver cursed.

"Yes," Charlie said, "that's how I feel."

"I can get off the ground without the gyroscopes," Bob mourned, "but I can't stay off it, an' I can't steer. It ain't going to do me no good to take off during the Jubilee aeronautical display an' crash right into the ground."

"You'll die," Oliver said.

"Yeah," Bob agreed, "an' I'll look a right dodo."

"We can help each other," Charlie suggested. "You can help me rescue my father, and I'm sure he'll give you the Pondicherry Articulated Gyroscopes, free of charge."

"And give us back the deposit?" Oliver suggested.

"Easy, Ollie," Bob urged, "it was already a good offer."

"And return the deposit," Charlie agreed.

"I'm not sure it's a good offer even with the deposit." Oliver said. "How are we going to get old Pondicherry back? This ain't some sweeping job, mate—the man's been kidnapped. Do we know where he is? Do we know who took him? What *do* we know—what's your name, again?"

"Charlie Pondicherry." Charlie held out his hand. They all shook. "Pleased to meet you."

"'Eaven-Bound Bob," Bob said. The light in the room was dim, but his eyes twinkled. "As you may remember."

"Call me Ollie."

"Chattelsworthy," Charlie said.

"Naw," Bob corrected Charlie, "'e ain't Chattelsworthy any more than 'e's a baronet. Some folk call 'im the Snake."

"My friends call me Ollie," Ollie said. "My friends and people that don't want to get on my bad side."

"Ollie." Charlie smiled. "If you prefer, I can just tell the police you were here tonight instead. Maybe they'd like to talk to you about the kidnapping." It was a bluff. The pouchy-eyed captain had said the kidnappers were policemen, so Charlie couldn't talk to them for sure, no matter what.

But it worked. "Tough one, are you?" Ollie said. "All right, then. What *do* we know, Charlie?"

"I saw it happen," Charlie told them. "A mustached man came. He had two hulders with him and a gang of men with swords, who all talked like Bob. The mustached man also talked funny."

"What do you mean '*also* talked funny'?" Bob objected.

"How did he sound?" Ollie asked.

Charlie searched his memory. "Like this," he said, and he tried to imitate the Sinister Man. "We have ze doctor."

"French!" Bob and Ollie exclaimed.

"Oh." Charlie had read all about France, with its Bourbon kings and its revolution, Napoleon Bonaparte and his march on Moscow, Monsieur Montgolfier with his hot-air-balloon airships, the loups-garou, and so on. "Is that bad?"

"The French are rotten." Ollie grimaced at his feet.

Bob shrugged. "Knowing 'e's a Frenchman'll give us something to 'elp us find 'im."

"Yeah, but it ain't a proper clue, is it?" Ollie said. "Did he leave any clues, Charlie?"

Charlie knew what clues were from detective stories. Clues were a rare kind of mud on the guilty man's shoes, or an exotic cigar's ash left at the scene of the crime, or ink on the thumb of an extortionist. He considered. "One of the hulders smoked, I think. That isn't much."

Ollie scratched his head doubtfully.

"It's something, though," Bob said. "We could go round to the tobacconists an' ask 'em if they sell to trolls."

"Have you got any idea how many tobacconists there are in London?" Ollie objected. "And how many jotuns that smoke?"

Then Charlie remembered what he had been intending to do when the boys had plunked down his father's chimney. "They left papers! Turn the lights on!"

The boys turned up the gas in the workroom and the reception room, and Charlie laughed.

"What is it now?" Ollie grumbled.

"You're both covered in black from head to foot," he said. "I didn't understand that before, but now I see that it's soot. From chimneys."

"Yeah, we're chimney sweeps; we ain't exactly surprised," Ollie admitted. "And you're dusted all over in white, like it's sugar and you belong on top of a cake."

Charlie laughed again. "I came through the ceiling a different way," he said, and he pointed to the hole above the reception room.

He wasn't sure why, but the fact that all three of them were dusted with powder and all three had come down through the ceiling pleased Charlie.

There was a broadsheet on the table in the reception room, crumpled and worn. They located another copy on a table in the workroom. In the corner sat a whole stack of them, tied together with string, new and crisp, looking ready for delivery. Ollie cut the string with his knife so they could compare the pages.

They were printed using worn type on cheap paper with ink that ran and bled. No two copies were exactly identical, but the words were all the same. The broadsheet read:

✳ !!! A warning to the SONS of APES !!! ✳

You have *trodden* upon the Elder Folk of this Island *long enough!!* Today we *remove* your Queen, like a *louse*—easily and in clean conscience—Tomorrow, we will *remove* you too, and *squash* you in our *invisible* fingers!!

✳ !!! FEAR the Anti-Human League and OBEY !!! ✳

Stories of kobolds living underground are likely cases of mistaken identity in which kobolds have been confused with ghouls or pixies. In Great Britain's cities, kobolds live mixed in human society and subject to human laws. In the countryside, kobold communities—variously called guilds, corporations, or partnerships—are generally located on waterways or highways, and especially at their intersection. Though this preference is clearly to be understood as a desire for commerce and a need to harness hydrodynamic energy in their machinery, it has likely given rise to the other persistent rumor about kobolds: to wit, that their natural habitat is beneath bridges.

—Smythson, *Almanack*, "Kobold"

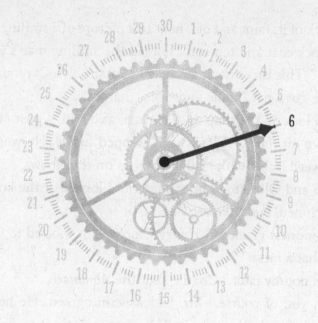

Neither Bob nor Ollie had ever heard of the Anti-Human League, nor had Charlie. He dragged several of his father's books downstairs and trawled through them, hunting for references. While he was at it, he looked for information on anything called the Iron Cog.

Nothing.

Bob and Ollie were no help. They dirtied a few pages of the *Almanack* and of the *New British Biographical Dictionary* before giving up. Then Bob fell to examining bits of machinery lying about the shop. Ollie mostly just scratched himself.

While Charlie was searching the books, he accidentally knocked the crumpled broadsheet to the floor.

Bending to pick it up, he saw that there was printing on

the back of it, faint and old, next to a picture of a smiling man in a frock coat and top hat. He read the smiling man's words aloud: " 'This isn't just a hat, my good man. It's a Cavendish.' "

"I've got a hat," Ollie said. "No, thanks."

The lock on the shop door clicked, and with a gust of cold predawn air, Henry Clockswain stepped inside. He wore his neat tweed jacket with leather patches on the elbows.

Bob and Ollie stood up straight and looked at the kobold. Bob grinned, but Ollie scowled.

"Goodness gracious," Henry Clockswain snorted to Charlie, "what a mess!"

"It's not my fault." Charlie shut the *Almanack*.

"Er, yes, of course," Mr. Clockswain agreed. He hopped from one foot to the other as if he was trying not to stand in the plaster dust that covered the floor. "I meant, well, goodness gracious!" The kobold smiled and shut the door. "And you are seeing . . . customers."

"Pfagh!" Ollie spat.

Mr. Clockswain looked up and saw the door owl askew on his brass perch. Tut-tutting with his tongue, the short clockwork engineer dragged a stool from the table underneath the owl and climbed up it. Standing on his tiptoes, he could just reach the owl.

"What are you doing?" Charlie asked. Something about the kobold's fussiness bothered him. The sheer normalcy of Henry Clockswain's reaction to the plaster dust felt . . . small. Charlie wanted to do something so urgently, his hands were shaking.

" 'E's fixing the door chime," Bob said.

Henry Clockswain only nodded, pulling a pair of pincers from his jacket pocket and gripping the owl with them, twisting it to push the clockwork back into place over the door.

"There's no time for that!" Charlie cried. "My father's been kidnapped!" He hopped down from his stool.

"*Kidnapped?*" The kobold spun around on the stool. His eyes blinked rapidly, he dropped the pincers, and if Bob hadn't steadied him with a hand on his shoulder, he might have fallen. "What happened? Shall I . . . er, call a constable?"

Charlie shook his head and tried to think. "No, the kidnappers might have been constables. Also, my bap was kidnapped by hulders, so talking to the bobbies won't do any good."

"That's right," Bob agreed. "Human crime, human coppers, Queen's Bench for the trial. Troll crime, trolls 'unt 'em down, tried at the Thing. Everybody knows that."

"Hulders!" the kobold squeaked. "There are hulders in Whitechapel?"

Bob might have a point, Charlie realized. What he needed was hulder help.

"There are hulders in Whitechapel," Charlie said. "And the one I want to talk to is in Tumblewain Close!" He gripped the table to steady himself. It felt like he was having an actual adventure, but it was only because his bap needed to be rescued.

And that was Charlie's fault.

"You can't go to Tumblewain Close," the kobold sputtered. His eyes blinked rapidly, and he opened and closed the pincers in his hand on empty air. "You don't know where it is. You've never left the shop. You haven't even got a map!"

Ollie snorted. "Who are you to tell Charlie he can't go?

Come on, mate." He screwed his bowler hat tightly onto his head. "I know the way."

Another fifteen minutes passed before they actually left. In the workshop Charlie covered his face and hands with the thick white cream that his father put on him every morning to protect him from the sun. The stuff felt gritty going on over the plaster dust, but it stuck and it covered his face. Bob watched attentively while he did it. Charlie didn't mind; he was starting to think of Bob as his friend.

"It's nice of you to help me," he said as he finished.

The chimneysweep aeronaut shrugged. "I need those gyroscopes. Besides, I've lost my own mum and dad."

"Is Ollie an orphan too?" Charlie put on his best jacket, which wasn't quite a peacoat, but was close.

"Naw. But I reckon 'e'd walk a mile to spit in 'Enry Clockswain's eye."

"What happened to make Ollie so angry with Mr. Clockswain?"

Bob laughed. "The first time we came into your dad's shop an' asked the kobold to build us the gyroscopes, old 'Enry couldn't sit still. The 'ole time we was talking, he kept balling up an' unballing a little rag in 'is 'ands."

"I don't understand."

"An' then one minute Ollie looks the other way, and 'Enry Clockswain reaches over with that rag and tries to *polish* Ollie. Tries to *clean* 'im."

This time they both laughed, and it felt good.

Charlie borrowed Mr. Pondicherry's John Bull, a short and

flat-crowned top hat with its brim smartly curled up over the ears. As a last touch, because he had sometimes seen his father dress this way for important customers, he tied a short white cravat around his neck.

As he looked at himself in his father's small dressing mirror, Charlie noticed his bap's pipe. The sight of it brought a sob from Charlie. He took the pipe and looked at it closely. The pipe had a short stem, and its round bowl was painted a dark cherry color, with golden panthers chasing each other around in a ring. Charlie tucked the pipe into his jacket pocket.

He would find his father and give him back his pipe.

"You look like soft cheese." Ollie cocked an eyebrow at Charlie when he emerged from the workroom. "I've got this urge to spread your face on a crumpet."

"Naw, 'e looks a right toff, 'e does," Bob disagreed. "With a very fair compression."

"Complexion."

"As I said."

"You ever been outside before, Charlie?" Ollie asked.

"All the time," Charlie lied. Soon he'd be strolling around Whitechapel like an ordinary boy. Not a boy at all, really: an *adventurer.* "I'm just sensitive to the sun, so I have to be careful."

"I'm coming with you," Mr. Clockswain said. He grabbed the lapels of his own coat and puffed his chest out, which didn't really make him look much bigger, especially since he immediately took to flicking wisps of lint off the front of his jacket. "You, ah, you'll need adult supervision."

"He didn't think so much about adult supervision when he was taking our money," Ollie observed to Bob.

"I mean Charlie." The kobold blinked. "I have a responsibility to Charlie and to his father."

Charlie took his father's spare key from the nail beside the door.

"Don't worry," he said to Queen Victoria as he straightened her. "I'll get Bap back."

They left. Charlie locked the front door and hung the key around his neck.

Ollie led the four of them down the Gullet. The pale blue sky above showed that dawn was imminent. Charlie squeezed his eyes shut as they passed through Lucky Wu's steam cloud, and then when he opened them again, he couldn't stop staring.

There were people on foot, opening shutters and sweeping refuse away from their doors. There were stern-faced buildings that steamed and clanked and smelled bad. There were shops of small tradesmen, where farriers or blacksmiths or velocipede men cranked up their fires, hammered on their anvils, and inflated their India rubber as they prepared to open for the day's customers. At the bottom of the lane, an immense iron-and-wood frame snaked through the sky over the roofs of buildings and baffled Charlie for a minute. Then he heard a shrill whistle and a grungy *chug-chug* and he saw a train pull into sight, and he realized that he was looking at Isambard Kingdom Brunel's famous Sky Trestle, the railroad whose tracks went over the rooftops.

Above that, tiny and dusty in a vast field of blue, Charlie saw zeppelins. They looked like flying whales grazing in the sky.

And there were elephants. Two of them, like big gray leathery walls with legs. Each was hitched to the front end of an enormous wagon piled high with casks and barrels. The wagons stood at rest in front of a tavern whose signboard read seven leagues under a pair of red boots. Four men unloaded the barrels and rolled them down an open hatch into the tavern's cellar. The elephants swished their tails and looked bored.

Charlie stopped to stare, but Bob dragged at his elbow.

"Come on, mate. Think of your old dad an' stay concentric."

"Concentrated," suggested Mr. Clockswain.

"'E knew what I meant."

Whitechapel whirled past in too many colors and smells to remember, and then Ollie stopped in front of an office building on a short cul-de-sac.

The sun shone against the tops of the walls now, pale but warm. It basted an egg-yolk glow over the top of a huge red-painted wooden front door and wide glass windows with shades drawn shut. Behind the window shades the building was dark. A steel nameplate on the door identified the occupant in bold copperplate type as GRIM GRUMBLESSON, LAW-SPEAKER.

"It's him you want, right?" Ollie asked. "Only troll in Tumblewain Close I know of."

"Yes." There was a pull-rope hanging down in front of

the door, and Charlie tugged on it. Inside, he heard the deep *clang-ng-ng* of a bell.

"It isn't too late," Henry Clockswain said. He rubbed his fingers together so much Charlie thought he might tie them in knots. "Bishopsgate is five minutes' walk. There's a police station there, and we can, er, ask for their help."

"Hmmph!" Ollie disagreed.

There was no answer. Charlie pulled the rope again. *Clang-ng-ng.*

Mr. Clockswain arched his eyebrows.

"Nothing," Bob observed.

"Maybe he ain't home," Ollie suggested.

Annoyed, Charlie reached out to grab the pull-rope again—and seized Grim Grumblesson by the front of his long, frilly yellow nightshirt.

The troll was yawning deeply. He smelled sour and vaguely meaty, and his eyes were half shut with sleep. "Told you," he rumbled, "I don't take milk."

"Mr. Grumblesson," Charlie said. "My father is Rajesh Pondicherry, of Pondicherry's Clockwork Invention & Repair."

The hulder forced one eye open. "The eyepiece," he grumped. "The Close-Reading Spectacles. It's early, isn't it?"

"He needs your help," Charlie said.

The hulder lawspeaker scratched his belly and turned to amble back into the building. Charlie followed. "Happy to help a respected local tradesman," the troll said, craning his neck and rolling back his shoulders with a loud crack, "but I don't know what Mr. Pondicherry can possibly need from me."

Charlie passed a huge coatrack and an open doorway to an office space full of books and tables. He found himself in a high-ceilinged hallway. There were various shut doors and a staircase leading up. The hall was deep in clutter. Muddy boots lay against the wall, and there were teacups and saucers stacked on the bottom steps, next to an empty wine bottle.

"Are you married?" Charlie asked. He knew it wasn't polite even as he said it, but he couldn't help it. "I mean, do you live alone?" He couldn't imagine anyone tolerating this much mess.

The hulder spun around and glared at Charlie. "Eh?" he growled.

Charlie staggered back under the hammer of those sparkling blue eyes. "I . . . I . . ."

"That it?" Grim Grumblesson demanded in a loud growl. "Your father want to marry a hulder woman? Who? Who is it, the little traitor?" He towered over Charlie, his face red and rough and angry. He smelled of animal. Charlie cowered.

The pixie clerk suddenly appeared between them. Her breeches and tricorn hat were gone; she wore a red dress with swirls of gold stitched into it, and red slippers.

Charlie hadn't seen her coming, and he stumbled back.

"'Tis time I left you, Grim," she piped in her melodious voice. "Sore subject," she whispered, winking at Charlie.

"No!" Charlie squeaked. "Nothing like that!"

Grim Grumblesson settled back and scratched himself again. "You look better than I feel," he harrumphed to the pixie.

"Aye. I drank less," the pixie explained.

"Don't congratulate yourself for being tiny." The troll disappeared through a big door. Charlie heard shuffling and scraping noises and thought the hulder might be getting dressed. "Very well," Grim Grumblesson called out, and then he grunted. "I have some business with Miss de Minimis here. When I return, in an hour or two, I'll come to your father's shop and we can see what help he needs. And I'll pick up the spectacles, as agreed."

The troll reappeared in the doorway. He had tucked his nightshirt into red trousers and pulled enormous brown boots over his feet. Charlie now saw that the hulder had a bull's tail to match his ears and horns.

Grim grabbed his yellow coat off the rack in the hall and shrugged into it.

"My father's been kidnapped," Charlie said.

Grim Grumblesson rubbed his chin. "Have you tried the bobbies?"

"It was trolls that did it," Ollie said.

"Odin's eyeball!" the hulder barked.

"And the spectacles?" Natalie de Minimis wanted to know.

"Taken as well," Charlie said.

The troll looked carefully at Charlie. "What other family do you have in London?"

"None," he said. "I have no other family in the whole world. Not that I know of."

"I . . . I've already suggested the police," Henry Clockswain said.

The hulder frowned, pulled his thick, matted hair back from his forehead, and settled his top hat down over it. "I can't cancel with Gnat," he decreed, "so you'll have to come with me. This won't take long; we'll look for your father immediately after, and on the way you can tell me everything you know."

"Why the delay?" Henry Clockswain's eyes blinked. "There is a police station just around the corner, and time is wasting!"

"*In loco parentis*," Grim Grumblesson said.

"Is that Hulder?" Ollie asked.

"It's Latin!" the troll snapped.

"What's it mean, then?" Bob asked.

"It means I'm dad now," the troll explained, "and we'll do as I say. You want to talk to the coppers, kobold, it's your choice. I'm not waiting around."

With strides five feet long, the hulder headed for the door.

Clicking his tongue against his teeth, Henry Clockswain followed.

Semihomo aliger (common names: pixie, fairy, fair folk, y tylwyth teg)—The pixies of Great Britain are slender, winged folk, averaging two feet in height. Their wings resemble insects' wings more than the wings of birds or bats, lacking feathers and being made of a thin, rigid membrane. Pixies can fly at tremendous speeds, and generally live in remote or hidden locations, in forests or underground.

—Smythson, *Almanack*, "Pixie"

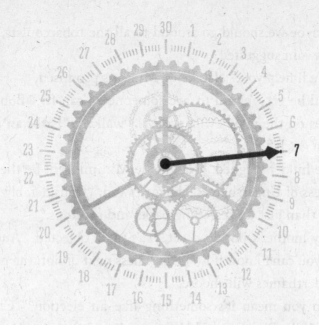

They walked, and Charlie told the hulder everything he had seen and heard: the Sinister Man, and the Iron Cog, and the Anti-Human League, and his father being called *Dr. Singh,* and THIS ISN'T JUST A HAT, MY GOOD MAN, IT'S A CAVENDISH, and the men with cutlasses who said they were policemen, and the two hulders, one of whom smoked. Henry Clockswain listened closely and watched with rapidly blinking eyes, and Charlie realized he hadn't taken the time to tell the story to the kobold.

"Scentless tobacco, hmm?" the hulder rumbled.

"Do you know him?"

"Doesn't ring a bell," Grim Grumblesson said, "but I'm not a smoker. But don't worry; there just aren't that many hulders in London. We'll find him."

"Maybe we should go around to all the tobacconists," Mr. Clockswain suggested.

"We'll help you," Natalie de Minimis promised.

"It'll be very 'elpful to 'ave someone as can fly." Bob kept his eyes on the pixie's wings as they walked. "Parks an' rooftops an' such."

The hulder laughed. "Natalie de Minimis will be the next Baroness of Underthames," he guffawed. "Considerably more useful than just for searching parks and rooftops."

"My mother's not dead yet," the pixie objected. "And besides, you can't know if I'll be baroness next or not; the people of Underthames will choose."

"Do you mean it's something like an election?" Charlie asked. "Like Parliament?" He remembered that the *Almanack* had been a little vague on this exact point, and had used words that Charlie didn't quite understand, such as *acclamation* and *charismatic leadership*.

"Something like that," she said.

"*Nothing* like that!" the hulder roared. A passing cart driver nearly fell out of his seat. "Parliament is secret ballots and whiskey barrels for the voters and political parties and platforms and greasy backroom deals! The passing of the barony is the clatter of spear on shield by the warrior throng; it's the cry of favor of the crowd for its chosen leader!"

Charlie could almost hear the cry of the warrior throng as Grim told it. "That sounds exciting."

"Sounds barbaric." Ollie scratched his armpit vigorously. "Sounds like something *Americans* might do."

"My people follow very old traditions," Natalie de Minimis said. "We're here."

Charlie had been so absorbed in the conversation, he hadn't paid any attention to his surroundings. Now he found that he was in a cobbled courtyard closed in by windowless brick walls. A narrow alley led into the yard, and a single large storm drain let the rainwater flow out, down, and away.

Charlie had read a lot about the sewers. There were rats down there, and worse. Ghouls haunted the empty places just at the edge of cities so they could eat other folks' garbage and their corpses and, Bap had suggested more than once, their lost children.

And sometimes they went down into the sewers.

"Where is *here*?" Ollie asked.

"One of the many doors to Underthames," Mr. Clockswain said. "It's signposted, if you know how to read the signs."

"It is?" Bob asked.

"Pixie gates aren't secret," the kobold explained. "They're just guarded."

The pixie floated over the storm drain and pointed down at it. "We've come by this gate so that you'll all fit."

Charlie looked at the storm drain. It was covered by a rack of iron bars, six inches apart. "I don't see how."

The troll cracked the knuckles of both hands, bent over, and grabbed the bars. "Stand away," he grunted, and heaved.

The grate came up from the ground, and Grim hoisted it over his head, with its surrounding wreath of cobbles. It left a hole in the earth at the troll's feet, neat and rectangular, like the trapdoor opening to a tavern's cellar. Charlie squinted to get a closer look. He saw stairs, and something else.

"The walls," he said. "They're glowing."

"'Tis gloom-moss," Natalie de Minimis explained. "We see perfectly well in absolute dark, but other folk don't, and this is a big-folk gate."

Charlie didn't remember any mention of gloom-moss in the *Almanack*.

"Shall we discuss the technical details later?" grunted the troll, who was still holding the slab of iron and stone over his head.

Charlie went first, with the pixie.

The kobold followed, and then, after some muttering and scuffing of feet, Heaven-Bound Bob, with Ollie the Snake on his heels.

Thud!

"Ouch," muttered the troll.

"Duck, Grim," the pixie called out.

Charlie heard wordless grumbling, the heavy boots of the hulder on the stairs, and the *whoomph!* of the gate being replaced.

The passage's rough walls and ceiling were covered with thick gloom-moss. The glow it gave off was a dull yellow, which seemed to come from inside the moss and shine through its surface like the glow of a lamp behind a lampshade. The gloom-moss glistened as if it were wet, but when Charlie touched it, he found it dry. He stepped carefully over a culvert that crossed the steps to carry any water flow off down a red brick–lined drain big enough to walk in. That must be the sewer. Charlie heard chittering and scratching noises from the sewer and wondered what could be making them.

Hopefully rats. He'd choose rats over ghouls any day.

Among the steady drips of water and with his companions' footfalls behind him, Charlie followed the pixie down. Centipedes the size of his fingers and roaches the size of his thumb scuttled out from under his feet as he walked.

"That's a pretty dress you're wearing," he offered.

"Aye, thank you," she agreed. "I'm coming home after a long time gone, and I'd like to impress my folk."

"How long was your grand tour?" Charlie asked.

"Two years," the pixie said. "That's standard. 'Twasn't really a grand tour, though. That's a custom of the wealthy English families, and 'tis Grim's little joke to call it that. There's a Pixie word for it, but it's no use me telling you, since you can't speak Pixie without wings, and half of spoken Pixie's too high-pitched for human ears to hear, anyway."

He hadn't read this in the *Almanack* either. "Like dogs and whistles, Miss de Minimis?"

She laughed, a very pretty sound like the tinkling of falling water. "That's not flattering, but aye. Don't you go whistling on me now. And please, call me Gnat."

"But you're the Baroness of Underthames!" It seemed outrageous to call a baroness just *Gnat*. "Or you will be."

Gnat shrugged. "No one here's a baroness yet. The best word in English for what I've done is a *walkabout*. That means a journey taken by the young natives of Australia to see the outside world. Sometimes in English pixies will call it the *tithe*, too, because a pixie goes when she's twenty, for two years of her life, which is a tenth. And then, *tithe* sounds a bit like the Pixie word for a journey."

"I'm on my walkabout now," Charlie said. "I didn't really mean it to happen, but it did."

"I did my tithe with Grim. Two years without going back. Two years with no contact with my home, even though I was but a mile away. I learned a lot about humans and hulders, and Whitechapel and London, and folk and the law. Hopefully all that learning, and a wee bit of experience, will add up to wisdom someday."

"Aye," Charlie said, and then he felt a little bit silly, but Gnat laughed and that made it okay.

"Hold!" barked a silvery voice below them. Charlie looked ahead and saw that they had come to a closed door without lock, handle, or knob. The door was large and set inside an arch of carved stones. Each stone was an ugly gargoyle face twisted into an expression of rage or hunger or menace. Each gargoyle's mouth was open, and into each stone tongue was carved a different rune. Charlie had never seen anything like it, even in books.

Eight pixies floated in front of the door, armed with shields and spears. The one in front pointed his spear in the new arrivals' direction.

"Hold, I said!"

"Hold, yourself, Cousin Hezekiah!" Gnat cried back. "I'm come home to my own mother's house after a full and successful tithe, and is this the welcome I get?"

Mr. Clockswain, the chimney sweeps, and Grim Grumblesson caught up to Charlie and the pixie and stopped.

"Natalie?" All eight pixies stared. "Can you really be Natalie de Minimis? What are you doing in the company of such a galumphing herd of uplanders, then?"

"And who are you, Cousin Hezekiah, to question me about my choice of companions? And why in Oberon's name are there so many of you, for just the one door? Open up, and let me and my friends in!" Gnat, who had seemed like a helpful and friendly girl in Pondicherry's Clockwork Invention & Repair, now fluttered with a fierce arch to her back and fire flashing in her eyes.

"Aye." Hezekiah sounded tired. "Aye, I've orders to take you to the baroness, and I suppose your friends will have to come too."

Hezekiah turned in midair and fluttered his wings in a twitchy pattern at the door. The gargoyle-tongue runes lit up all at once. The door swung open with a rush of air, and Charlie thought he heard the gargoyle heads whispering to each other.

"Goodness gracious," said Henry Clockswain.

Hezekiah led the way. Charlie felt a sharp pang of remorse, realizing that he was likely getting farther from his father with every step. But once Gnat had met her mother the baroness again, Charlie reassured himself, he'd return to the surface with an army of flying pixies, and they'd find Mr. Pondicherry in no time.

And then he promptly lost his train of thought.

The gloom-moss disappeared beyond the doors. The walls

of the vast caverns Charlie now entered were studded with jewels of every color. There was light—he couldn't see where it came from, but it was there—and it spun and flashed in every gem, filling Charlie's vision with rainbows and whorls and stars and streaks of joy.

In and among the dancing lights Charlie saw nests. They looked just like birds' nests: piles of thatching woven together like giant cups. Peeping up over the edges, he saw, were pixie faces. Pixies flew through the air, too, above the nests and high in the caverns and around the edges.

Every pixie dressed like Gnat. Shoe buckles, waistcoats, kilts, hose, and tricorn hats on the male pixies, with long hair in a braid; brocade shoes, close-bodied gowns, jacket bodices, panniers, and hoop skirts on the females, with long hair piled up above their heads. It was like a fancy-dress party of winged insects.

"Goodness gracious!" exclaimed Mr. Clockswain.

Charlie and his party followed a stone-paved road that crawled through and beneath the teeming cloud, through several caverns, across a stream of water, and through a field of glittering green gemstones. At the top of a small mound of stone beyond squatted a circle of pillars, half again as tall as Grim Grumblesson and broken off at the tops. It looked like a Greek temple that had lost its roof. At the far end was a simple stone chair, pixie-sized. Here Hezekiah barred the company's way with his spear.

In front of the chair hovered a strange cast of characters, posed in a scene. It took Charlie a moment to figure out what they were up to. "Tableau vivant," he murmured. "They're making living art."

He'd heard his father mention tableau vivant, but he'd never understood quite what it would look like.

The pixies all posed together to look like a painting. A pixie in a pink cape, who looked a lot like Gnat, hovered above the others. She confronted a shy pixie in a blue toga, with sad eyes, who stood on the ground and turned his shoulder. Behind Pink Cape stretched a procession of revelers holding joints of meat and small snakes and tambourines. A stuffed dog and two purring leopard kits on chains completed the scene. They all held perfectly still, and Charlie wondered what painting they were imitating.

A crowd of pixies had gathered around. Some of them fluttered low to the ground and others higher, even directly overhead. Charlie was standing inside a living bubble formed entirely of pixies.

Almost all of them armed with spears.

The tableau actors held their pose.

Grim shuffled from one foot to the other.

Crack! A paving stone under the troll snapped in two.

"Agh!" Pink Cape threw her hands up in exasperation. She fluttered down and threw herself into the seat, and the other actors all relaxed. All except for Blue Toga, who stayed on the ground and kept his back partly turned to Pink Cape.

"Cousin Elisabel," Natalie said to Pink Cape. "You're in my mother's seat."

"My old auntie's dead, Cousin Natalie," said the seated

pixie, "and the seat is my own now. Have you returned to make a claim, then?"

Gnat's wings fluttered a little faster, and Charlie thought he heard Grim Grumblesson mutter under his breath. Blue Toga looked at Gnat, and Charlie saw a glimmer of hope in his eyes.

"I've no wish but to come back to my own home in peace, Cousin Elisabel," Gnat said, "and see my fine cousin Seamus. I'm no one you should worry about, no one special at all, just a pixie come home from her tithe. I've not come to make a claim today."

"Good." Elisabel gestured with her hand to the spear-wielding crowd. "Lock her up, her and all her uplander friends."

It is common knowledge that the rats of London are of an unusual size. There is, however, no evidence that they are sentient or possess the power of speech, and it is ridiculous to suggest that rats should be treated as one of the folk of Britain.

—Smythson, *Almanack*, "Rat"

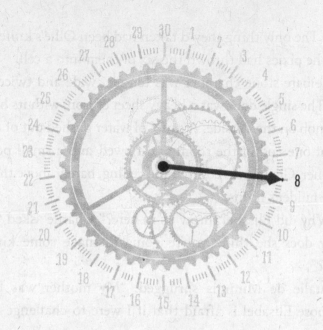

"Sorry, Ollie. Sorry, Bob." Charlie hung his head between his knees. "If you hadn't tried to help me, you wouldn't be in this mess."

"Help *you*?" Ollie snorted and jerked his thumb at Bob. "Help *him*, more like! Wants to be famous, wants to be a big fancy aeronaut! Ha!"

"Easy, Ollie," Bob urged his friend. "You see the markings around the door?"

"Yeah." Ollie slumped. "They've got a ward up. No magic in here."

Charlie didn't quite understand the other boys' words, but Ollie sounded defeated.

A squad of pixies with spears had surrounded and searched

them. The only thing they'd taken had been Ollie's knife, and then the pixies had thrown the six of them into a cell.

The bare stone chamber was ten feet wide and twice that long. The single door was a heavy sheet of iron, with its hinges and knob on the outside. A canal of water gushed out of a clay pipe at one end of the room and flowed into a small pool at the other. Glow-moss covered the ceiling, barely above the tips of the hulder's horns.

"Why did Elisabel throw us in here?" Charlie asked Gnat. "Why does she think you're going to make some kind of claim?"

Natalie de Minimis shrugged. "My mother was loved. I suppose Elisabel is afraid that if I were to challenge her, I might get some support."

"And would you have challenged her?" Charlie wanted to know.

"I have the right to; that's what worries her. The baronesses of Underthames have been ladies of the de Minimis family, my grandmothers and great-grandmothers and so on, since Boudicca herself decided she'd had enough and it was time to start skewering Romans."

"Boudicca was a pixie?" Charlie was surprised. "I thought she was a Celt."

Gnat smiled. "Aye, don't believe everything you read in books, Charlie."

"They gone now?" Grim asked.

Gnat flitted to the door, looked through its slit window, and listened. "Gone."

Grim grabbed the door with both hands and pushed. He pulled and he twisted; he slammed his big shoulder into it with a boom.

The door didn't budge.

Charlie's shoulders slumped when he saw that the enormous troll couldn't shake the door, but the hulder wasted no time. He crossed the cell to the canal. Water entered the chamber through the clay pipe at one end, crossed the floor in a ditch into a pool at the other, and then exited through a grate in the wall. With a single pull, Grim ripped off the grate, sending splinters of stone and mortar and drops of water whizzing around the room. The chimney sweeps and the kobold rushed to look at the tunnel Grim had exposed, while Gnat stayed listening at the door.

Charlie squinted at the dark opening. It was the mouth of a narrow underwater passageway. He had read enough books to know that the way to get out of a prison cell was to dig a tunnel. It was pretty lucky to be thrown into a cell that already came with a built-in escape route.

"It's no good," Henry Clockswain announced. He'd picked up the grate and was fidgeting with it, poking his fingers through each of the grate's holes in turn.

"What do you mean, *no good*?" Ollie demanded. "It's a tunnel; there's water flowing through it; it has to go somewhere!"

"Goodness gracious, yes!" the kobold agreed. "But it's a tunnel full of water—there's no air! And, er, look how tight it is! This might go twenty miles with nothing to breathe, all the way to the sea. You'd be out, and, ah . . . cold comfort that would be to you."

"We could stop all the water coming in," Charlie said. "That would leave the tunnel dry."

"Stop it? What do you mean, like with a dam?" Bob asked. "But the water's got nowhere to go; it'd just spill around whatever we use to block it an' keep going."

"'Tis no twenty miles," Gnat said. "It flows past the rest of the prisons, which won't be more than a few hundred feet. Then it joins up with other streams that all go out into London's sewers. You'd be able to get out of the water there, for certain."

"A few hundred feet!" Mr. Clockswain was almost yelling, his voice like a whistle. His long fingers twisted the buttons on his jacket with nervous energy. "It may as well be twenty miles! To use this tunnel, you'd have to be a fish, or . . . or something!"

"Or something," Bob agreed. He looked at Charlie with furrowed eyebrows.

"Footsteps!" Gnat hissed from the door. Grim shoved the grate back and they all scrambled away.

A hedge of spears sprang in through the door as it opened, with grim pixie faces behind it. The hedge parted, revealing the pixie youth who had worn the blue toga in the tableau vivant. Now he wore breeches, hose, buckled shoes, and a tricorn hat. The spearmen retreated, and the door shut.

Gnat listened at the door for a few moments before she said anything. "Cousin Seamus." Her voice was sad and tired, but there was a faint trace in it of something else. She spoke quietly, almost in a whisper. "So you've not forgotten me completely, then."

"I've not forgotten you at all, you silly girl," he answered, his voice also very quiet. The way he said *silly girl* made Charlie think he meant something else, something much nicer. "I'd sooner forget my own eyes."

"Did Elisabel kill my mother?"

Seamus shook his head. "'Twas the rats," he said. "They attacked six months ago, killed your mother and a great many other warriors."

"And did no one think to tell me, then?" Gnat asked.

"That's the tithe, isn't it? We couldn't tell you." Seamus shook his head. He looked at the door, then lowered his voice even further. "But maybe we did wrong. We've been at it against Scabies and his horde ever since. Elisabel fought like a wild woman when the rats attacked, and got chosen baroness for it when your mother died. She's kept us safe since, but we're in a state of war."

"I'd noticed."

"And besides, no one but your mother knew for certain where you were."

Gnat looked around at her companions. "Am I a dead woman, then?" she asked. "And if Elisabel kills me, will that satisfy her, do you think? Will she let my friends go free?"

"I wouldn't take my freedom from someone who killed my friend," Grim Grumblesson snarled.

"*I* would," Ollie said.

Seamus shook his head. "I don't know, but I'm afraid she has plans for you, Natalie de Minimis. She only let me come down to see you because . . . because I'm her betrothed, and I've a soft spot for my cousin Natalie."

Gnat was silent for a few moments. "A one-year betrothal?" she asked.

"Aye. Agreed today."

"I've got to escape," Gnat concluded.

"Aye."

"And I've got to challenge her. I don't like her sitting on my mother's seat, and I'll not let her marry you, Seamus. You're my own true heart."

"That I am." Seamus smiled. "But you can't challenge a living baroness just because you want to. Besides, Elisabel is loved too. She keeps Underthames safe. You'd be mad to challenge her directly, just come back from your tithe as you are."

"Aye," Gnat agreed. "I'll have to make something of myself, and fast."

"Three mighty deeds," Seamus said. "That's what makes a hero; that's what makes a warrior all of Underthames can love. A woman who had done three mighty deeds could challenge the baroness for her seat, and for her betrothed."

"Can you give me any aid in escaping from this pit?" Gnat asked.

Seamus shook his head. "They watch me too close. You've got my heart, Natalie de Minimis," he said, "and my faith, and all my best wishes, but I'm afraid that's all I've got to give you."

Gnat grinned recklessly. "Not even a kiss, then?"

"Aye." He smiled, but there were tears in his eyes. "I've got a kiss for you yet."

Charlie turned his back, and heard the door shut when they were done.

"Rats," Gnat said, deep in thought.

Ollie snorted. "That's putting it mildly."

"Next time they open the door, we attack," Grim suggested.

"But there are too many of them," Mr. Clockswain said. He shook with nervous energy, twisting his buttons. "They're tough fighters, and, er, they're armed and we're not. Besides, they know they've got a troll in the dungeon. They're never going to send a force down here that's small enough that we can overpower it. They may never send down any force at all. They could just leave us here to rot." One of his jacket buttons popped right off, and he stared sadly at it in his palm.

"You have another idea?" The troll glared at the little kobold.

"We could dig another tunnel," Charlie suggested. He imagined himself digging with a spoon, or one of the big brass buttons on the front of the hulder's coat. They could throw all the dirt into the stream, and it would be washed away. He wondered how far they could dig in a year, if they took turns and never stopped. Maybe they would tunnel into another cell, and find other prisoners they could join forces with.

His wildly galloping imagination pulled up short. Of course, he couldn't wait a year. His father had been kidnapped.

"Naw, I think we should use the tunnel we've got," Bob suggested. He had a sly grin on his face, and he looked at Charlie. "It's a perfectly good tunnel. We've just got to figure out 'oo can 'old 'is breath the longest."

"I'll go," Charlie volunteered.

"*I'll* go," the pixie contradicted him.

"No," the hulder said. "I'm still dad here, and Pondicherry's boy doesn't go." He climbed out of his long yellow coat and began tearing it into strips.

"Hey!" Charlie objected. "You don't get to tell me what to do."

"Nor the pixie," Grim continued, ignoring him. "The water will ruin her wings, and she knows it. And whoever goes, we tie a rope around him, so we can pull him back if we need to." He looked at Mr. Clockswain, like he was daring the kobold to volunteer.

The kobold took several steps back.

"Fair enough," Bob said, "but I've got a feeling that maybe Charlie 'ere can 'old 'is breath longer than any of us can. I've got a feeling 'e might be able to 'old 'is breath a surprisingly long time."

"Yeah?" Ollie asked.

"'Ere's what we do." Bob smiled reassuringly at Charlie. "I'll cover your mouth an' nose with my 'ands, an' Ollie will start counting. When it starts to feel unconditional, you just raise your arm an' we'll stop."

"Uncomfortable," Ollie corrected his friend.

"Right." Bob covered Charlie's mouth and nose with his hands.

"One . . . two . . . three . . ." Ollie started counting. Bob's hands were tight on Charlie's face. His fingers felt surprisingly delicate.

"One hundred . . . one hundred one . . . one hundred two . . ." Charlie felt fine.

"Two hundred fifty-three . . . two hundred fifty-four . . ." Charlie still felt fine. Grim Grumblesson had finished knotting together a rough rope out of the strips of his coat; his jaw had dropped, and his mouth hung open. Ollie's eyes bugged huge, and the pixie's wings fluttered like a hurricane. Mr. Clockswain rubbed his thumb in a circular motion around his detached button so hard Charlie thought the button might snap.

"Three hundred . . . three hundred one . . ."

Bob took his hands away.

"'Ave I made my point?" he asked the others.

"I feel fine," Charlie said. He'd never tried to hold his breath before. "Three hundred. Is that good?"

"How is that possible?" Grim looked bewildered.

"Charlie 'ere is a very special boy."

"Do I get to do it now?" Charlie asked. "Or does anyone else want to see how long he can go?"

Gnat shook her head. "Nay, my boy," she said, "no one here is going to hold his breath any longer than you've done."

Grim handed the end of his strip rope to Charlie. "Very well. You are a special boy, Charlie Pondicherry, and a brave one. Tie this around you."

Charlie fastened the rope around his waist in a neat bowline, tight against his body. He knew his knots; he'd learned them from one of his father's books, *Practical Sailing for Boys*. "What do I do? What am I looking for?"

"As soon as you can get out of the water, do," Gnat told him. "And then you'll have to come back and let us out. Can you do that?"

"Aye, I can," Charlie said, and this time he didn't feel silly for saying *aye*.

"Just remember," Gnat said, "you're used to being the little one, around your father's shop and his customers. Here you're a giant."

Grim Grumblesson harrumphed.

"Aye, and the hulder's a giant's giant. But look, Charlie, you'll not be able to count on being small, so you'll have to be smart . . . understood? Can you tell a good lie?"

"I'm not a liar!" Charlie protested, but then he nodded. "Yes, I know how to tell a good lie."

"Good, because you'll not be able to sneak about unseen. When anyone challenges you, tell them you're about the business of the Baroness Elisabel de Minimis. If they interfere with you, they'll have to answer to her. Be bold."

"I'm about the baroness's business!" Charlie snapped fiercely, practicing. "Do you want to explain yourself to the baroness?"

"Excellent." Gnat patted Charlie on the shoulder.

"But won't they know the baroness put me in prison?" Charlie asked.

Gnat nodded. "Aye, they may. But for all they'll know, she may also have let you out and sent you on her errand in the meantime. Trust me, Charlie. Be bold."

"I'll let the rope out slowly," Grim said. "Pull twice if you've found a way out of the water and are leaving the rope behind. Pull three times if you're in trouble, and I'll pull you back."

"Twice when I'm done. Three times for trouble." Charlie repeated. He grinned. This was an adventure. It almost made him forget that he was trying to rescue his father. For good luck he patted the bulge in his coat pocket made by his bap's pipe.

"Good luck, Charlie," Heaven-Bound Bob said.

"Good luck," the others echoed.

Charlie handed his hat to Grim and slipped into the water.

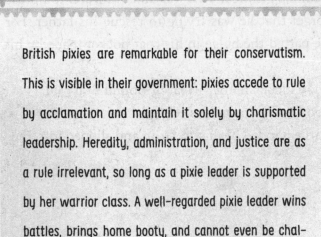

British pixies are remarkable for their conservatism. This is visible in their government: pixies accede to rule by acclamation and maintain it solely by charismatic leadership. Heredity, administration, and justice are as a rule irrelevant, so long as a pixie leader is supported by her warrior class. A well-regarded pixie leader wins battles, brings home booty, and cannot even be challenged to single combat unless the challenger has sufficient heroic status in her own right.

—Smythson, *Almanack*, "Pixie"

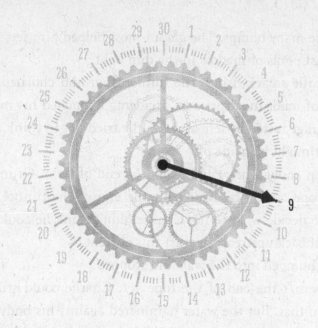

The water was cold. Charlie ducked under the surface and let the current suck him into the tunnel.

At first he closed his eyes. He immediately crashed against the sides of the tunnel, so he opened them again. He could more or less make out his surroundings. The gloom-moss grew down in the tunnel, too, even underwater. It looked different, more like a shapeless see-through sack with a light burning inside. And the light . . . the gloom-moss whizzed by his face too fast to be sure, but he thought the flames were shaped like tiny, dancing people.

He went headfirst. The rope slowed him down, but not very much. The tunnel was rough, and he pushed his hands out in front of him so he could keep his head from banging into the many bumps. The gloom-moss helped him see, but it also cast pools of shadow in the dim light.

Charlie smacked into the tunnel floor and churned up a cloud of mud. In surprise he accidentally opened his mouth. The sludge tasted rotten, and Charlie tried not to think about what it might be made of.

Soon enough he would reach the end of Grim Grumblesson's rope, and if he hadn't hit the end of the tunnel, he'd have to decide what to do. Charlie didn't think he could pull himself back upstream against this current.

He bumped into the wall and stopped.

It wasn't the end of the rope yet; Charlie could still feel slack in that. But the water hammered against his body, pinning him to the stone, and Charlie couldn't tell where the current went. He groped around with his hands but failed to find the way forward. He peered through the dark water too, but it was dirtied with silt now.

He wondered whether he should have been counting as he went. He knew he could hold his breath to at least a slow count of three hundred. Had swallowing all that mud squeezed out some of the air?

Charlie flailed with his hands and feet, banging against stone.

The water had to go somewhere, though. Charlie forced himself to be calm; then he held his hands out, felt where the current dragged them. He tried to follow the water, twisting his body to get into what looked like a tight corner, and the current pulled him through.

He plunged, straight down, and then suddenly leveled out again.

He careened off another tunnel wall, and cracked the back of his head against the stone. It hurt, and Charlie clapped one hand on the injured spot—

and then the rope caught on something.

The loop jerked at Charlie's waist and held him still.

The flow of water rushing around him felt very strong and sounded very loud. Charlie tried to look back to see what had happened, but the water battered him in the face and he couldn't see anything.

Three times for trouble, Grim Grumblesson had said. Charlie wrapped his fingers around the rope and gave it three hard pulls.

He waited.

Nothing.

He must be getting close to three hundred by now. He felt banged up and frightened, and of course he wouldn't be able to hold his breath forever.

He pulled on the rope three times again.

It wasn't just himself he worried about. Charlie didn't know what the Sinister Man wanted from his bap, but it must be something terrible. And if Charlie couldn't get out, what would become of his friends?

He pulled three more times.

Nothing happened.

He thought he felt something slither across his leg.

Charlie had to do something. He couldn't think of a better plan, and he knew he was running out of time.

He untied the knot.

The current rushed him away.

Charlie tumbled down the tunnel with his hands covering his face, scraping and banging against all the walls. His shoulder plowed through a patch of gloom-moss and knocked free several of the glowing sacks. They rushed with him down the tunnel. Charlie hoped that he hadn't just made the last and worst mistake of his life.

Another turn, and this time he collided with the tunnel wall with the full force of the water.

He whooshed off again instantly. How long had he been underwater now? A slow count of four hundred, at least. What had Grim Grumblesson done when the rope had gone slack?

Thud, into the wall again, this time face-first. The current snapped him around at a terrible angle, and Charlie was sure for an instant that his neck would be broken. Then he was snatched away by the stream.

He hurt all over.

The tunnel opened, and he was hurled into open space.

Charlie fell. He saw dim yellow light around him.

"He-e-e-elp!" he shouted—

and went *splash!* Down on his belly into a pool of water. It stung. Charlie had seen his bap tenderize a piece of lamb by pounding it flat with a spiky hammer. He knew now how that lamb must have felt.

This pool was much bigger than the tunnel. Charlie thrashed with his arms and legs, trying to remember how boys managed to swim in books he had read. Whatever it was those boys did, Charlie didn't figure it out—he sank.

His feet touched bottom. There was gloom-moss in this

chamber too, including clumps floating on the surface of the water—the moss Charlie had dislodged with his shoulder. Charlie stopped kicking and looked around.

He stood at the bottom of a pool built of brick. The water was dark and cloudy, and it stank. He realized he was in the sewer, and then he had to try hard not to think about it anymore.

A ladder of iron rungs set into one wall climbed up out of the pool. Charlie took big bouncing steps over to the ladder and dragged himself out. The rungs were rusted and a couple of them were missing, but he managed to scramble over the gaps and throw himself onto the lip of the pool and lie there.

The air felt good on Charlie's face and in his mouth. He lay still and enjoyed it for a few moments before eventually opening his eyes.

He was at the bottom of a well. The shaft was circular, and built of red bricks. Spouts of water poured out of holes in the walls above him and splashed into the cistern below. He counted at least ten streams, and he realized immediately that he had no idea which one he'd come through. Water flowed out of the well in a calm river, and he also saw passages that came down to the well by brick stairs.

Charlie was totally turned around. He had no idea which way to go to get back to the cell and his friends.

First things first. Charlie stood. He hurt, but he could still move, and he scooted along the lip until he could get under some falling water that didn't look brown. It wasn't a bath, exactly, but he felt much better after he had stood in the spray a while and was more or less clean. He inspected himself while he was at it; he was still wearing his jacket and shoes, but his cravat was gone, along with several buttons of his shirt.

He heard noises.

Footsteps. Scratchy, shuffling footsteps. And a soft chittering sound.

Charlie dropped to his bottom and slithered back into the pool. The water was soupy and dark, but he let himself go under.

He would wait out the new arrival.

Charlie kept his eyes open and looked up. Silhouettes arrived at the end of the cistern. They looked like hunchbacks, with big legs like he'd seen on pictures of Australian kangaroos. There were three of them, and the chittering sound definitely came from them. They turned and shuffled along the lip, shimmering and slipping in Charlie's watery brown vision.

Charlie turned slowly in place so he could watch the silhouettes. They didn't move like people. They humped along leaning forward, and sometimes touched hands or knuckles to the ground. Once or twice Charlie thought he made out the flicker of a swishing tail behind them.

Also, the three creatures were carrying something in their hands. Maybe buckets.

They stopped, exactly in the spot where Charlie had stood to clean himself off in the falling water.

They stood and held the things in their hands over their heads.

Charlie shifted his position a little bit and squinted. They *were* buckets.

The people—or maybe *things,* because when they squatted and held the buckets over their heads they looked even less human than before—filled their buckets with water. Very quickly, long before anyone would have reached a slow count of three hundred, they finished.

Charlie waited until the intruders had turned and were going back up the way they'd come, and then he climbed out of the water again. He slipped to the steps and listened.

He heard chittering and shuffling and whimpering and the occasional sniff.

Charlie risked a peek around the corner and saw the backs of the three figures just as they disappeared up the stairs. They were covered with patchy gray fur; they waddled; their big ears and twitchy noses shifted from side to side. They snuffled and they squeaked, and long tails dangled behind them.

They were rats.

Really big rats. Two feet tall, or maybe taller. The size of pixies.

Charlie thought that rats had a good sense of smell, and he wondered why they hadn't detected him. It must be because of all the water. There was the stink of the sewer to mask everything, and Charlie had washed himself off in the clean stream.

The rats and their buckets disappeared out of sight, and Charlie was left wondering what to do.

He only wondered for a moment. Then he started climbing the stairs, up, toward the surface. Up, to where his friends lay in prison.

Up, on the heels of the rats.

Although the sewers of London attract their fair share of overimaginative and unsubstantiated stories (see, e.g., "Rat"), it remains true that the brick labyrinth beneath our capital is a dangerous place, full of potentially deadly encounters for the unwary (see, e.g., "Ghoul," "Will-o'-the-Wisp," "Shaitan," and "Corpse Candle").

—Smythson, *Almanack*, "Sewers"

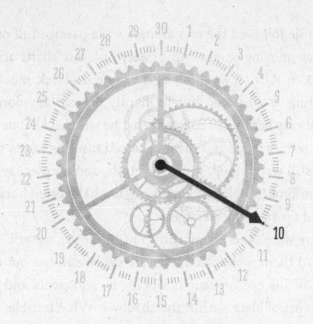

Not all the passages were well lit. Some were very gloomy indeed, with only the occasional patch of glowing moss to show Charlie where to put his feet. More rarely, a shaft of light pierced the darkness from above. Charlie squinted up these brilliant lightning bolts and wondered how far belowground he really was, but he had no way to tell, and he had to keep moving or lose the rats.

Charlie wasn't sneaky by nature, but at night in Pondicherry's Clockwork Invention & Repair he had to keep the noise down so his bap could work. He was used to stepping softly, toes first, and not bumping into things. Here in the sewers, where there was no wood to creak underfoot and betray him, it was even easier.

Charlie followed the rats along a wide passage full of clotted, slow-moving sludge, up a steep, narrow shaft, across a wide room. All of it was built of the same red brick, moldy and crumbling. It all stank, but he hardly noticed anymore. His path quickly became so complex that he worried he'd never be able to retrace it. He and the rats passed running water, falling water, still water, mud, muck, rubbish, and corpses, as small as storm-broken starlings and as big as a half-rotten horse that jammed up an entire passage.

There were other living things in the sewer, as well. Charlie heard them more often than he saw them, but out of the corner of his eye he caught ripples in still pools and shifting patches of black within the shadows. What terrible, blind, stinking things could live down in this choking stench? Charlie shuddered.

He began to see other rats. They crossed his path, sometimes ahead of him and sometimes behind. He was in a city of rats, on a rodent highway. The rats moved in the same direction, and many of them carried things. At first he tried to squint and get a closer look, but when he saw that one held a hunk of mold-crusted meat, he decided he'd rather not know.

Being sneaky seemed almost not to matter. More than once he stood within a few feet of a rat, right in front of its face and lit up clearly by the glow of gloom-moss. The rats did nothing. The rats didn't even sniff at him, just clicked their big yellow front teeth and kept going on their way. He understood why they might not *see* him; he had read that rats had very poor eyesight. He was being as quiet as he possibly could, so he thought he knew why they couldn't *hear* him too. But why couldn't the rats *smell* him?

Charlie hugged the darkness and moved on tiptoe. Should he walk away from the direction in which the rats were headed? After all, the rats were the pixies' enemies, and they couldn't possibly be his friends.

But if he walked away from the rats, into the darkness, he had no way to get himself out of the maze. He considered the possibility of just jumping into the next big stream of water he crossed and letting it carry him out to sea, but there was no guarantee that it would work. He might end up trapped against iron bars deep underground. Or he could be crushed and battered to death. Or he could simply be stuck underwater long enough to finally drown. Or maybe something dark and nasty in the water would eat him, or maybe he'd end up breakfast for a ghoul.

Clang-ng-ng!

Charlie jumped at the sound, and the rats around him went crazy. They shrieked, jumping over each other and pawing at their ears. Charlie pressed his back against the bricks and waited while they calmed down.

It must be their big ears. The rats had sensitive hearing.

Eventually the rats continued on their path. Charlie continued with them.

At least if he followed the rats, he was going *somewhere*. He was going where *they* were going. Wherever that was. And if it was true that the rats were always attacking Underthames, shouldn't he eventually be able to follow the rats back to the pixie home?

The rats ahead of him scampered up a ladder and disappeared through a hole in the ceiling. Through the opening Charlie saw a grayish light that wasn't gloom-moss glow. He felt a small thrill of excitement at the thought that he might be almost at the surface, and he poked his head through.

"Loki's spats!" he gasped. Using Grim's curse made him feel bigger than he really was, which he needed.

Because he was looking into a big room, swarming with rats.

It was like a great hall that had been carved out of a rubbish heap. Thin lines of gray light showed that the ceiling was made of boards. He must be out of the sewers and in the cellar of a building, maybe a warehouse or a dance hall. The walls were still brick, and they were nearly hidden by piles of junk. Charlie saw broken boards with nails sticking out of them, shattered crates, piles of dirt-encrusted pipes, stacks of withered newspaper, and rusted-out machine carcasses. Water dripped from the beams overhead and trickled down the walls like the sweat on his bap's face when he was concentrating.

He climbed into the hall, watching his surroundings. The near end of the chamber was littered with heaps of things. Charlie saw *his* rats set their buckets down among the stacks and continue on. There were other buckets and pipe ends and broken pots full of water. There were heaps of fruit, the rotten and the moldy and the good all piled together. There was a mound of something that Charlie identified as meat, and he turned his head away. Rats continued to deposit things in the piles and creep past Charlie.

He was standing at the refreshments table. Of a meeting of rats.

Charlie picked up a short piece of heavy pipe for a weapon. Then he looked for a hiding place.

He found room enough to crouch inside the big husk of a furnace. All the gauges and doors had been stripped off, and the furnace sat rusting and empty. For once Charlie was happy to be on the small side for a boy.

The rats chittered and scratched in a teeming knot of fur and tails. He had followed the rats hoping to get somewhere, and where he had ended up was a place with a lot more rats.

He might have made a serious mistake.

But if he could just find a way to sneak out past the rats, up to where the light was coming from, he'd be aboveground and back in Whitechapel. He still had clues to follow up on. He didn't need Grim Grumblesson's help to interview tobacconists, or to find the Anti-Human League, or to look for a Cavendish hat.

He stopped himself.

No, he needed to rescue his friends.

He was about to creep out of his furnace shell and back down the ladder to retrace his steps when he heard a voice. "My brothers, welcome!"

The voice was scratchy and squeaky. Charlie peeked out.

The rats sat on their haunches in twitching rows, each with its nose in the air and snuffling frantically. Something exciting must be happening. Beyond the rats, in front of them, was a platform built of wooden crates.

On top of the platform stood a gray rat. It was taller than the rest and had long, ugly scars streaking down its face. Both its eyes were milky white, and one was ruined by a scar that cut down from its forehead and continued onto its neck and belly. The scarred gray rat stood with its back straight, looking more like a little furry man than an animal. It wore a bit of twisted wire about the crown of its head, and it held a long sharp stick in its paws.

It was the rat on the platform that had spoken.

"My brothers," it squeaked again. "Thank you for coming!"

The rats chittered. Charlie hunched his shoulders to try to cover his ears. The echoes in the hall were deafening.

Charlie was stunned not just by the noise, but by the words. He wondered if all of Whitechapel's rats spoke English. And then he wondered why they would bother—why would a rat speak to other rats in English, when it could speak to them perfectly well in Rat?

Maybe there was no such language as Rat.

"You all know *me*," the scarred rat hissed. "And you know how much I love our friends the *bugs*."

A very loud chittering burst from the crowd. It sounded a lot like laughter. Dust sifted down from the ceiling, shaken free by the noise.

"Today we have a special guest," the rat continued. "My favorite bug—my *very* favorite *fairy*, that is—has come to visit. She has a few words to share with us."

The scarred rat scraped backward out of the way, making room for someone else to join him on the platform. That second person flew up in a snap of bright butterfly wings.

It was Elisabel de Minimis, the Baroness of Underthames.

Charlie tried very hard to hold still. Gnat had told him that pixies saw perfectly even in complete darkness, and Elisabel was looking more or less directly in Charlie's direction. If she recognized Charlie and shouted a warning, the rats would finish him off in seconds.

"Thank you, Scabies," Elisabel said. She was gracious and calm, even though she was surrounded by rats. This was why the scarred rat was speaking in English. Rats must not speak Pixie, and pixies must not speak Rat, so they spoke to each other in the language of the uplanders. *In English,* he corrected himself. "And thank *you all,* too, my handsome sisters and brothers," she added, speaking to the crowd.

The rats hunched and trembled.

"You've done everything I asked," Elisabel went on, "and I thank you."

Murmurs.

"Mind you, I've let you kill some people you'd been wanting to kill for a good long time." Elisabel said this like it was a funny joke. Charlie remembered Seamus saying that when the rats had attacked Underthames, they had killed the old baroness. Elisabel must be talking about her own aunt's death. Charlie was a little sick to his stomach.

Chittering. It sounded like approval.

"Now, I've got to ask you to be patient for a wee bit yet.

For a while, Scabies'll lead you against my people, and there'll be fighting, and it may get to feeling like you're not making the progress you expected. I've come today as a sign of good faith, and to warn you that's how it'll go. I don't want you to be surprised."

The scarred rat, the one Elisabel had called Scabies, nodded and snarled. The other rats fidgeted, scratching the ground and each other. Charlie felt like Elisabel was building up to something.

"On the other hand, my fine furry brothers, I also don't want you to be bored." Elisabel de Minimis raised one hand and waved.

Rats at the back rushed to a wall and dragged several wide boards out of the way. Behind the wood there was a ragged hole in the crumbling brick, and out of the hole advanced several ranks of pixies, four at a time, with spears in their hands.

A great shriek rose from the throng. "Wait!" Scabies barked. "Shut up and wait, all of you!"

The rat hubbub calmed down, but the rats still hissed and hopped from one foot to the other and shook their claws. They looked and sounded like water skittering around on a hot frying pan.

The pixies moved forward, spears raised. More pixies followed, some with spears and some holding the ends of fine chains. Charlie realized that the troop was leading prisoners of some kind. This might be his chance to escape. The rats were distracted. He looked at the distance separating him from the ladder down into the sewer and got ready to run.

The first of the prisoners came into view—

It was Heaven-Bound Bob.

Charlie's chimney-sweep aeronaut friend had chains around his neck and hands, and he stumbled, pulled along by the pixies as he walked.

Behind him came Ollie, Mr. Clockswain, Grim (hunched over to fit beneath the ceiling), and finally Natalie de Minimis.

"You see?" Elisabel smiled at the crowd. "I've brought you a little gift. I do hope you're hungry."

Generally speaking, shape-changers can assume one particular nonhuman form, or a limited range of such forms. Oral tradition, to be treated with some skepticism, suggests that some individuals may possess the power to assume multiple shapes.

—Smythson, *Almanack,* "Loup-Garou"

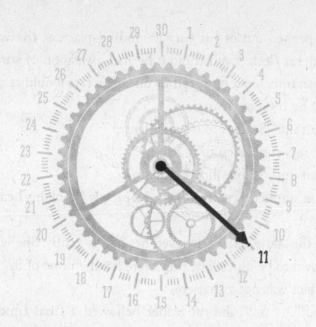

The rats went berserk.

They slipped over and under each other; they scratched; they barked like dogs and yowled like cats. Grim Grumblesson balled his fists and hunched even lower as he walked. Charlie's other friends stuck close to the big hulder. Ollie and Mr. Clockswain looked worried; Bob looked defiant; Gnat looked angry. The pixie spearmen held their trembling spears ready, but the rats held their position.

Charlie tightened his grip on his metal pipe.

The room spun about him. He'd been hit more than a few times in his life, by Mickey and Skip and the Bruiser, but he'd never hit back, not unless you counted throwing dirty laundry. He wasn't a fighter. Bap didn't want him to fight.

He peeped out of his furnace hiding place at the wall of howling rat flesh. Even though he had a weapon of sorts, he was outnumbered a hundred to one. The rats would tear him apart if he tried anything.

"Shut up!" Scabies roared. "Silence!"

The rats continued to rage.

"Shut up!" Scabies howled again.

Grim stared down at the rats. He slowly shook his head and then spat.

On the stand, Elisabel waved her hands gently. She wanted the crowd to be quiet, but they were having none of it.

Scabies was not as patient.

"Shut . . . up!" the rat leader bellowed a final time, and shoved his spear through the nearest rat.

The sudden spurt of blood and the death squeak of the impaled rat hushed the room. The rats weren't calm, Charlie saw. Their eyes bulged, and some of them foamed at the muzzle.

They were on the brink of madness, and only fear held them back.

The pixies were on the edge too. Charlie could see their hands shaking.

"That's better." Scabies sniffed, and jerked his spear out of the dead rat.

Everyone was silent and still, and everyone was also ready to jump.

This was Charlie's moment. He raised the pipe over his head and slammed it against the wall of the furnace.

Bong!

The mound of rats erupted like a volcano, spewing at the pixies. The pixies yelled and charged the rats. Spears and teeth flashed. Charlie's own head nearly burst. The ringing of the furnace was immense inside the hall, but it was loudest of all for Charlie, who was standing inside the furnace itself.

"No!" Scabies hollered.

Charlie struck again.

Bong-ng-ng!

"De Minimis!" he heard Gnat shout. "De Minimis and Underthames!" The words sounded far away, and in between him and the voice was a vast gulf full of crying seabirds and crashing thunder.

Bong!

Charlie struck a third time. His head spun. Trying not to lose his grip on the pipe, he staggered out of the furnace.

Chaos.

Pixies and rats stabbed and bit each other in a frenzy of blood. Scabies and Elisabel de Minimis shouted at their followers, but Charlie couldn't hear them anymore. The noise was too loud, or his ears were ringing too much; he couldn't tell the difference.

Grim Grumblesson charged. His pixie keepers fell away, turning to fight against the rampaging rats. With a single yank, Grim ripped from their grasp the chains that held him. As Charlie watched, he wound them around his hands like big silver knuckle-dusters, and then he laid about him with fists the size of hams. Each blow pounded a rat flat into the ground or threw a pixie across the hall.

Suddenly Charlie's friends were free and moving.

Gnat fought at Grim's back with a spear, and Ollie and Bob fought with sticks. Mr. Clockswain cringed in Grim's shadow. The hulder plowed through the battle with purpose in his eyes.

He was coming for Charlie.

Charlie waved and almost fell over. He was dizzy, but he wasn't afraid.

Three rats jumped on Grim from one side. He bellowed and snapped his arm, throwing two of them against the wall. He grabbed the third in his fist.

Three more rats rushed at Grim from the other side while he struggled. Gnat impaled one with her spear through its chest and then flipped through the air to kick a second in its teeth. With her red-and-gold skirt and green wings flashing in the dim light, she looked like a kite out of control.

Ollie kicked the third rat away and hit it with his stick until it ran.

"Everything all right, mate?" Bob yelled.

Charlie nodded and smiled to show he was fine. He almost fell over, and Bob steadied him. "I don't want to die," Charlie said. He meant to say it in a brave way, to show his friends that he was determined to live. He was embarrassed when it came out sounding frightened.

"Don't worry," Grim Grumblesson bellowed. He butted the squirming rat in his fist with both horns, then tossed the limp creature to the floor. "We're leaving now."

The hulder bent at the knees and looked up at the ceiling. Dust and speckled light sifted down through the boards just over his head.

"Rrraarraaagh!" Grim roared. He kicked up to his full height and punched both his fists through the ceiling.

Wood fragments and dust rained down around Charlie.

"You first!" Grim yelled. He tossed two more rats aside and grabbed Bob, then threw him up through the hole. The room above was light in a grayish, rainy sort of way.

"Stop them!" Charlie heard through the ringing of his ears. He looked across the surging tide of rats and saw Scabies and Elisabel de Minimis, both dodging fighters and headed his direction.

"And now you!" Grim bent and grabbed the kobold. Mr. Clockswain yelped but didn't resist, and Grim tossed him up through the ceiling too.

Gnat pulled her spear out of a rat and cast the crumpled furry body aside. She fluttered her wings and rose into the air to meet her cousin's charge.

"Here comes the boy!" the hulder yelled over his shoulder. He seized Charlie.

Charlie got a good close-up view of the dust and splinters in the troll's matted hair, and smelled Grim's sweaty-animal smell, and then the dark confusion of the basement hall disappeared.

He vaulted up into a new space and landed hard, but on his feet. He staggered a few steps to one side, and then Bob and Henry Clockswain caught him.

"Easy, Charlie," Bob murmured.

The noise below still rioted in Charlie's ears. Without warning, Ollie the Snake hurtled up through the hole. "Aaagh!" He hit the floor hard and rolled.

Charlie tried to look around, but Bob was already dragging

him away. They were in another big room, this one with a high ceiling and tall windows. The light through the windows was pale, and outside, Charlie heard the thump of rain. Long wooden benches filled most of the room. At one end the floor was raised and there was a lectern. Behind the lectern there was a piano, and on the wall a large, plain cross.

It must be a church.

"Come on, Ollie!" Bob called. "Catch up!" Charlie's hearing was still deadened, but his vision had almost stopped spinning. Bob dragged him toward the back of the church, where Charlie could see big wooden doors out to the street on the right-hand side and a staircase on the left.

Stairs that went up and also stairs that went down.

"I was helping!" Charlie yelled, but Bob kept dragging him. "I hit the furnace! I could have helped more! I could have bit someone!"

"You still can," Bob said, and he stopped suddenly. "You might 'ave to."

Charlie looked where Bob was looking and saw what Bob saw.

Rats.

Rats spilling up the stairs and onto this floor. Lots of them. They were between him and the door.

"Windows!" Henry Clockswain yelled. "Quick!"

Bob was fast, but Ollie was faster. He sprinted to the wall, where a dark wooden cabinet stood under the windows. The bottom of the windows was seven or eight feet off the floor, but if the boys could get on top of the cabinet, they could get at the glass.

Ollie squatted and made a stirrup with his hands. "Go, Charlie!" he shouted. When Charlie put his foot into Ollie's hands, the other boy grunted. He almost slipped, but then managed to hoist Charlie up. He landed at the same time as the kobold, thrown by Heaven-Bound Bob. A cloud of dust erupted around them, and Mr. Clockswain sneezed.

The rats rushed their way, shrieking.

Charlie looked down at his chimney-sweep friends. Ollie crouched. "Off my back, Bob!"

Bob took two running steps and planted his foot on Ollie's shoulders. He jumped, and the other boy stood at the same time, and Bob sprang through the air and landed on top of the cabinet.

Creak! The cabinet shifted unnervingly but Bob didn't stop. He let his momentum carry him forward; he raised his arms to cover his face with his elbows—and crashed through a window, out into the rain and onto the street.

"What about Ollie?" Charlie yelled, and he looked down again.

Ollie was gone.

In his place there was a long, yellowish snake, coiled and rearing. A hood of scaly skin flared out to either side of its head, with dark dots on it. Charlie recognized it as a cobra. His father had told him stories about cobras in the Punjab. Cobras were very dangerous.

The rats recognized it too. They bounced to a stop, howling and baffled. The cobra snapped at them, scaring them back, but didn't bite.

Charlie thought he smelled the sweet stink of rotten eggs.

"Go!" Henry Clockswain yelled. He didn't sound fussy at all. He pushed Charlie through the window.

Bob helped his landing with both hands, steadying him so he kept his feet. A moment later the kobold plunked to earth beside them. The rain beat down on them heavily. His ears still rang. They stood on a cobbled street. Charlie saw the church, and something big and foul-smelling that might have been a tannery, and a pub. The street wasn't crowded, but the faces he did see looked startled.

Bob started pulling him quickly away from the building.

"The others!" Charlie objected. He looked back at the shattered window he'd jumped from.

"We can't help them!" Henry Clockswain cried.

"Ollie'll be right along," Bob said. "An' there's nothing we can do for the rest."

Even as Bob spoke, Ollie appeared in the window. He hit the ground running and sprinted after them.

"Ollie!" Charlie shouted. Bob pulled him faster.

"Run!" Ollie shouted back.

Behind him the big wooden doors exploded. Splinters and dust blew out in a cloud, and Grim Grumblesson punched through like a runaway train. He was covered in rats. He ran, batting them away with his fists. When one leaped from his thigh to his chest, snapping with its teeth at his throat, Grim snatched it and squashed it flat against the redbrick side of a building.

The people on the street who had been staring at Charlie screamed and ran.

Behind and above Grim flew Gnat. She was still holding on to her spear, but only barely. There was blood on her dress, and one of her wings beat more slowly than the other. Still, she flew, and she pried rats by their tails off the hulder and tossed them into the street.

More rats, a wave of them, rushed up to the empty door—but there they stopped. They gnashed their big teeth, they shrieked and howled, but they didn't follow their prey outside.

Tired and beaten and bloody, Charlie and his friends ran through the cooling rain. They were much the worse for wear, but they were free.

The Fellows of the Royal Society of London for Improving Arcane Knowledge, commonly known as the Royal Magical Society, is Britain's premier association of learned magical practitioners. The society, often abbreviated the RMS, was founded in the days immediately following the Great Fire of September 1666. Although minutes of the organizing meeting are not publicly available, it is generally believed that the founding impulse of what was originally called simply the Fellows of the Arcane Society of London was the belief that unskilled spell casting had been responsible for the fire, and a desire to limit or license the use of magic in Great Britain.

—Smythson, *Almanack*, "Royal Magical Society"

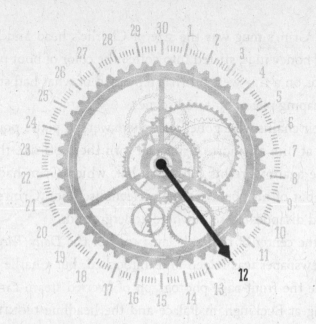

"Didn't go quite like I expected," Grim Grumblesson observed.

"Ouch." Gnat tried to straighten her left wing, and couldn't do it.

"Broken?" Ollie asked.

"Sprained a flying muscle in my back," the pixie said. "I expect it'll still work, more or less, but it hurts like Mab's own blisters."

They sat in the Port Royal Coffeehouse, all dark wood and smoke-greased glass. Outside hung a signboard with the portrait of a privateer. Charlie recognized him from his twirled mustachios, second chin, and bulging eyes as the famous Henry Morgan. Inside, china teacups and old belt buckles hung from hooks set into the ceiling beams and high on the walls. Charlie sipped a hot cocoa; his friends had tea or coffee. Grim's mug was the size of Charlie's head and had a pint of honey in it, stirred into coffee the color of boot polish. Crumbs on a tray were all that remained of what had started as a heaping pile of buttered scones.

Their chains were gone; once there weren't pixies pointing spears at him anymore, Grim had torn them off like thread. Charlie again wore his John Bull hat, which Grim had produced out of his pocket at the coffeehouse door. Grim's own hat had disappeared somewhere underground.

In the center of the table lay a copy of the *Daily Telegraph*. The newspaper was folded and untouched, but Charlie could still see the front-page photograph of liveried steam-carriages arriving at Buckingham Palace and the headline DIGNITARIES ARRIVE FOR THE GARDEN PARTY. A column below the main story and to the right was headed TENSIONS MOUNT OVER CUBA, BOERS.

When he wasn't actually drinking, Charlie left his mug resting on a brass disk sunk into the wood of the table in front of them. Though the wood was cool to the touch, the plate was hot.

Bob nudged Charlie in the shoulder and pointed at the brass plate. "'Ot water," he said. "Pipes 'idden inside the table, I reckon."

"Could be a spell," said Ollie.

"Bah." Bob shook his head. "Isambard Brunel, I reckon. That bloke made all the best things."

Charlie tried not to stare at Ollie the Snake. Charlie found that he felt strangely envious. The chimney sweep had a special talent, and he had secrets. Ollie caught Charlie not staring and gave him a hard look back that seemed to say *don't tell*.

Charlie nodded and sipped his chocolate.

Ollie's look softened, and he squeezed Charlie's hand as he leaned in to whisper. "Thanks, mate. I thought I was rat food there for a minute."

"Charlie," Grim said, "I'm sorry."

Charlie remembered the troll hurling him up out of the rats' lair to save his life. "What for?"

"For the delay," the troll explained. "I thought our trip to Underthames would be a short one, and that we'd soon be out and on the trail of your father's kidnappers."

Charlie nodded. "I know you didn't expect to get captured . . . and the rats."

"True." Grim's voice was a solemn rumble. "But I regret it."

"So let's get to work," Ollie said. "Time to help my mate Charlie."

Bob slapped Charlie on the shoulder, and Henry Clockswain nodded.

"Right," Grim Grumblesson said. "Let's see this handbill you were talking about."

Charlie brought out the broadsheet and unfolded it on the table. It had survived his underwater journey, but the ink was running and barely readable.

⥲ !!! A warning to the SONS of APES !!! ⥲

You have *trodden* upon the Elder Folk of this Island *long enough!!* Today we *remove* your Queen, like a *Louse*—easily and in clean conscience—Tomorrow, we will *remove* you too, and *squash* you in our *invisible* fingers!!

⥲ !!! FEAR the Anti-Human League and OBEY !!! ⥲

"Hmm," the kobold said, smoothing the paper over and over with his long fingers. "Er . . . not very impressive, is it?"

"'As something 'appened to the queen?" Bob asked.

"Not unless it happened while we were underground," Grim answered. Outside the Port Royal, the rain was ushering in a dark evening. "Nothing we can do about it. Stay focused on the client."

"Charlie's dad," Ollie clarified.

"Mr. Raj Pondicherry, alias Dr. Singh." Grim turned the broadsheet over, looking at one side and then the other. "Bad print job," he pronounced. "Amateurs. I've never heard of any Anti-Human League."

"Nor I," Gnat agreed.

"I haven't either," Henry Clockswain added. "They sound like complete nutters to me."

"Nor have I heard of the Iron Cog. We'll follow up on all those leads tomorrow, when we can get into a library, or maybe a bookshop." Grim scratched his rough chin. "Tobacconists will all be shut now too."

"Do we 'ave to wait until tomorrow?" Bob asked. "What about the 'ats? Cavendish, innit?"

"Anxious, are you?" Gnat teased the chimney sweep with a grin.

"I'm worried about Mr. Pondicherry's safety," Bob said. Then he added, a little embarrassed-looking, "an' the Jubilee aeronautical is the day after tomorrow."

"Yes," Grim agreed.

"Aren't there hulder police that can help us?" Charlie asked. "Lawspeakers?"

"I *am* a lawspeaker," Grim snorted.

"I know," Charlie said. "I mean . . . more lawspeakers."

Grim shook his head. "If we need more help, I can raise the hue and cry. That means I declare an emergency, and I make a deputy out of any troll we can find. Or another hulder could do it on my authority, as long as I bless it afterward."

"Better check to make sure your deputies ain't smokers first," Ollie said, a little sourly.

"'Tis Cavendish hats for tonight, then," Gnat pronounced. "To see if they've a connection with the Anti-Human League, or the Iron Cog."

"Kidnappers!" Charlie spat out the word like a curse.

"What do we do, just ask these 'atmakers if they're 'atching an evil plot?" Bob asked.

"Cavendish will likely be closed for the evening," Grim said. "So we're going to break in."

"We'll want weapons." Ollie scratched his belly. "Just in case. And Gnat's pixie friends took my knife."

"I saw a velocipede shop across the street," Grim said. "It may still be open."

Henry Clockswain scrambled to his feet and dug into his trousers pocket. "Let me, er, pay for the drinks. You know, to say thanks. I'll be right behind you."

The velocipede shop owner was a stout man with a walrus-like mustache, standing on the doorstep to lock up. When Grim opened his enormous wallet and started producing five-pound notes, he changed his mind.

"What interests you this evening?" he asked, sliding behind the counter. Velocipede wheels and pumps hung on the wall behind him, along with other ironmongery. Inside the glass counter lay rows of weapons. Charlie had never been inside a velocipede shop before, and he knew they carried a wide range of tools, but he was still a bit surprised to see so much fighting gear. There were knuckle-dusters and billy clubs and guns and knives, and things that he didn't recognize but that looked fierce and cruel. "We have the latest velocipede models." He waved stubby fingers at a velocipede in the corner, which had an enormous front wheel and a tiny back one. Charlie moved to look at the velocipede, but Grim stepped in front of him.

"Guns," Grim said. "Something big for me, and something smaller. For a kobold. And powder, shot, and caps. And something suitable for the lads and the pixie." He gestured at the walls, and Bob and Ollie set about examining clubs and knuckle-dusters. "Do you have a good clasp knife for the boy?"

"I only get a clasp knife?" Charlie demanded. "I'm not a baby." It was his quick thinking that had saved all the others when they were in chains in the church basement. A clasp knife wasn't even a weapon; it was for whittling.

"You're not a baby," Grim grunted, "but you're . . . young. Bob and Ollie are older."

"How do you know?" Charlie balled his fists.

Grim turned to the sweeps. "Boys, how old are you?"

"Fifteen," Bob said at once. "Orphaned since I was six an' on the street since I was nine."

Ollie shrugged. "Dunno. I ain't an orphan, as far as I know, but I ain't seen either of my parents in donkey's years, and they never told me."

Grim looked back to Charlie. "And you?"

"I don't know." Charlie looked at the floor. "My bap never told me."

Grim Grumblesson snorted. "Petition quashed. That means *no*, in lawyer speech. You get a knife, if there's a good one to be had. A decent knife is all a fellow really needs, anyway."

The shopkeeper did have a good knife for Charlie. It was a locking clasp knife, with a bone handle carved to look like a mermaid. Opening and closing it a few times made him feel grown-up. For Natalie de Minimis, the shopkeeper reached under the counter and produced something that made the pixie smile from ear to ear: a spear, Gnat-sized and iron-tipped. "We have occasional dealings with the folk of Under-thames," he explained with an air of pride about his twitching mustache.

Bob chose a sword. It was short and slightly curved, with a blade along only one edge. Charlie thought it looked Japanese, but it suited Bob anyway when he tied the scabbard to his belt. Ollie picked an umbrella.

"That's a surprising choice," Bob said.

Ollie hefted it. "It's heavy, mate. And the end is pointed. And besides, it feels . . . English."

Bob nodded his approval. Then the chimney sweeps spent several minutes swaggering around the shop, catching glimpses of themselves in mirrors.

Charlie watched with wide eyes as Grim sorted through a rack of guns, choosing a small pistol called a Bulldog for the kobold just as Henry Clockswain himself reappeared through the door. Then the shopkeeper passed Grim a hulder-sized firearm. The mustached man needed both hands to hold it up. "The Webley Eldjotun," the merchant beamed. " 'Fire Giant,' the name means. Six hundred caliber: not a beast in Britain it won't drop in a single shot."

"What about an elephant?" Charlie asked.

The shopkeeper chuckled. "Elephant's a beast in Britain, isn't it?"

"I'll take them all," Grim chortled, sighting down the enormous pistol at a red velocipede in the corner. Then he looked at Ollie's umbrella. "And accessories, and rain slickers."

While the shopkeeper wrote out a receipt, Grim loaded his pistol. Charlie watched, fascinated. The troll poured powder from a new powder horn into five of the six chambers of his pistol, then pressed in a neat round bullet. Next he flipped the gun over and tapped in five firing caps. Henry Clockswain did the same, though he dropped three bullets on the floor in the process, two of which rolled under the counter and disappeared.

"Hammer on the empty chamber," Grim admonished the kobold, showing him what he meant with his own giant pistol. "Accidentally goes off in your pocket, someone will get hurt. And keep the gun dry, or there's no point in having it."

The shopkeeper produced Grim's change and receipt and showed his last-minute customers into the evening rain.

Charlie and his companions all wore the new rain slickers: bulky coats made of oiled brown paper. The slickers smelled funny, but they kept the rain off with a soothing *thump-rat-*

a-tat-thump. Charlie tried to imagine a melody to go along with the drumming, or the words of one of his father's many stories.

They all walked, even Gnat. Her wings were folded neatly against her back under her tiny slicker, even smaller than Charlie's. To keep up with Grim's enormous steps, she ran.

Charlie followed the troll. He didn't know any of the buildings they passed or the streets they crossed, and he could barely guess at even the nature of the places that whizzed by him.

He thought he heard rats. When he turned to look back at the chittering sounds, he seemed to see big rodents scampering to hide in every shadow. He told himself he was being silly. London was a big city, and a dirty one. No doubt there were a lot of rats, wherever you went.

They were getting closer to the river.

He knew at first because he saw more and more men who looked like sailors, with canvas trousers and tattoos and ribbons braided into their caps. Many of the buildings about him were public houses catering to the men of the sea: the Siren Sisters, the Calypso's Island, the Admiral Benbow. The muddy, fishy, oily stink that clogged his nostrils must be coming from the Thames.

"What is this place?" he murmured out loud.

"Wapping," Ollie said.

"'Old your breath," Bob added. "We all know you can."

"Shush," Grim Grumblesson growled. "We're here. Cavendish Hat Factory. And warehouse."

They stood in a cobbled street lined with tall wooden

buildings, its air thick with the smells of animals and coal. The street was wide, but not wide enough for its traffic; Charlie was surprised at how busy it was. Big wagons ground up and down the cobblestones, pulled by horses or llamas or buffalo or, in a few cases, puffing out smoke and steam and churning under their own power. They rubbed wheels with each other while their drivers cursed and wrestled for position. Men unloaded crates and barrels from the wagons into the tall buildings, or loaded barrels and crates back up in the other direction. Many yellow gaslights still burned in the street's windows, but at least half the buildings were dark.

Grim pointed to a warehouse that stood in the elbow of the street. Over its wide front doors hung a board with the image of a black top hat painted on it, worn by weather to mud gray.

"How did you know how to find this place?" Henry Clockswain asked.

Grim laughed. "When you've got a size-twelve head and need holes in the brim," he chuckled, "you have to go straight to the factory!" He rubbed his head as if remembering his own missing hat. "I also know all the shoemakers."

Gnat shouldered forward. "I'll just have a wee look, then," she volunteered. "We can't go in blind."

Grim scratched his head. "Brave lass, Natalie de Minimis," he acknowledged, "and I know you'll have three mighty deeds under your belt in no time at all. But you're hurt. We'll do without a scout this time and just all go in together. We're ready." He patted the bulge in the rain slicker where his hand-held cannon lurked at his belt.

"Nay, you can't forego a scout," Gnat insisted. "There may be an ambush." She looked angry.

Grim nodded slowly. "Or maybe not," he said. "Might just be an accident that broadsheet was printed on the back of a Cavendish advertisement."

"This might be nothing," Henry Clockswain agreed.

"Aye. Or it might be a trap." The pixie folded her arms across her chest.

"We'll go," Bob jumped in. "Ollie an' I will. We know roofs an' climbing; this'll be easy-peasy for us."

"We will?" Ollie asked, but Bob shot him a look that shut him up. "Yeah, we will."

"An' we'll take the boy along too," Bob added. "Come on, Charlie, come with us to 'ave a look-see. A *butcher's,* like they say where I come from."

Charlie jumped at the chance. He'd show Grim he was as brave as the other boys. "A butcher's?" he asked.

"Butcher's hook, look," Ollie explained.

"Will you hold my hat?" Charlie held his bap's John Bull out to Grim. He didn't think it would stay on his head long if climbing was involved.

Grim scratched his head, but he accepted the hat. "If you want to go, Charlie, you can. Just remember, boys, be careful."

Pseudopan cadavercenans (common names: ghoul, gallu)—Ghouls are an import to Britain from the eastern lands of the empire. They are to be found today in London, principally around the graveyards of the city, though reports indicate that they are increasingly a problem at slaughterhouses as well. Possibly due in part to the vicinity of the Smithfields butchery, St. Bartholomew's and other East End hospitals employ teams of ghoul wardens, who patrol nearby alleys and sewer openings with light, fire, and scattergun to prevent the abduction of patients.

—Smythson, *Almanack*, "Ghoul"

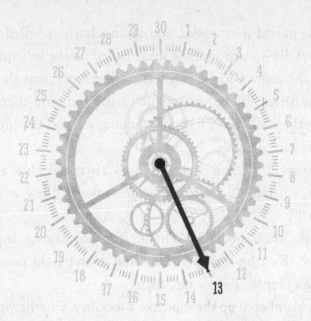

"You ever climbed anything, Charlie?" Bob asked. He looked up a lead drainpipe that snaked its way down the side of one of the warehouses, gushing gray water onto a pothole it had pounded into the cobblestones.

"No," Charlie admitted. The thrill of volunteering had passed, and he couldn't help noticing that the pipe went up the height of three stories. He patted the clasp knife in his pocket to reassure himself, which was ridiculous. He wasn't going to get into a knife fight with the pipe.

Ollie was muttering something under his breath and crossing his eyes.

"I've got a feeling you'll be a natural," Bob assured him. "Just keep your eyes on me an' do as I do. An' don't look at the ground."

Ollie puffed into smoke, and again Charlie smelled rotten eggs. In Ollie's place a yellow snake coiled on the wet stones. It wasn't the cobra Charlie had seen earlier, but it was the same color. It hissed, flicked its tongue in and out, and then slithered to the wall. With its body winding around the pipe, the snake began to climb.

"I knew it!" Charlie said. "That's amazing! He's a loup-garou . . . snake . . . He's a were-snake! Ollie's a shape-changer!"

"Yeah," Bob nodded. "Thanks for not saying anything about it. 'E's a bit sensitive, old Ollie. Don't want nobody to think 'e's French. Follow me, then."

Bob clambered up the pipe like a monkey. Charlie wrapped his own fingers around the lead and followed. Bob was right; climbing was easy. He followed Bob's instructions and kept his eyes pointed upward.

He didn't look down even when he heard chittering and scratching sounds in the alley below.

In no time at all he watched Ollie the Snake slither over the lip of the roof, followed by Bob. When Charlie arrived at the top, Bob and Ollie both reached down and pulled him up. Ollie was a boy again.

"I ain't French," Ollie said.

"I didn't say you were," Bob agreed affably. "It don't matter what your dad might 'ave been, anyway. You're as good a subject of 'Er Majesty as any Micklemuch ever born."

"Shut it," Ollie told his friend.

Charlie looked at Ollie.

Ollie stared back.

Charlie started slowly. "You think you might be French, because shape-changing is French magic."

Ollie spat. "Some people think that, but they're wrong."

Bob scooted close to Ollie on his other side. "Too right, mate."

"Yeah," Charlie agreed. "But what if they weren't? Would it be so bad, to not be English?"

As he spoke, Bob on the other side of Ollie waved his arms to try to make Charlie stop talking. When Charlie was finished, Bob held his breath; he looked like he was waiting for an explosion.

None came.

"It's like this," Ollie said. "You've got your dad, right?"

"Bap."

"Yeah. And the shop, and so on. And Bob's got family, or anyway he *had* family, when he was young, and he remembers them. Robert, and, uh . . ."

"Alice," Bob said.

"Alice." Ollie looked Charlie square in the eye. "And he's got his aeronaut schemes. Not me, mate. I've got nothing. The only thing I remember about my parents is them abandoning me. So I grew up without them, in St. Jerome's House for Wayward Youth by Gray's Inn. I grew up English, and a Londoner. Ain't nobody taking that away from me."

Charlie decided to change the subject. "What do we do now?"

All around them stretched a mountain range of peaked

rooftops, covered in shingles. The black tar and the gray lead of rain gutters and the shadowy canyons between the buildings mirrored the sky above, which was a sheet of dark mottled iron. Rain hammered down, *thump-rat-a-tat-thump,* and streamed off the shingles. Pigeons huddled under eaves and cooed their objections.

"We walk very careful," Ollie told him. "And we don't fall."

"I'll go first." Bob stood and led the way. Charlie followed, and Ollie came third.

They crossed the rooftop, then a second, then stopped on the flat peak of a third. "That's the Cavendish," Bob said, pointing. "Only there's a bit of an 'ole between us an' it."

The "hole" was another alley. It was narrow, only six feet across, but it would have to be jumped. On the other side the roof was steep and slippery.

"I can jump that." Charlie tried to sound confident.

"You know, I can see a spot on the back of your head where you got banged up," Ollie observed.

"Am I bleeding?" Charlie asked, and felt the back of his skull. There it was, a dent the size of his thumb. He didn't feel any blood, and there was no pain. It must be where he had hit his head in the underwater tunnel.

"We can fix it," Bob said calmly, "an' you ain't bleeding."

Bob jumped first, then Ollie. When they were sitting on the opposite roof, Ollie muttered something and *poof!* turned into a yellow snake again.

"Come on, Charlie!" Bob gestured at Charlie to jump.

Charlie stepped forward off the peak of the rooftop and

trotted down its steep side, picking up speed as he went. At the edge, he pushed off with one foot, sailed through the air, arms flailing—and crashed flat onto his belly on the shingles on the other side.

He smiled up at Bob, and Bob smiled back. "See?" Bob said. "Nothing to it. You're a natural-born chimney sweep, Charlie Pondicherry."

Then the shingles slipped loose, and Charlie slid into the abyss.

"Charlie!" Bob grabbed at Charlie's fingers but missed.

The rain gutter banged Charlie's knees and then his belly as he rattled over it. He grabbed at the lip of the roof—

missed—

fell—

looked down into the rushing darkness—

and was caught.

Something wrapped around Charlie's wrist and stopped him with a jerk. His arm felt like it might rip out of its socket, and he heard a groan of metal overhead, but he didn't fall.

Charlie looked up. Ollie, in snake form, was wrapped tightly around Charlie's forearm and also around the rain gutter. He was a strong snake, Charlie thought gratefully.

"'Urry up an' climb!" Bob hissed. Charlie couldn't see the other sweep. He couldn't see anything past the rain gutter but the stormy evening sky.

The gutter groaned again and bent. Charlie dropped six inches.

He climbed. Quickly Charlie got one hand and then the

other onto the straining rain gutter, and he hoisted himself onto the roof. Bob grabbed him by the shoulder and pulled him into an angle formed by a window gable.

Ollie the Snake slithered up to join them, and in a puff of stinking smoke he was himself again. "Ow!" He clutched his stomach.

"Thanks, Ollie," Charlie said.

"You're surprisingly heavy," Ollie complained.

Bob patted Charlie on the shoulder. "'E's just a good 'ealthy lad."

"Huh" was all Ollie said.

Bob scooted around the gable to the window. "Locked," he announced, after trying to pull it open. "Can I borrow your knife, Ollie?"

"I ain't got a knife anymore, remember?"

"Use mine," Charlie said. Bob opened the blade, slid it down between the two halves of the window, and quickly unlatched it.

"You'd think a businessman would be a little more careful with 'is place of business," the sweep commented. He gave Charlie back his knife with a wink, and the three boys climbed in.

The top floor of the factory was a storeroom. There were drums with the word OIL stamped on them and brass pipes and boxes of gears. There were stacks of lumber and metal rods. There were spare pistons and blades and pulleys and springs, all spilling out of open boxes.

Light came up from a stairway against one wall.

The boys stripped off their rain slickers and dropped them in a pile by the window.

"I don't see anything here." Charlie shrugged.

"What are we looking for?" Ollie asked.

Charlie shook his head. "Clues. I don't know. Anything about the Anti-Human League, or the Iron Cog, or my father."

"Or the Articulated Gyroscopes," Bob added. "Except first we 'ave to scout this place out, see if it's safe for the others to join us."

"What about 'Nobels Extradynamit'?" Ollie asked. He stood over a stack of short, stiff paper tubes in a dark corner of the attic room, squinting to read the labels pasted on them. "Hold on. 'Blasting powder,' it says?"

"I don't think they use blasting powder for making 'ats." Bob picked up one of the tubes and examined it. A short fuse was stuck into one end of the tube.

"Looks like a firework to me," Ollie said. "Or a bomb."

"Right." Bob pocketed it. "We'll just borrow one, to discuss it with the 'ulder. Anything else up 'ere, gents?"

There wasn't. They crept down the stairs.

The stairs brought the boys down to a small mezzanine floor and a series of catwalks inside the big main room of the factory. Dim light came from gas sconces in the walls and pillars on the factory floor, all turned down low. Street noise from outside—the rattle of wagon wheels on the cobbles, and the barking of warehouse men—echoed inside Cavendish Hats.

The main floor was divided into four parts. One part was

underneath their feet: a room separated by walls from the rest of the floor. Charlie wondered what could be inside until Bob pointed down and nodded wisely. "Office," he whispered, and Charlie nodded back. A second quarter of the floor was taken up by piles of hat components and a third by stacks of finished hats.

Between the components and the finished product squatted the machine. It looked like a giant brass insect skeleton with a hundred arms, each arm ending in some sort of tool used to assemble hats. A disturbingly large number of the arms ended in blades, but there were also pincers, chalk fingers, open pipe mouths, cloth buffers, blocks of pumice stone, steam jets, and things Charlie couldn't immediately identify. The long body of the insect wound back and forth across the room and was made of spinning wheels, flexing pistons, pumping bladders, and a central track of upright rods like a spinal column. When the machine was turned on, Charlie guessed, hats were assembled on rods at one end of the spine and then passed along, buffed and precision-cut and folded and shaped by the various tools as they went, until they ended in the stacks of finished headgear. The machine wasn't on, but the beast seemed to be only sleeping: from somewhere in the middle of the works a faint plume of steam curled up into the air.

"I don't see how that thing could use tubes of blasting powder," Ollie mused.

"Maybe it doesn't," Charlie murmured. "Maybe the powder is for a bomb."

Bob pulled Charlie to the floor. The chimney sweep put his delicate-fingered hand over Charlie's mouth and whispered in his ear. "'Ush, Charlie, we ain't alone."

Ollie lay down too. Charlie nodded, and then the three of them crawled to the edge of the mezzanine. Charlie poked his head up the tiniest bit so he could see down onto the floor below.

Bob pointed, and Charlie followed his finger.

He was right; they weren't alone.

Charlie now saw the big double doors that must be the front entrance, across the room by the finished hats. On either side stood men with naked cutlasses in their hands. Charlie quickly counted four, crouched in the shadows and behind hats.

One was the big man with the pouchy eyes, the one who'd been called captain. Charlie shuddered.

There were more men with cutlasses by a back door, and others by a window. They all hunkered down to hide from the view of anyone coming in by the front door.

"The pixie was right," Bob whispered, "it *is* an avocado."

"Do you mean an ambuscado, Bob?" Ollie asked.

"An ambush," Charlie offered.

"Yeah." Bob scratched his head. "But what 'ave the Cavendish people got against us? I don't even wear a Cavendish." He tugged on the chin straps of his aviator cap. "I wear a bomber. An' what 'ave they got against the queen?"

"Maybe that's the problem." Ollie snickered. "They're angry you and the queen of England ain't wearing their hats."

"Maybe Cavendish is owned by, I dunno, trolls or something. And they can't stand humans, so they formed the Anti-Human League, an' they're going to kidnap the queen."

Ollie pointed at the men around the door with his umbrella. "Only those are humans. The story don't seem right, does it?"

"Maybe it's me," Charlie guessed. "Maybe they were unhappy that I got away the first time, so they left the Cavendish Hats broadsheet to bring me here."

The other boys were silent for a moment. "That sounds less crazy the longer I think about it," Bob admitted. "Except it seems an unusual caper for an 'at manufacturer."

"Well, that's our clue, anyway," Ollie said. "The kidnappers have something to do with the hat people, and the hat people have a big pile of blasting powder and a gang of toughs with swords. Too dangerous to lie around here all night, old sons; let's get up top and get back. We've got to warn the others. Maybe Grim can round up a gang of hulders like he said, and we can come back in the morning."

Ollie backed away a few inches. Bob stayed put.

"I don't think I can wait until morning, Ollie," he complained. "I've run out of time. Day after tomorrow is the Jubilee an' the flotilla an' the display. I need the gyroscopes, an' I need 'em now."

"I know, Bob," Ollie agreed. He looked sadder and more sincere than Charlie had ever seen him. "Only I don't know what to do. Let's tell the troll anyway and see what he says."

Crack!

Charlie and the chimney sweeps fell flat to the floor again.

"I think that was the door," Ollie whispered.

Creak.

"Right." It was Grim Grumblesson's voice. "Told you the door was no problem, Clockswain. Now let's find out what happened to our boys."

"Ambush!" Bob yelled at the top of his lungs.

Kobold magic-users are also called *brownies* or *redcaps*.

They are said to specialize in chaos, bad luck, and curses.

The practice of brownie magic is illegal in Great Britain,

except by license issued jointly by the Royal Magical

Society and the Home Office. Fortunately, brownies are

extremely rare.

—Smythson, *Almanack*, "Kobold"

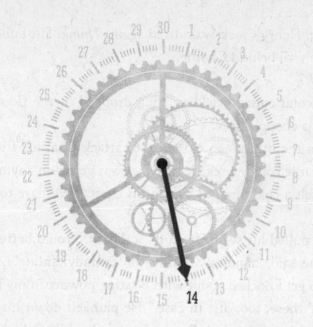

Bang!

Smoke curled up from the kobold's pistol.

Cutlasses flashed.

BANG!

Grim's Eldjotun roared like a lion. The nearest charging swordsman crumpled backward. Charlie's eyes opened wide, and he dropped lower to the floor.

"De Minimis and Underthames!" Gnat zipped to the attack. She shot up into the air, nearly straight, and then dropped like a hawk back into the battle. Even though she wobbled, she was very fast. Spearhead-first, she slammed onto the shoulders of the captain. He staggered sideways, swatting at Gnat and dropping his cutlass.

Bang! Henry Clockswain fired again. *Thunk!* His bullet bit into the wall behind Charlie.

BANG!

A second cutlass-wielding thug dropped to the floor. He fell like a chopped tree.

Then the other men closed in to attack Charlie's friends, and Charlie couldn't see clearly what was going on anymore.

He felt a cold lump of fear in his chest. "We have to help them!"

Bob pulled his sword from its scabbard. "You'd better 'old this," he said, handing Charlie the Extradynamit. "I don't want to get knocked about with blasting powder in my pockets. An' these, too, just in case." He plunked down his little wooden box of matches. But he hesitated, while Ollie hefted his umbrella like a club.

Bob and Ollie were just as afraid as he was. They were bigger than he was, probably older, and more experienced. They were chimney sweeps and burglars, a shape-changer and an aeronaut, but they were still boys.

The men standing at the factory's other entrances charged to join the fight. Grim ripped a curled sheet of metal off the hat machine. Slinging it over his arm like a shield, he turned to face his attackers.

BANG!

A window shattered, and the hat-making machinery let out a *gong!* as a bullet from the Eldjotun pounded a dent into one of its steam tanks. The attackers' swords flashed yellow-white in the gaslight. Grim swung his big gun like a club now, and scooped men away from him with his improvised shield.

Bang!

Mr. Clockswain fired again. Charlie wished that Henry Clockswain were a better shot, because as far as he could tell, the kobold hadn't hit anything. On the other hand, Charlie didn't *really* want to see any more people shot. He just wanted his friends to escape.

"Kill the troll!" one of the men shouted.

Five men rushed Grim Grumblesson. He swung with his gun and knocked one aside, then scooped his shield beneath a second and hurled the man straight up into the air.

"Aaaagh!" the flying man screamed, until he came down— *crash!* And flattened one of his friends.

The other two stabbed at Grim. Charlie saw red flowers of blood sprout on Grim's white shirt and turn the yellowish rain slicker into a greasy brown. Charlie felt ill.

BANG!

One of Grim's attackers dropped. Reinforcements swarmed him.

"Come on, Ollie!" Bob hissed. "It's now or never!" He jumped up and sprinted down the stairs.

Ollie followed Bob to the edge of the mezzanine, but there he took a different route. Stepping onto the railing, he hooked the curved handle of his umbrella over a cable that stretched at an angle from the ceiling down to the front doors. Leaning out over the fight, he slid down, faster and faster—the captain stood at the bottom of the stairs, with swords in both hands, grinning as Bob charged him—and at the last second Ollie raised both his feet and kicked the man right in his pouchy eyes.

The captain went down, and Bob and Ollie both charged into the fray.

Gnat dodged and dived and danced like a mad, wobbling ballerina. The men she fought staggered and bled, but they didn't give up. Then one of them caught Gnat with a big swing of his sword. It wasn't a direct hit, just the tip of the cutlass nicking the pixie, but Natalie de Minimis was little. The blow sent her spinning through the air.

"Gnat!" Grim bellowed, and he was stabbed again. He had lost enough blood to kill any human, but the troll was as big as a bull. He waded through the tide of his attackers, knocking aside cutlass blows to get to his fine-print clerk. He raised his big gun again, and a cutlass swipe knocked his aim wide—

BANG!

Grim's bullet blew a crater in one of the factory walls, shattering a gas sconce on the wall. All the lights in the room snuffed out. Pounding and grunting sounds told Charlie that the hulder was still fighting.

Charlie wanted to be as brave as the chimney sweeps, but all he had was a rotten little knife. It was one thing to crawl around in the sewers alone; that hadn't been so bad, really. Dirty and stinky and lonely, but no worse than that. And hitting the furnace with a length of pipe hadn't been any great act of heroism; it was just what had to be done.

It was another thing entirely to run straight into gunfire.

Charlie patted around on the floor and found the tube of blasting powder and the box of matches. He pushed open the box and drew a match out, to be ready. Just in case, Bob had said.

Chaos raged inside the front doors. Charlie started to be able to see in the shadows; the night outside was gloomy, but it wasn't black. Bodies twisted and flailed; metal drew *clang!* from metal.

Bang! Bang!

Charlie couldn't tell who was firing the shots.

BANG!

That was Grim, of course. In the muzzle flashes Charlie saw an attacker collapse. He also saw Bob trading sword blows with a cutlass swinger until Ollie stabbed the man in the back of one knee with the umbrella and he fell. Gnat was still airborne, though she moved like she was dizzy. Grim had attackers crawling on him like barnacles on a ship, so he charged the hat machine itself. Men screamed and fell off him as they were stabbed with hatting scissors and knives.

Charlie began to hope his friends might win.

He noticed a soft, steady hiss, barely audible under all the fighting sounds.

Then a rattle from the hat-making machine dragged his attention away. He peered into the gloom and found that his eyes had adjusted.

"Watch out!" he yelled. He meant to yell, at least, but it came out as more of a squeak. "Watch out! Trolls!"

Two hulders charged. They had been hiding among the arms and pistons of the machine, and they had been the source of the steam, Charlie now realized. He had thought the machine was emitting small amounts of steam while it idled. In reality, he now saw that it must have been the smoking jotun, the one with the scentless tobacco.

Grim turned, flinging off an attacker with one arm and throwing the man into a wall. Two others still clung to him and pounded, one on his shoulders and one wrapped around a leg. He looked like a grown man wrestling children.

Grim lowered his head and charged.

Bang! Bang!

Henry Clockswain crouched in the corner, firing. Gnat fluttered her wings, grabbing a man's shirt and pulling it up over his face while Bob punched him repeatedly in the stomach. Charlie didn't see Ollie for a moment, and he worried that his friend was down, but when he saw one of the thugs stumbling around in circles, slapping at his feet, he realized what had happened.

Ollie was in snake form and was tripping the man.

Crash!

Grim and the first hulder rammed horns-first into each other, like giant billy goats. The noise was almost as loud as the gunshots, and then they grappled, arms locked on shoulders, each trying to throw the other to the floor. For a moment Charlie's heart lifted at the sight of his mighty friend in action.

Then the second hulder collided with Grim. He rammed

his head and his big bull horns into Grim's chest, under his arm. Grim Grumblesson stumbled back, bellowing in anger and pain. His arms windmilled, he tried to regain his balance, and the second hulder punched Grim in the face.

Grim fell. Charlie's hopes fell with him.

"Grim!" Natalie de Minimis shouted.

Bang!

Ollie, Bob, and Gnat were still tripping, stabbing, punching, and dodging. The trolls lumbered in their direction now, though, and Henry Clockswain stood near the door, fidgeting with his weapon and dropping bullets to the floor in his efforts to reload.

Charlie struck one of the matches against its box. He couldn't bring himself to throw the explosive directly at anyone, but he thought that if he threw it close, he might frighten his enemies. He could do that much to the men who had kidnapped his father and hurt Grim Grumblesson.

He lit the fuse on the tube of blasting powder, raised it over his head, and hurled it at the hat-making machinery—

and as the sparking, *fitz*ing stick of Extradynamit wobbled through the air toward its target, Charlie remembered the hissing sound he had heard, and it occurred to him to wonder whether it might be gas—

KABOOM!

The Extradynamit exploded within the brass arms of the machine. Rods and plates flew in every direction. Charlie ducked. The building shook, wheels spun, levers dropped, and what was left of the machine coughed into motion.

Scissor arms snipped, blades swooshed through the air, and pincer hands grabbed for raw materials that weren't there. The machine was missing parts now, and it was off-balance. Arms swung in the wrong direction. Top hats and hat parts began to spew from the output end of the machine, piling on the fighting trolls like huge black snowflakes.

The air over Charlie's head burst into flame.

He ducked. Feeling the heat on his skin, he covered his face with his hands. The stink of scorched hair filled his nostrils, and he hurt all over. When he uncovered his face and looked again, the scene had changed.

The two hulders were flapping their arms to ward off the flurry of hats that threatened to cover them, dodging brass mechanical attacks and staring at the fire overhead. Grim took advantage of their distraction and dragged himself onto his feet. He backed away slowly and stiffly, but he was moving.

Charlie's other friends still struggled, but it looked like they might be winning. Charlie saw Ollie wrapped around one attacker's legs in the form of a heavy constrictor while Gnat swooped in sideways to kick the same man in the stomach. Bob chased a now-unarmed man around the floor with his sword.

All around the factory, a ring of flame sprouted. Patches of fire burst here and there through the wood of the walls.

Charlie ducked as a long brass arm, out of control, swung over his head.

"Rats!" he heard Bob shout. Charlie looked down and saw

the rodents, a horde of them. They flooded through the front doors, sweeping away the fighters.

And a man in a black cloak was coming up the stairs.

The Sinister Man.

In his hand he held a long pistol.

Few things are as devastating, in a dense urban environment such as London, as fire. It is for this reason that Sir Robert Peel, in addition to organizing London's police force, chartered and funded its fire brigades, the so-called *fire bobbies* or sometimes *firemen*.

—Smythson, *Almanack*, "London"

The Sinister Man raised his pistol. "Be a good little thing. Come with me."

Being called a *little thing* was worse than being treated like a baby.

"Clock off!" Charlie yelled.

He threw the matches. The little wooden box hit the Sinister Man in the chest and fell to the floor, and the Sinister Man only laughed.

Charlie noticed again the cog-shaped pin holding the man's cloak in place. "What does the Iron Cog want with me?" he asked. It was an attempt to buy time.

The Sinister Man arched one eyebrow. "What has your maker told you of the Iron Cog?"

Maker? Little thing? Charlie felt uncomfortable and confused, but he had no time to think about it.

He ducked as the mechanical arm swung past him again. It was a sturdy piece of gear, built to move heavy things from one side of the factory to the other. Now its pole was knocked off-kilter and the arm swung in a big circle, swooping down fast and low over the mezzanine floor and then gliding higher and slower at the far end of its orbit.

"What does the Iron Cog think it knows about me?" Charlie tried to grin confidently, like an adventurer would. Like Bob grinned.

The Sinister Man pointed his gun at Charlie's head. "No more questions! Come with me now, or you're scrap!"

The arm swept down again, and Charlie grabbed it with both hands.

Bang!

He had to shift his stance to grab the swinging arm without being knocked down, and that movement was just enough; the Sinister Man missed. He lurched forward and reached for Charlie with his free hand, but the mechanical arm brushed Charlie over the edge of the mezzanine floor—

bump! against the railing—

and high into the air.

The Sinister Man stumbled against the railing but didn't fall.

Pulled away from the burning walls, Charlie immediately felt cooler. For a moment the floor below and the building around him spun in a kaleidoscope image of brass and orange. He held on tight.

The arm reached the top of its swing, and he slowed down.

Bang!

The bullet whizzed by him in the air. On the mezzanine floor the Sinister Man pointed his pistol at Charlie again.

Charlie looked down to see if there was a safe space below, but all he saw was a tangle. Long brass poles swung, pistons pumped, and steam hissed out in constant rushing streams. The rod-studded spine writhed and buckled off its track, and the tool-holding arms swung wildly in all directions. If he dropped into that chaos, Charlie would be chopped to pieces—as well as chalked and polished with pumice.

He tightened his grip.

Bang!

The shoulder of Charlie's jacket twitched as the bullet nicked it, just at the edge.

Charlie gulped. He scrambled, trying to get out his knife without letting go of the arm, wishing again that Grim had gotten him a pistol.

The arm was starting to pick up speed again and rush downward, and Charlie was a sitting duck. The Sinister Man would get a point-blank shot or would simply knock him off the arm by force.

Then he saw Heaven-Bound Bob, sprinting up the staircase to the mezzanine with something big and floppy balled up in his hand. Behind him came Henry Clockswain and Grim Grumblesson. The hulder was walking backward, a black silhouette against the flaming wall. Gnat zipped through the air about the troll's head.

They were moving backward because they were fighting

a wave of rats. Gnat knocked them off the staircase's hand-rail and skewered the few that slipped past Grim with her spear. The troll kicked with his feet and swung his pistol like a club.

Behind the rats came the other hulders, and men with swords. At the bottom of the stairs the pouchy-eyed captain shouted and pointed at Grim, sending his men up to attack.

The Sinister Man saw Bob rushing him and swiveled around to aim his pistol. "Stop right there!" the Sinister Man shouted.

Bob threw the thing he had balled up in his hand.

Bang! The Sinister Man shot him. Bob staggered and fell—

but the thrown object kept going. It unraveled in flight, like string, and wrapped itself around the Sinister Man's neck.

Charlie swung back down. The offices below the mezzanine floor were burning, and it would only be moments before that fire would chew its way up. The Sinister Man dropped his gun and staggered back. Ollie, in snake form, was wrapped around the Sinister Man's neck.

Charlie picked up speed, racing toward the low point of his orbit.

The Sinister Man scratched at the snake with his fingers, trying to rip Ollie away.

Charlie raised his feet and kicked the Sinister Man in the chest. Then he let go and dropped to the mezzanine floor.

The Sinister Man flailed his arms and slipped backward, bumped against the railing, and tumbled, falling over into the flame.

Charlie shoved one hand out over the edge of the mezzanine, just in time to catch Ollie, who was a boy again, by the back of his peacoat.

Ollie was falling, and he was heavy. Charlie threw one arm around the railing and tried not to be dragged into the fire. Ollie bounced, and for one second Charlie thought he would be forced to drop his friend into the hungry flames below. He felt like his arm would be ripped from its socket, but he gritted his teeth and held on.

The Sinister Man shouted and disappeared into the blaze.

"Cripes, Charlie, but you're strong!" Ollie muttered.

Charlie chuckled. "Just a good healthy lad, ain't I?" He braced himself with his feet and managed to drag Ollie back, up onto the mezzanine floor.

The three boys all clambered to their feet at the same moment. Bob was bleeding from a wound in his shoulder, but he had a big grin on his face.

"Run!" Henry Clockswain shouted. The kobold staggered up out of the staircase. Fire licked up all sides of the mezzanine and the walls like golden-orange curtains. The catwalks that led away from the mezzanine floor and around the factory were all burning, or had already burned away.

K-k-k-kranggggg!

The mechanical arm that Charlie had just ridden finally twisted off its axis and collapsed into the floor. It crushed squealing, chittering rats beneath it. Charlie smelled the burning fur and flesh stink of their deaths and felt sick.

Grim Grumblesson stepped back onto the mezzanine.

Beyond him a wall of rats gnashed its many teeth and shrieked in anger.

"Up the stairs!" Charlie shouted. He ran, and his friends followed.

Cre-e-e-e-eak . . . CRASH!

The floor of the factory below gave way. All the spinning arms collapsed into the cellar in a jumble of brass and flame.

Charlie looked over his shoulder as he popped up into the top floor. He saw fire everywhere, and behind him a struggling line of people and beasts that wanted out of the flames. His friends were first, and then the rats, and last the hulders and cutlass men of the Iron Cog.

Charlie picked up the pace.

The flames had not yet reached the attic, but the heat had. Still, even this air was better than the furnace blast of the factory below, and Bob and Ollie both sucked in big breaths. Charlie rushed for the box of Extradynamit.

"Don't mess with that stuff now!" Bob yelled in a strangled voice. "It's too 'ot in 'ere—might go off in your 'and!"

Charlie ignored his friend's warning. He wasn't a baby.

He grabbed a stick of the blasting powder and rushed back to the stairs. Looking down the stairwell, he saw Grim Grumblesson's shoulders squeezing through. The rain slicker was gone, and Grim's back was sweaty and marked with blood.

When Grim had stepped far enough back that Charlie could see the black, swarming rodents and the orange fire in front of him, Charlie threw the blasting powder. He tossed it as far past Grim as he could, down onto the mezzanine.

KABOOM!

Rats squealed and flew away in all directions. Grim staggered back but kept his feet.

"Come on, Charlie!" Ollie called from the window. "We've got to get out!"

With the rats off him for a moment, Grim thundered up the stairs. Gnat buzzed fiercely around him, spear in hand.

Charlie looked out the open window. Bob and Ollie and Henry Clockswain had already jumped across the gap to the adjacent rooftop, and they waved at him to join them. Grim turned to face the stairs and began loading his gun.

"Come on, Grim, we have to go," Charlie urged.

Grim kept working. When he had taught the kobold to load his pistol, it had been a slow exercise. Now Charlie saw that the hulder really did know what he was doing. He poured the grains of powder in with practiced and casual speed and then thumbed in six of the gun's huge bullets and caps in no time at all.

He finished loading the gigantic Eldjotun and raised it just as the Iron Cog's hulders poked their heads up out of the stairwell. In the darkness, with orange light blazing up from below, their bulls' horns and shaggy hair made them look like devils.

Charlie noticed that a wisp of smoke was curling up out of the first hulder's coat. That didn't make much sense, though, unless maybe the troll had stuck a lit pipe into his coat pocket—

BANG!

The hulder ducked as Grim fired. Grim took two steps closer and fired again.

BANG!

"Aye, Grim, the lad's right," Gnat urged her boss. "And you've got to come now, or we'll burn with the factory!"

Grim's face twisted. Charlie climbed out the window and onto the roof. The rain had stopped, but the shingles were wet. There was bare wood exposed where Charlie had landed earlier.

BANG!

Grim fired again and then squeezed into the window frame. For a moment it looked like he wouldn't fit. He grunted and pushed, and the wooden frame around the window cracked in several places. And then he fit through just fine.

Across the alleyway, Bob and Ollie backed away from the edge. Mr. Clockswain huddled with them.

"'Urry up!" Bob shouted.

Rats squealed again in the attic behind Grim.

"You first." Grim nodded at Charlie. His eyes bulged and his mouth twitched.

Charlie turned and rushed down the rooftop, easily jumped over the alley, and then scrambled up to join Ollie and Bob.

"Come on!" he yelled to Grim.

Grim nodded, but something was wrong. He held his head stiff and chewed his upper lip with his tusks. He didn't look down.

He was afraid of heights.

There was noise inside the building. Grim turned, pointed his gun back inside the window, and pulled the trigger.

Nothing happened.

"Now!" Natalie de Minimis shouted. She poked Grim in the rump with her spear.

Grim lunged forward onto the slope of the roof. He hit it hard, and shingles scattered beneath his feet as he started to slide.

Charlie saw faces at the window, but he had no attention to focus on them.

Grim Grumblesson was tumbling toward the abyss, and his eyes were closed.

It is also not the case that kobolds eat only or principally goat flesh. It is true, however, that kobolds have been known to saddle and ride goats, or to employ goats to power mills by muscle. This fact is likely, specialists in koboldry inform us, the source of the folktale of billy-goat brothers who successively avoid being eaten by telling the troll under the bridge to wait for the oldest and largest brother, who upon his arrival promptly butts the troll into the river. This story clearly has no connection, in any case, with the folk known as *troll* in Great Britain.

—Smythson, *Almanack*, "Kobold"

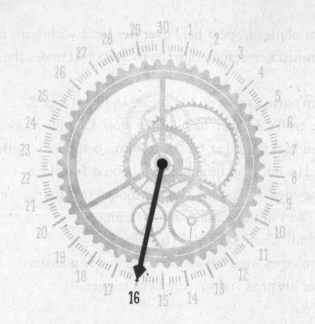

Charlie sprinted down the slope toward his troll friend. He didn't have time to think.

Across the alley, shingles sprang into the air around Grim's heavy boots. Grim plowed twin furrows in the rooftop as he slid.

Charlie jumped.

"No!" Bob shouted.

Gnat buzzed through the air in front of the hulder—and Charlie slammed shoulder-first into Grim's chest. The troll fell backward, air whooshing out of his lungs from Charlie's blow. Charlie saw his friend's eyes open in astonishment, and then they crashed together onto the rooftop . . .

. . . and kept sliding.

Gnat plunged, spear held over her head with both hands. She jammed her weapon into the rooftop, just under the troll's armpit.

Grim's arm caught on the spear, and he stopped.

The troll's sudden halt didn't stop Charlie motion. He tumbled backward, but grabbed Grim's belt buckle with both hands. His body, and the hulder's booted feet, hung together over the edge of the roof. Charlie looked up at Grim and saw hulder faces in the window above them.

"Grim!" Charlie yelled. "The window!"

Grim's eyes were screwed shut again. He pointed the Eldjotun over his head and squeezed the trigger.

BANG!

His shot went wide. The bullet gouged a head-sized chunk of wood and shingle out of the peak of the roof, several feet to one side of the window. But the threat and the noise were enough to make the hulders disappear.

With the faces gone, Charlie saw orange light through the window. Smoke billowed up in the alley below him. It reminded him of the Gullet, and Lucky Wu's Earth Dragon Laundry, only here the air stank of fire and blood. If Charlie fell, he would not survive.

"Grim!" He grabbed the troll by the front of his shirt.

Grim kept his eyes squeezed shut. "Shoot again?"

Gnat zipped in close to the window, still off-balance due to her sprained wing. She took a peek inside and flapped back abruptly, just in time to avoid a tide of rats. The rodents surged around and over Grim, some turning left and right to race away in the rain gutter and others tumbling into the abyss. Charlie and Gnat fought to batter the rats aside. Grim helped, swinging his gun about blindly.

"They're getting away!" Charlie heard Gnat's high, silvery voice over the rat shriek. Through puffs of smoke he saw the shadowy outlines of hulders and men slinking away across the rooftops.

The rat tide continued, but suddenly a booted form crashed into the rooftop beside Charlie and Grim. It was Bob, with Ollie in snake form wrapped around his neck. Rats squealed as he kicked them aside.

"Ow! That's 'ot!"

Poof! The rotten-egg smell was lost in all the other smoke and in the sewer stink of the rats, but Ollie took his human shape again and dropped on all fours to the shingles. "Ow!"

"Grim, stand up!" Charlie yelled.

"I can't!" the troll bellowed. "My feet are dangling!"

"Open your eyes, you big oaf!" Ollie shouted.

"I can't!" the troll roared again.

Bob met Charlie's gaze through the smoke. "The blasting powder is in the attic," the aeronaut reminded him. "It's going to explode."

"If the roof don't just cave in first," Ollie grumbled.

Charlie scrambled up the troll's chest. He grabbed Grim by one shoulder and pulled. "Help me," he begged. Bob and Ollie grabbed the other shoulder, and they all tugged together.

"I'm too big!" Grim wailed.

But with all three boys hauling, he budged.

The wave of rats was past. The smoke hung around them thick as cobwebs, and everyone but Charlie was coughing.

"Use your hands!" Charlie yelled at the hulder.

"Hurry up!" Gnat shouted. "The flames are into everything!"

Grim Grumblesson pushed with his hands, and the boys pulled, and with a big heave they managed all together to drag his legs back onto the roof. The troll stumbled to his feet, but his eyes were still closed. He weaved back and forth.

"Come on!" Ollie stepped up the rooftop, took a few steps' run, and jumped across the alley. Bob followed.

"I can't open my eyes!" Grim wept. "Go!"

"Gnat!" Charlie yelled. "Hold his eyelids!"

The pixie pounced on the troll's shoulders. Wrapping her legs around her friend's horns, she reached over his heavy forehead with both arms and grabbed handfuls of troll eyelashes. Grunting and throwing her back into it, she pulled open Grim Grumblesson's eyelids, revealing bloodshot yellow orbs and twitching blue irises.

Charlie caught Grim's gaze. The troll coughed, and sweat streamed down his face.

"Follow me!" Charlie slapped Grim in the belly to make sure Grim heard him.

The hulder nodded, quick and nervous. He still wasn't looking down.

Charlie trotted several steps back up the rooftop. Smoke curled from the soles of his shoes, which felt like they were on fire. He waited a second, and then Grim stepped up behind him. The troll was puffing like a train.

Charlie started running down the slope.

"De Minimis and Underthames!" Gnat yelled. The rooftop shook as Grim thundered on Charlie's heels.

"Pondicherry's of Whitechapel!" Charlie cried in response. Then he jumped. The alley was invisible below him. He sailed blindly into smoke, and when he smacked into a rooftop on the other side, it was almost a surprise. The shingles hurt his hands and knees, but at least they were cool.

"*Mutatis mutandis!*" Grim yelled behind him.

Charlie heard a huge *whoosh!* as the troll jumped—

and then a *CRASH!* as he hit the roof and smashed right through it.

Bob and Ollie grabbed Charlie by the back of his jacket and dragged him down into the hole Grim had just created. The others coughed and spat, and the air got even cooler and suddenly tasted like sawdust. Charlie could see almost nothing, and he tried to stop.

"Is everyone here?" he called.

Bob and Ollie dragged him along. "Keep running!" Ollie yelled in his ear.

Ahead in the darkness, Gnat shouted directions. "Left! Right! Stop!" Then a door opened, yellow light flooded the room, and Charlie could see again.

KABOO-OOM!!!

A hot wind whipped around Charlie's ears. Burning wood rained down through the hole through which they'd entered and fell on stacks of lumber that filled the room.

"It ain't over yet!" Bob hollered.

Again they ran.

The building caught fire around them. It was a sawmill, with giant jagged-toothed circular-saw blades and chain belts heavy with lumber. As Charlie rushed out the front door and into the street, the wall sconces behind him exploded into jets of flame. Gas, he thought. He ran faster.

A bucket brigade of men in shirtsleeves threw water on Cavendish Hats. Other men ran down the street, banging on the door of every building whose lights were out. Bells ringing at the end of the road announced the arrival of a fire wagon. Some of the fire bobbies, men in black rubber capes and steel helmets, spilled from the wagon, unrolled the stiffening hoses, and pointed them at the burning buildings.

Charlie and his friends ran right through the crowd of shouting firemen, who charged in the opposite direction with axes and ladders over their shoulders. They ran down the street, turned a corner, and kept running until Grim pulled them all into the shadows under a Sky Trestle station, where Charlie's friends puffed and sweated and Ollie muttered things Charlie couldn't quite hear.

When he had finally caught his breath, Grim Grumblesson spoke. "Charlie Pondicherry," he rumbled, "you are a very special boy."

"I thought you'd see it my way," Bob said to the troll. He laughed and clapped his right hand on Charlie's shoulder. Bob's left arm hung at his side.

Charlie looked around at his friends. They were singed, battered, and out of breath, but they were alive. "Thanks." He smiled.

"I think we ought to tell 'im," Bob said.

"No," Henry Clockswain objected. "There's nothing to tell, Charlie."

"What?" Charlie asked. "Is it something about Bap ... about my father? Did we find another clue?"

"It's nothing about your dad," Bob said to Charlie, and then he turned to Grim. "Look, wouldn't you want to know, if it was you?"

"I dunno," Ollie said. "If he wants to keep a secret, let him."

"Your secret's already out, my boy," Gnat told Ollie.

"I ain't French."

Charlie looked around at his friends. There was a secret that everyone knew but him.

"I'm not keeping a secret," he said. "I don't know what you're talking about."

Grim rumbled thoughtfully.

Henry Clockswain folded his arms across his chest. "I'm not going to tell Raj Pondicherry's son anything that Raj Pondicherry didn't want to tell him himself."

"Thing is, Charlie," Grim Grumblesson said, ignoring the kobold, "you're a very special boy."

"Thanks," Charlie said again.

"Get to the point," Ollie muttered.

"You're so special, I don't think there is another boy like you." Grim furrowed his heavy brow. "You're strong. Excellent balance and coordination. You can hold your breath a long time."

Charlie nodded. "True," he agreed. He tried to keep his

expression modest, but he couldn't help poking his chest out a little bit.

"Thing is," Grim continued, "I think you could hold your breath forever, if you wanted to."

Charlie shook his head. "What?" All his friends watched him closely.

"I think you could hold your breath forever," Grim explained, "because your father . . . *made* you that way."

"That's not right," Charlie objected. "A *person* isn't *made*." This was as bad as the nonsense the Sinister Man had said to him. It was the same nonsense, in fact; the Sinister Man had called him a *thing* and said he had a *maker*.

"I didn't say you weren't a *person*," Grim said quietly. He dug into a pocket and handed Charlie back his bap's hat with a look of apology; the brim of the hat had a hole punched through it. Charlie put the John Bull on and pulled its brim low over his eyes.

"You have a mother, Charlie?" Ollie asked.

"You 'ave a birthday?"

"Do you need to eat and sleep?" Gnat stood on a low brick wall, resting her wings.

Charlie shook his head. It wasn't right. It couldn't be right. Raj Pondicherry was his bap, his father; he had always said he was Charlie's father, and he had always treated Charlie as his son.

It just couldn't be true.

Overhead, brakes squeaked as a train puffed slowly into the station. Charlie looked up at the train to avoid meeting his friends' eyes. The station was lit by gas flames flickering inside pole-mounted bulbs, and Charlie could see the train clearly enough. Through the slats of the Sky Trestle he watched the brass piston arms connecting each wheel to the next pump, in and out in a hiss of vapor.

The sight of the piston arms and the steam looked strangely familiar to Charlie. They reminded him of something, and he tried to think of what it could be.

"Look at yourself in the mirror, Charlie," Bob said gently. Charlie only half heard his friend.

"The hulder!" Charlie snapped, realizing what was niggling at his thoughts. "The hulder who smokes scentless tobacco!"

"Charlie . . . ," Ollie said. "Don't go ducking the issue."

"Yeah, mate," Bob agreed. "Everybody thinks you're a good lad, whether or not you're the real thing. I mean, the *natural* thing."

"No, listen! One of the hulders who kidnapped my father let off fumes, remember? Smoke that I couldn't smell."

Grim frowned. "You saw him smoking a pipe."

Charlie shook his head. "I *thought* he was smoking a pipe, because he let off smoke. All I *actually* saw was the smoke. And he was at Cavendish Hats tonight. And I saw the smoke again, but I didn't see any pipe. Did you see one?"

Grim frowned deeper and shook his head. "It was dark, and then everything was on fire and covered with rats. Also, lots of people were hitting me at the time."

"What are you talking about, Charlie?" Gnat asked.

Charlie pointed up at the train, even though the pistons

weren't in sight anymore. "What if the smoke wasn't from a pipe at all?"

Grim smacked himself between the horns with the palm of one hand. "You mean, what if it was steam from a mechanical arm?"

"Yes," Charlie agreed. "Exactly. Or leg, or something. Is that possible? Can people have mechanical parts?"

"That's the 'ole discussion we were just 'aving, Charlie," Bob murmured.

"It isn't a leg; it's an arm!" Grim thundered. "No wonder it hurt so hard when he punched me!" He shook his big head, then squatted down to get face-to-face with Charlie. "Remember I told you there aren't many hulders in London?"

Charlie nodded. "That's why you want to become a human solicitor. To get more business."

Grim shrugged. "Well, there's a troll in London with a mechanical arm. Rough troll, a criminal. A notorious troll. I don't know him personally, but I know how we can find him."

"'Ow's that, then?" Bob asked. "London's a big place."

"Easy." Grim looked annoyed. "He drinks milk."

Trolls are farmers, and their cuisine consists generally of meat dishes and bread. Their principal sweetener is honey, which they also use to brew the mead for which troll social gatherings are famous. Trolls shun milk, cheese, and other dairy products.

—Smythson, *Almanack*, "Troll"

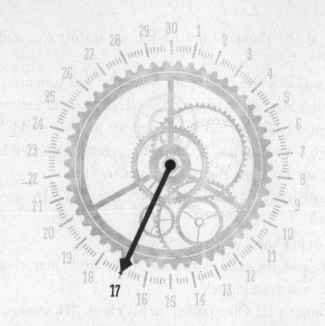

Grim paid for them all, trading shillings with a slot-mouthed automaton for copper train tokens. Charlie stared at the bell-shaped token vendor while Grim worked with it. Its face was a slot to take coins below a vertical brass plate with distances and prices stamped on it. There were buttons to the side of the plate by which Grim chose the distance he wanted to travel, and an arm on the side he pulled when he'd inserted enough money. The vendor whirred softly as it digested the coins, each stamped with the profile of Queen Victoria, and clicked as it spat into a tray farther down tokens marked with the face of the engineer Brunel.

How could Charlie's friends think this token vendor was a closer relative to him than his bap? Charlie felt gray and empty at the thought, and he leaned against the wall for support.

He was closer to finding his father, he was sure of it. The Cavendish Hats clue had led to the warehouse and back to the one-armed troll who had kidnapped his bap. He couldn't see it all yet, but a picture was coming together. Charlie felt hope.

But was Raj Pondicherry his bap, after all?

Charlie couldn't believe he was just a thing. He *wouldn't* believe it.

He didn't know *what* to believe.

"I'm glad the train is running this late." Charlie said it mostly to distract himself.

"Course it is." Ollie puffed up his chest. "This is London. The Sky Trestle don't stop for a little darkness."

Once they had their tokens, the redbrick-and-brass station was quiet. Here, too, the light came from gas sconces set into the walls six feet off the ground. Brass pipes crawled around the room at the floor level, probably circulating hot water so the station would be comfortable even in winter. Charlie was just noticing that the same pipes also seemed to operate the latch that opened windows to cool the station when their train arrived.

"Let's have a look at your arm, then," Ollie said to Bob as they climbed up the short ladder and found seats on the wooden benches of the train.

Thud!

"Ow." Grim rubbed his head where he'd banged it on the top of the train's door. The other passengers in the car all tried not to stare at the troll.

No one noticed Charlie.

"Nah." Bob refused, and he pulled away when Ollie reached for his shoulder. "It ain't nothing." But his arm hung limp at his side, and the aeronaut poked a finger tenderly around his own biceps.

Grim sank onto a bench with his eyes shut. "Tell me when we get there," he rumbled.

Charlie looked out the window as they rode back to Whitechapel. The Sky Trestle rested on the tops of buildings or rode on columns just above them. Arriving at and leaving stations, the train rolled slowly. In between, it hurtled like a comet. Charlie pressed his face to the cold glass of the window and forgot about everything until Gnat pulled him away because they had reached their destination.

The station's steps dropped down in front of a length of stone castle wall, right where a broad street narrowed to crawl between two ancient stone towers and under a portcullis. "This is Aldgate," Grim told him. The troll was visibly relieved to be down from the elevated train tracks, and his eyes were open again. He pulled Charlie close to his side and pointed up the road. "Whitechapel High Street. We're almost back to my place."

The city streets were dark and wet. Charlie didn't see any hulders or pixies on the short walk to Grim's rooms. He did see a dwarf wagon, big-wheeled and gold-painted. It rested in the mouth of an alley, and two dwarfs sat beside it, tending a small fire in a ring of uprooted cobblestones. A large cat with tasseled ears curled around the fire opposite them, and all three of them watched a bird roasting on a spit over the flame.

The dwarfs' gold earrings and green silk scarves shimmered in the firelight, and Charlie shuddered, remembering the dwarfs of the Iron Cog who had covered up his bap's kidnapping.

Tumblewain Close was mostly dark, with a puddle of yellow light around Grim Grumblesson's door, thrown from a lamp high in the wall above. "Going to draw some water for a bath." Grim turned the key in the lock. "Anyone else want to wash up?"

No one else did, so Grim plodded up the stairs alone. The chimney sweeps collapsed on soft chairs in the office and instantly fell asleep, Ollie with his bowler hat over his eyes and Bob after buckling the chin straps of his bomber. Charlie hung his bap's hat on a hook in the hallway wall.

Henry Clockswain stopped by the door, twisting his toes in the ground. "My, er, garret's around the corner," he said. He held up the button he'd accidentally twisted from his own jacket and smiled apologetically. "I'll fix this, and I'll be right back." The kobold slipped out into the yellow lamplight.

Charlie stood in the door, holding it open and watching Henry Clockswain disappear down the close. He badly wanted to run out into the darkness and . . . do something. He shoved his hand into his pocket and wrapped his fingers around his bap's pipe. The feel of the rounded bowl in his hand instantly brought memories of his bap puffing smoke in the reception room with clients, or over a bubbling pot of chicken curry in the workshop.

"I'd give you a penny for your thoughts," he heard Gnat say, "only I don't carry pennies on my person. I find them too large to be convenient."

Charlie kept his hand on the pipe. "I don't know what my thoughts are. Only I feel like I should be with my father. Or home. Or something."

"It's been a long night, Charlie, and we're doing all we can," the pixie said. "Now come inside."

Slowly, Charlie obeyed.

Natalie de Minimis perched at a high stool beside Grim's desk and made faces while she arched her back. The stool was just the right height to give the pixie access to the desktop, and it sat next to a stack of papers with miniscule writing on them.

Charlie sat down, still secretly holding the pipe. "I'm sorry about Seamus," he said. "And Elisabel. And your mother. That's a very hard way to end your tithe."

"Aye, 'tis. And I'm sorry about your father."

"I don't see how I can ever find him. London is so big."

Natalie de Minimis rested a tiny hand on Charlie's shoulder. "You're not alone."

Charlie nodded, then tried to change the subject. "I thought you were very brave at Cavendish Hats," he offered. "I mean, the way you did all that fighting! And then you saved Grim."

"Nay, 'twas *you* who saved the big fellow." The pixie shrugged. "Well, perhaps we all did it together."

"Maybe. I was thinking that tonight you've performed one of your three great feats."

Gnat laughed. Her laughter sounded delighted, but also tired. "Oh, were you? The Battle of Cavendish Hats, was it, and its great hero Natalie de Minimis?" She threw her hair back and struck a pose, one hand pointed at the sky as if she were a military statue, holding a sword.

Charlie nodded.

"Well, I thank you. Sadly, I think it'll not be up to the expectations of the good folk of Underthames, and that's who I need to satisfy. Three great feats'll be like"—she searched for examples—"three mighty beasts slain, or three magical items recovered, or three lost princes rescued."

"That sounds exciting," Charlie said. "It also sounds hard."

"Aye," Gnat agreed. She winked. "But I've got a year to do it, and I'm my mother's daughter."

"What about the rats?" Charlie asked. "Elisabel and that big rat with all the scars, Scabies, they were plotting. Can't you just . . . I don't know . . . *tell* people about it?"

Gnat nodded slowly. "I could. But I'd not be believed by most people, because Elisabel is the baroness, and she's saved Underthames from the rats, or at least they believe she has. And you would come with me and be another witness, and so would Grim and the lads. And you'd not be believed either, because you're not pixies."

Charlie shook his head. "I don't understand. You can't tell a . . . a fairy judge, or something?"

"There is no judge in Underthames," Natalie de Minimis said. "There is only the baroness."

"So you have to become the baroness." It was a strange way of thinking, but Charlie was coming to understand. "And to do that, you have to challenge Elisabel. And to do that, you have to perform three great feats."

"Aye," the pixie said. "I've got my people as well as my love to save. So I've got to slay three dragons." She looked Charlie up and down and nodded at the hallway and the stairs. "You might consider Grim's offer of a bath, you know. You've been in the sewers, and you're a bit of a sight."

"What about you?" Charlie asked. "Your clothes got dirty, too."

Gnat looked down at her red dress, which was quite bedraggled. "Aye," she agreed. "But I think I may wear this a little while yet."

A bath sounded good to Charlie, so he climbed the stairs. He finally let go of his bap's pipe as he knocked on the only shut door in the upstairs hallway.

"Come in!" Grim roared.

Compared to the wooden tub and spigot of hot water in the corner of the workroom of Pondicherry's Clockwork Invention & Repair, the bathroom was luxurious. There were two tall windows with thick white curtains, and green carpet covered the entire floor. There was an enormous flush toilet in one corner and a sink with hot and cold faucets in another. In the center of the floor rested a big brass tub full of soapy water.

In the tub sat Grim: big, paunchy, and muscular, with a skirt of soap bubbles around his waist. His hair was white and sudsy too, and he was scrubbing away at his scalp with all ten fingers. He was humming something, but the tune didn't sound cheerful. It sounded fast and nervous.

The troll's body was covered with cuts and bruises. To Charlie's astonishment, the wounds were healing so fast he could actually see them close and disappear.

"You can have the tub next, if you like," Grim offered.

Charlie nodded and went to the sink. Over the basin hung a large mirror, and he inspected himself. He was filthy. His fingernails were black. His hair was matted and thick with chunks of something he hoped was mud. His clothing was caked almost black.

And his skin was bronze.

He had always thought of himself as having his father's complexion, but now he saw that wasn't true. His bap was brown-skinned, like a chestnut. Charlie's complexion was metallic in color, coppery red. It could be human skin, he thought, but it might be something else. He prodded his own face. He didn't feel like metal, not quite, but now that he was thinking about it, the flesh of his face didn't feel like normal human flesh, either.

Was the Sinister Man right about him? Was he just another thing, just a device like the Articulated Gyroscopes?

"The creams," Charlie murmured to himself. "Bap was hiding what I look like from other people." His voice hardened. "But I'm not a *thing*."

"No!" Grim barked. "No, Charlie, you're not." The troll stood up and wrapped a towel around himself. "We're all made somehow, Charlie. However you were made, you've got a father who loves you, and you're very much a person. You're a *very special boy*, Charlie Pondicherry."

Charlie wasn't sure he was convinced, one way or the other. Machines could move, and they could certainly look like people, but Charlie felt like much more than a machine. If he really was a . . . device, like his father's owl or Lucky Wu's sparrows, how was he able to see? It was true, he'd never really needed much food—maybe he'd never needed any food, it occurred to him, but he shook the thought off—and he could hold his breath a long time, but . . . Did the Sky Trestle token dispenser smell passengers as they approached it? Did it taste the coins that were pushed into its slot?

There were too many questions, and Charlie just couldn't face them right now.

"Anyway, I've got a bap," Charlie said. He remembered the sight of his father being dragged away in a collar by the Iron Cog's hulders. "We've got to rescue him. We've got to find the troll with the piston arm, and find out why the Cavendish Hats people took my bap and why they want me, and what all the blasting powder was for."

"All those things," Grim agreed. "Just as soon as you take a bath. You're so dirty, beggars would be embarrassed to have you."

Charlie bathed and washed his own hair and gouged mud out of his ears and scrubbed his fingernails without thinking very much about what they were made of. When he had finished, Grim had somehow laundered and dried Charlie's clothes, and Charlie got dressed again in his coat and John Bull. He decided not to ask Grim if he had any creams for Charlie's skin.

He felt like a new boy.

Grim looked like a new troll. He wore a tightly knotted white cravat and white kid gloves. He had clean, pressed red trousers and a matching red waistcoat, and a fine chain across his stomach hinted at the enormous gold watch that he pulled out and consulted once as he dressed. Over it all he hung a yellow coat, a mirror of the one he had turned into rope in the prisons of Underthames. His hair gleamed with oil and was tied with a gold ribbon in a queue down his back, poking out underneath a brand-new top hat. He showed Charlie the label: the hat was a Cavendish, and they both laughed. Grim's breath even smelled minty, and after he rubbed his tusks with some sort of thick paste, they were white as china.

Henry Clockswain had returned, and sat quietly dozing in a chair in the office, wearing a clean shirt and coat, with all its buttons. Ollie rubbed his eyes and looked about when Charlie and the troll woke them all up. "Here now, what's this? Are we going to the palace and someone didn't tell me about it?"

"Why do you care?" Bob laughed. "It ain't like you'd dress up or anything."

Ollie spat in both hands and combed his hair with his fingers. Bob just unbuckled his bomber cap. At Grim's reminder, both boys checked their weapons. When the kobold announced that he'd lost his gun in the fire, Ollie only sneered.

Grim produced three loaves of bread, a brick of butter, and four apples from his larder, and they were devoured in seconds.

At the last moment Bob disappeared into the bathroom for a few minutes. He came out grinning and winding his injured arm in small, slow circles. "Just exhuming my injury," he explained.

"Examining?" Charlie suggested.

"Yeah. It ain't too bad."

They set out again.

Charlie had lost track of time. There was no sign of the sun yet, so he thought it must be the early hours of the morning. It took fifteen minutes of waiting and fruitless waving, but finally Grim hailed a hansom cab by flagging it down with a white handkerchief, and they all climbed in. The cab was a wide, two-wheeled carriage, pulled by a crusty gray rhinoceros, with a window on each side and open in the front. The cabdriver stood on a little platform at the back, with his reins running over the top of the roof and down to the draft animal's bit and bridle. The rhinoceros strained at its harness and scuffed at the cobblestones as it waited for its passengers to get aboard.

"Where to?" the cabbie shouted through his thick scarf.

"Limehouse!" Grim barked. "St. Arnfinn's Lane, if you know it."

"Disgusting!" The driver spat. "And with kids, even!" But he cracked his whip, and the rhino snorted into motion.

"Where are we going?" Charlie asked.

"Back into the stink," Ollie muttered.

"Everything stinks," Bob said. His chin straps bounced against his cheeks. "An' every*body*. Except Grim and Charlie, now. Welcome to London."

"The, ah, dairies," Henry Clockswain said. He folded and unfolded his hands repeatedly.

"The dairies," Grim agreed, and then they both fell quiet and stared out opposite windows. Charlie was squished in the middle, so he looked over the trotting rhinoceros at London as it flashed by.

Two policemen passed going the other direction. They rode zebras and carried cutlasses at their belts, and Charlie recognized their dark blue uniforms with short capes and buttons. He shrank into the seat of the hansom cab to hide, but neither of the policemen noticed him.

The streets became darker. Charlie saw fewer long coats, and more tunics and togas and robes. Then he began to see hulders. Not many, and some of them staggered like they were sick, leaning against walls and even falling to their knees.

The hansom turned down a smaller street and stopped. "St. Arnfinn's," the cabbie grumbled.

The street was unpaved and muddy. The buildings looked like shops, with iron bars dropped in front of the windows for the night. There were no signboards, but hitching posts stood in front of many of the buildings. Large horses waited, tied to the posts, along with a couple of zebras and even a yawning tiger, all saddled and hitched.

The lane reeked of animal sweat and dung, and something else. Charlie sniffed a moment and thought about it.

Sour cheese. St. Arnfinn's Lane smelled like sour cheese.

He saw no humans, and only a few hulders. The trolls moved slowly, or lounged against the street's brick walls in silence.

"Thank you." Grim paid the cabbie, they all climbed down, and then the rhinoceros pulled the cab away.

Grim approached one of the idling trolls. The other troll

was bigger than Grim, and mostly hidden behind a shabby black coat and scarf. "Looking for Egil Olafsson," Grim snarled, and tossed a coin to the hulder. "The one they call One-Arm."

The troll caught the coin and bit it. He squinted at Grim and then nodded at an open doorway across the street. Grim nodded back.

"Of course it would have to be *that* one," Grim said to nobody in particular. He sighed, shifted his belt, tucked his shirt in, and lifted his hat to tease a few strands of hair back into place with his fingers. Then he patted Charlie on the back. "Follow me, Charlie. And brace yourself."

Female trolls may be slightly more difficult to identify. Their tendency to be taller than the average human and their almost universally fair hair may assist a sharp-eyed observer in spotting them, but the unmistakable mark of a hulder woman is one she shares with the males of her species: all hulders have long, cowlike tails.

—Smythson, *Almanack,* "Troll"

Charlie shuffled into the darkness on Grim's heels. Past the troll's flapping coat he saw a glimmer of dusty yellowish-green light. Then he and Grim punched through a curtain of bones knotted into leather thongs, which made Charlie think of a spider's web. He shuddered, and entered a small room with a standing desk.

Behind the desk stood a woman, and she was beautiful. She was tall, taller than Charlie's bap, though not nearly as tall as Grim. Long blond hair tumbled around her face and was pinned back by a tortoiseshell comb over one ear. Her eyes twinkled as blue as Grim's even in the flickering yellow-green light. Cherries shone on the cheeks and in the smiling lips of her cream-white face.

"Grim Grumblesson," she said. "I hope you left your high horse tied to the hitching post outside."

Grim growled, a low, purring, throaty noise that made Charlie step back. "Something *wrong* with caring about the future of my *people*, Ingrid?"

"Is there something *wrong* with having a little *fun*?" the woman countered.

The light to Charlie's left winked out and back on again. Surprised, he turned to look at it. He was even more surprised to see that the light came from an insect. The bug was the size of his fist, and it was all abdomen, like an aphid or a tick—Charlie had seen pictures in *Insects of the Isles*, a dog-eared tome in his bap's library. *Insects of the Isles* didn't mention any aphid or tick this big, though, or any that cast light. The insect's abdomen glowed a sickly yellow, with just a hint of green.

The bug was free, and crawled slowly along the wall of the room. Charlie reached out to touch the bug with one finger—

and it flew away, *shup-shup-shup-shup*, three or four feet to a new perch on the wall.

Charlie looked around. The room was lit by nothing but bugs, fifteen or twenty of them, all slowly creeping around with their lights winking.

The rest of Charlie's friends stopped just inside the door. Ollie muttered something Charlie couldn't make out.

"Some kinds of fun are out of bounds," Grim ground out slowly.

"Dairies aren't illegal," Ingrid countered. Another thong curtain behind her parted, and a man strolled out. He wore a cravat, waistcoat, and top hat, and he was tall, with big muttonchop side-whiskers. Long hair tied in a queue down his back made him look a little like Grim, though a human version. In his hand he swung a cane with a large metal knob at the top. He slapped the knob into the palm of his other hand to punctuate his sentences.

"Anything wrong, darling?" he asked. *Slap.*

A glowing bug scuttled onto the desktop, and Ingrid brushed it away. "I don't think so, Sal," she said. "The law-speaker here was just telling me he doesn't like our business."

"Grim Grumblesson." *Slap.* "Well, I reckon I already knew what Mr. Grim Grumblesson thought of my business." *Slap.* "The two things about my business that Mr. Grim Grumblesson might like to keep very firmly in mind are that my business ain't illegal and my business . . . is *my business.*" *Slap!*

Grim trembled. Charlie was afraid the troll was going to explode, but when he spoke, his words came out measured. "I'm not here about your dairy, Sal. I'm here to help this boy." He patted Charlie on the shoulder, and Charlie smiled his best smile.

Ingrid's harsh expression melted into something warmer. She looked touched, and something else. Sad, maybe.

Sal shook his head. "If you're looking for an orphanage, this ain't it. Try the nuns up the street."

Grim growled. "I'm here for Egil One-Arm. Give him up, and we'll have no trouble."

"I don't know no Egil One-Arm." *Slap.* Sal stepped a little closer.

"And if we did know him, he isn't here," Ingrid added. The warm expression was gone.

"And if he was, we wouldn't tell you anyway." *Slap.* "'Cause if there was a jotun here named Egil, he'd be a customer, and that'd make him *my . . . business.*" *Slap. Slap.*

Grim's voice rumbled low. "Egil Olafsson, called One-Arm, is a criminal. That makes him *my business.* You can let me in, Sal, or I can raise the hue and cry. If I come back here with a dozen honest hulders who aren't milkers, there's no telling how much *accidental damage* they might do to your disgusting . . . *business.*"

Sal's face twitched in the yellow-green light. *Slap!* Ingrid looked from Sal to Grim and back again. Just in case, Charlie slipped his hand into his jacket pocket and wrapped his fingers around his clasp knife.

A glowing bug dropped from the ceiling onto the desktop. It landed belly up and lay there with its legs twitching.

"Fine. We'll do this the hard way." Grim turned to leave.

Sal swung his cane—

splat!

The glowing bug on the desktop exploded. It left behind a yellow-green phosphorescent puddle and a few bits of insect carapace. Charlie swallowed.

"You win, lawspeaker." Sal looked at Ingrid and smiled a greasy smile. "*This* time." He turned and disappeared into the back.

Ingrid pointed at another curtain to her right.

Grim nodded and led the way. Before he turned and lost sight of her, Charlie thought he heard her murmur, "Poor kid."

In the dark hallway beyond, lit by just one bug crawling slowly along the ceiling, Gnat flitted to Charlie's side. "Ingrid used to be married to Grim," the pixie whispered.

"Oh," Charlie said. "Grim was married to a human woman?"

The pixie shook her head. "Ingrid's a hulder. All hulder women look like her. Many human men desire them in marriage."

Charlie thought back to what he had read about hulder society. "The *Almanack* didn't mention that."

The pixie shrugged. "'Tis a sensitive point."

The hall turned, and they began trudging up stairs. "You must have the second edition," Grim said, barging into the conversation. "Smythson wrote a lot more in the first edition, but some of us went and had a conversation with him. We persuaded him that certain sufferings were private and didn't need to be printed for all the world to read about."

"You heard us," Charlie said.

"I've got big ears. And we weren't married. She decided that settling down wasn't really the life she wanted. Said she couldn't see me as a father, and didn't want to see herself as a mother."

"If she's a milker, you're better off," Ollie sniffed.

"She's a milker," Grim agreed. "And she likes human men. Like far too many of her sisters do."

The stairs ended in a hallway, with thong-curtained doorways on each side. The sour-milk smell was stronger up here, and mixed in with it was a stink of animal sweat and other bodily fluids. This was what it would smell like inside a latrine in the middle of a cow pasture next to a boarded-up cheese factory, Charlie thought.

"This is work for smaller folk than you, Grim," Gnat said. She zipped through the nearest curtain.

Grim shuffled to a halt and drew his pistol. He checked its caps and turned its cylinder to move the hammer off the empty chamber. Bob and Ollie followed his lead; Bob struck a martial pose with his sword, and Ollie opened and shut the umbrella twice. Charlie unlocked his clasp knife and held it in his hand, blade pointed at the floor.

"May I ask . . . why the insects?" Charlie was starting to imagine them crawling over his own skin.

"Glowbugs," Grim said. "When you're dealing with milkers, you want to minimize the fire hazards."

"I don't like this. We could still call the London police," Henry Clockswain squeaked. "They can't *all* be bad. We're stirring a pot of bees here."

"No," Grim croaked, his voice like the brakes of a train. "This is *really* none of their business."

Gnat emerged from a curtain. "He's in here."

"Follow me, lads," the troll said. "And watch out for the arm. It packs a wallop."

Grim burst through the curtain, and Charlie followed right behind. The room was square and hot, with tall shutters closed over the windows. In the center of the room was a long, low, wide platform. It was carved of wood and looked like a bed without a mattress, raised off the floor to the height of Charlie's knee. The sides of the bed were solid, and they were carved with a dense network of images. Charlie thought he could make out dancing, drinking, and feasting in the carving work. Not human, though. Trolls.

On the bed lay a troll. He was huge, maybe even bigger than Grim. His eyes were open, but they were rolled back into his head and twitching. His snaggletoothed mouth gaped wide. Thick drool slid down his check and puddled under his neck. He wore a white film of milk like a mustache on his enormous upper lip.

Beside the bed a clay pitcher sat on a heavy chair. Over the back of the chair hung the troll's large coat.

Charlie could see the troll's right arm clearly. It was brass from shoulder to tip. Its shoulder and elbow were ball joints, and the arm ended in another ball, with three pinching claws like grotesque fingers. Charlie saw the shoulder joint clearly, because the troll's chest was covered only in a filthy sleeveless undershirt; the ball of the shoulder seemed to be permanently attached to the troll's flesh with brass bands that wrapped around his chest. It wasn't a prosthetic, like a pirate's wooden leg—the device was part of Egil One-Arm. The rest of the troll shivered, but his arm lay still and slowly piped thin jets of steam out its ball joints.

This was the hulder whose face Charlie hadn't been able to see while he kidnapped Charlie's bap. This was the troll from

Cavendish Hats who had knocked Grim Grumblesson down with one punch.

Grim stood over Egil One-Arm with his Eldjotun pointed at him.

Charlie stared. "This is terrible."

"Milk makes trolls sick," Ollie explained.

"Yeah," Bob agreed, "only some of 'em like it."

"Or they don't have the strength to quit." Grim's voice was somber. He pointed his pistol at Egil One-Arm and squeezed the trigger.

BANG!

Smoke poured from the gun. Egil sat up, eyes rolling wild and unconnected in his head. His mechanical arm didn't sit up with him; it fell to the floor with a loud *clang-g-g!*

Grim had shot Egil's arm off.

"What?" Egil bellowed. "Who's there?"

"Stay back," Grim warned the boys. "Bob, watch the door." He bent and picked up the severed arm. Its claw clenched and unclenched spastically.

Bob stationed himself by the exit, sword in his good hand.

Egil slapped himself on the side where his arm had been. "What happened?" His eyes were starting to roll in the same direction. "Where's my arm?"

"Got your arm right here," Grim said. He reached forward with the mechanical arm and pressed it against Egil's face. The claws clenched, squeezing Egil's forehead and cheeks. "The bad news for you is I'm in a foul mood today. The good news is I think you can tell me a few things that will cheer me up."

"O where have you been, my long-horned lad,
These seven years and more?"
"O I'm come to hold you to heart-sworn vows
You granted me before."

"Speak to me not of heart-sworn vows;
They'll bring you only strife.
Mistake me not for one of your herd,
For I am a farmer's wife."

"Your farmer may plant wheat and rye,
But be you not beguiled;
However many beds he carve,
He'll never plant a child."

—Francis James Child, *The English and Scottish Popular Ballads,*
Including Certain Lyrics of Britain's Ancient Folk, No. 72

"I won't tell you nothing!" The claw on One-Arm's face squeezed, and the hulder grunted in pain. Blood trickled around the fingers of the claw.

Grim twisted the arm. His face was full of fury and hatred. It was the ugliest Charlie had ever seen his big friend, and he lurched back. "The kidnapping!" Grim yelled. "What do you want with Raj Pondicherry?"

"Ram off!" Sweat poured off Egil One-Arm's face.

"Cavendish Hats!" Grim thundered, twisting again. His hat tumbled off, and he squashed it with a heavy boot. "Why the explosives? What are you doing? Who's paying you, you worthless scum?"

"Milk yourself!"

"The Iron Cog!" Grim rumbled, and gave such a twist to the arm that Egil nearly fell off the bed. "The Anti-Human League! Who are they and what do they want?"

Egil One-Arm attacked.

He spun inward and smashed his left forearm against the mechanical arm, wrenching it out of Grim's grasp. With the backward twist of the same movement, he slammed the shoulder end of the mechanical arm against the Eldjotun, just as Grim raised it to fire.

BANG!

The bullet chomped a hole the size of Charlie's chest right in the center of one of the shutters. The gun sailed through the air in one direction, while the arm released its death grip on Egil Olafsson's face and went spinning in the other. With its first twirl, the arm banged into Natalie de Minimis, slamming her to the floor.

Egil sprang forward. He rammed his head, horns first, into Grim's forehead. Grim staggered back.

Bob yanked his sword from his belt and charged. Ollie was right behind him, the tip of the umbrella in his hand and the curved handle swinging through the air like a lasso.

"Milker!" Grim bellowed.

"Rat!" Egil leaped forward again. He plowed shoulder-first into Grim's chest, knocking him down.

Charlie took a swipe with his clasp knife at One-Arm's heel, but missed. Then the two trolls were thrashing on the ground in a thicket of fists and boots and horns, and he was afraid to try again. He didn't want to stab Grim by accident.

Bob slashed at the tumbling trolls, but his attacks were tentative. Ollie was bolder, and managed to hook the umbrella handle around one of the hulders—Charlie wasn't sure which one—but then the trolls rolled over, and the sudden motion hurled Ollie across the room.

Charlie had to do something. Even with one arm, Egil was winning, and however frightening Grim might have become here in the dairy, he was still on Charlie's side.

As Charlie looked for Grim's gun, he met Henry Clockswain's gaze. "I'll get the Fire Giant," the kobold told him; "you get the arm!"

Charlie scrambled for the corner. The big brass arm shuddered and twitched at the base of the wall like a wounded snake.

Charlie hesitated. Could it be true that he was really no more than this arm? No more than the mechanical songbirds in Lucky Wu's Earth Dragon Laundry, or the Articulated Gyroscopes?

It couldn't be.

"Thor's hammer!" he heard Grim shout.

Charlie picked up the arm. It was so heavy, he was surprised he could get it off the floor. But Charlie ignored his doubt and lifted, and found that he could stand and hold it very well.

He was, after all, very strong.

And that made him feel bad. Maybe it was true: he wasn't his bap's son.

BANG!

"Aaarrgh!"

Charlie spun around in time to see Grim Grumblesson crash to the floorboards, one white kid glove clapped to his chest. Red welled around Grim's fingers, and the hulder struggled to rise onto one elbow.

Bob crouched against the wall with Henry Clockswain. Charlie couldn't see the aeronaut's sword, and he didn't see Ollie. Gnat lay on her face, back arced in pain and wings fluttering.

One-Arm stood over the lawspeaker, the Eldjotun in his single fist. Egil's shaking, spastic eyeballs looked even scarier in the yellow-green light of the room's glowbugs.

Egil thumbed the hammer back on Grim's hand-cannon. "Let's see if you got any bullets left, you stupid toff."

"No!" Heaven-Bound Bob shouted.

He threw Ollie in snake form.

Egil turned just in time to take the incoming serpent right in the face. Ollie was a constrictor again, and he wrapped around the troll's neck as he hit.

"Ayyyayaaaaaayaaagh!"

In a puff of smoke and stench of eggs, Ollie became his boy self again. He was still wrapped around Egil One-Arm's head, but he jerked back, straightening out and snapping his body as he hollered and fell to the floor.

"Ow," Ollie moaned.

Charlie saw blood on Egil's snaggled tusks and a low, cunning grin on his lips. "Serves you right, you stupid French git." He kicked Ollie, who rolled across the room and plunked against the wall, clutching his stomach.

Bob crouched to look at his injured friend.

Grim struggled into a sitting position. He was gasping, and the puddle surrounding him, black in the dim light, was frighteningly large. The room reeked with the ripe stench of blood.

The troll lawspeaker held up a hand and pawed at the air in Egil's direction. His swipe fell several feet short.

Charlie's heart sank.

"Where was I?" One-Arm rumbled. "Oh, yeah."

He raised the Eldjotun again, pointing it at Grim's head.

Charlie charged. "Pondicherry's of Whitechapel!"

He tucked the mechanical arm's shoulder up into his armpit and held it like a lance, like he'd seen in his father's big illustrated copy of Malory's *Le Morte d'Arthur,* about King Arthur and his knights of the Round Table. As Charlie galloped across the room, the fingers clenched, unclenched—

Egil snorted and turned to face Charlie—

clenched, unclenched—

Egil pointed the gun at Charlie and frowned—

clenched, unclenched—

"Pondicherry's!" Charlie yelled again, and jumped.

Too late, Egil One-Arm tried to dodge. Charlie adjusted his own aim as the troll slipped sideways, and rammed the mechanical arm into Egil's crotch.

Clench.

"Hrooooowwwwwwghaaaagh!" Egil roared.

BANG!

Charlie's John Bull hat was whipped off his head by the

hurricane force of the six-hundred-caliber bullet. His scalp burned; he yelped, but he didn't fall down or let go. Pride kept him on his feet.

Egil One-arm dropped the gun, went slack, rolled his eyes up into his head, and toppled to the floor.

Charlie dropped the arm. "Yes!" he shouted.

Henry Clockswain ran forward to check Egil One-Arm.

"Charlie!" Bob hollered. "Your 'ead's on fire!"

Charlie smelled a bitter stink, so bad it cut through the cloying sweet-rotten-bloody smells that choked the air of the little room.

No wonder his scalp hurt.

"It's the gunpowder! It was so close, it lit you on fire!"

Charlie's head burned. He raced around the room, looking for anything to put out the fire. On his second circuit, Bob grabbed Charlie by the arm and diverted him toward the hall.

"Milk!" Charlie gasped. "Water! Something!"

"No time!" Bob snapped as they pushed through the curtain into the hall. "Keep a secret," the aeronaut chimney sweep hissed, "or else!"

Bob whipped off his leather bomber and clapped it down over Charlie's head. Charlie felt the flames smothered instantly.

Then Bob's hair fell down to his shoulders. It was long and curly and brown, and even in the dark it shone.

And he noticed, as if he'd never seen them before, that Bob's lips were heart-shaped and sweet.

And his fingers were gentle on Charlie's cheeks, clamping the hat down and saving him from the fire.

Charlie nearly fell over, and he couldn't believe he hadn't seen it before.

Bob's hair was down to *her* shoulders.

Heaven-Bound Bob was a *girl*.

It is debated whether the species commonly called *ghoul* ought to be considered a folk. Herbert's researches (1822), as well as the memoirs of the American military doctor Buchanan (1867), suggest a species devoid of tools, culture, and even language, so these subrational and illiterate creatures are best considered beasts, like carrion-eating, hairless chimpanzees.

—Smythson, *Almanack*, "Ghoul"

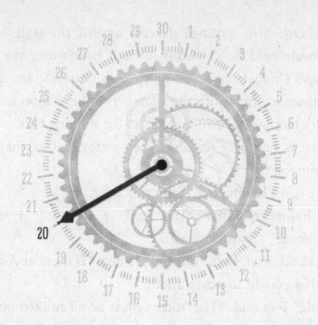

"Keep a secret," Bob hissed again. She piled her hair back under her bomber cap. For good measure, she buckled the chin straps. "Do it for a mate. You know I just saved you from burning up; don't you even think about saying nothing to nobody about me being anything but a lad."

"Bob?"

Bob sighed. "Roberta. Roberta Alice Micklemuch. But the odds ain't good with any orphan in life on the streets, an' they're longer still against a girl. You call me Bob, you 'ear?"

"Bob." Charlie could barely speak. "Your hair . . ."

"Yeah. Don't really want to *be* a boy, do I?"

"Does Ollie know?"

Bob shook her head. "Keep a secret." She led Charlie back into the milking room.

Egil One-Arm slumped dazedly against the wall. Henry Clockswain held Bob's sword in both hands over the troll. Ollie and Gnat struggled to help Grim Grumblesson sit up. Grim thumbed caps onto the chambers of his Eldjotun.

Egil's mechanical arm lay still on the milking bed.

"That is one ugly seafood," Bob swaggered as she came back into the room.

"I've had a rough day," Grim said.

"Nah, I mean old One-Arm 'ere."

"Seafood?" Charlie asked.

"Seafood bowl, troll," Ollie explained. "Is there anybody in the hall we ought to worry about?"

"Nah," Bob said. "The 'ulders must be all milked out, an' Ingrid an' Sal are minding their own business." She laughed. She looked completely different to Charlie now, and he had a hard time not staring.

"Right." Grim put one arm against the wall and lurched to his feet.

"Careful, Grim," Ollie said.

Grim pointed his big pistol at Egil One-Arm and thumbed back the hammer. "Last chance, dirty milker," he growled.

"The Jubilee." Egil still looked dazed. "They wanna replace the queen."

"The Anti-Human League?" Bob asked. "Replace 'er with what, a troll? A kobold? A dwarf? 'Ow on earth could anybody get away with that?"

Egil laughed. "No such thing as the Anti-Human League. They're gonna blow something up. I don't know, maybe Parliament. And then they're gonna kill Pondicherry. Dump his body at the scene. Blame it all on the Anti-Human League, but it's a fake. The explosion is to distract everybody, so they can get at the queen."

Charlie sat down sat down so he didn't fall down.

"Who are *they*, milker?" Grim snarled. "Stop talking in riddles."

Egil hesitated. His eyes rambled over the room. "The Iron Cog. The Frenchman. I do what he says, and I get paid. *He* talks about the Iron Cog."

"The French!" Ollie spat on the floor.

"What do they need Pondicherry for?" Grim pressed.

"Replace the queen, isn't it? Only Pondicherry knows how to make the inside bits right. So they need him to make the fake work." Egil shook his head. "That's what I hear from the Frenchman."

"That doesn't make any sense," Ollie complained.

"Rule Britain," Bob said. "Makes enough sense to me."

Charlie shuddered. "The garden party."

"Goodness gracious!" Henry Clockswain gasped. "You don't think they'll use this replacement queen to . . . er, er, murder all those foreign leaders, do you?" Charlie wasn't sure who the kobold was talking to. "Prince Bismarck, and the Emperor Franz-Joseph, and the Italian king?"

"Humberto," Bob said. No one corrected her.

"That would mean war." Grim's voice was quiet and sad.

One-Arm shrugged. "My job was get Pondicherry, then get his boy."

"Freya's frisky tail!" Grim cursed.

"Why Charlie?" Gnat asked. "Why would you want the boy?"

"They want to inverse interfere 'im," suggested Bob.

"Reverse engineer, you mean," Henry Clockswain said. "Take him apart to, ah, see how he works. You might be right. Sounds like the Iron Cog, whoever they are, are building a fake Queen Victoria. Sounds like they haven't quite figured it out yet. Maybe she's a clockwork creation."

"Like Charlie," Ollie said.

"I'm a boy," Charlie insisted. He desperately wanted it to be true. Especially now. "If they take me apart, I'll die."

"Nobody's taking you apart," Grim reassured him, "unless they take me apart first."

"The Frenchman's at Waterloo," Egil One-Arm volunteered. "Down with the trains, there's a maintenance door. It's at the end of platform thirteen. He's got a, a . . . a place . . ."

"A lair," Grim suggested. "A hideout. A safe house."

"Yeah," Egil agreed.

"Pitcher of milk, Bob," Grim instructed the aeronaut. She nodded and slipped out into the hall.

One-Arm licked his lips. "What you gonna do?" he asked.

"Who else is at this lair, besides the Frenchman?" Grim asked.

"Nobody."

"Not a gang of men with swords?" Gnat asked. "You sure? Not any more trolls like yourself, either?"

"Policemen," Charlie said.

"Yeah," Egil admitted. "Off-duty coppers and toughs like me. He hires us when he needs us. So unless he has some job going on I don't know about, he should be there alone."

Grim pulled his watch from his waistcoat. "Nearly morning," he announced. "The Jubilee and the progress flotilla and the garden party and everything else are tomorrow."

"The bar exam is *today*," Gnat said softly.

Bob returned, holding a pitcher in each hand.

"Yes." Grim laughed. "It is. But the examiners will be happy to accept my fee again next year." He sighed. "I don't think we can count on any help."

"I see now that we can't, er, go to the police," Henry Clockswain agreed.

"Can't raise the hue an' cry," Bob pointed out, setting the pitchers down on the milking bed. "It ain't an 'ulder affair, is it?"

"There'll be no help from my cousin Elisabel. Nor from her rat friends."

"On the other hand," Grim said, "if we act now, we catch the Frenchman alone. We rescue Raj Pondicherry and we stop the Iron Cog from replacing the queen with some sort of . . . of . . ." He looked at Charlie and flailed.

"Machine," Charlie finished for him. "Assassin." Bob put her hand on his shoulder.

Grim nodded, then picked up one of the pitchers. "Right, you," he snarled. "Drink up!"

He poured both pitchers down Egil One-Arm's throat. One-Arm drank eagerly, the milk glugging deeply in his throat and overflowing, spilling down his chin and onto his shirt. As Grim dropped the second empty pitcher, One-Arm let out a long rumbling belch and collapsed. They left him leaning against the wall and slobbering on himself.

When they walked through the front, Ingrid looked up with something on her face that might have been relief. The room was dimly lit, but Charlie thought her lip was bleeding and the cherries on her cheeks were smudged.

"Grim . . . ," she said softly.

Grim kept walking.

When they emerged into St. Arnfinn's Lane in the gray predawn light, the big troll sighed heavily, removed his crumpled top hat, and ran his fingers through his hair. It had escaped its queue in the fight, and he managed to chase some of it back into place.

"Sky Trestle will be running," Ollie said. "That'll take us straight to Waterloo."

"'Ome," Bob laughed.

"You live at Waterloo Station?" Charlie asked.

"Nah," she answered, "but close by. An' I keep my wings there, to be ready for the flotilla. They're in a locker."

"The boy," Henry Clockswain said to Grim. "He's been put into enough, ah, danger already tonight. We can take him to his father's shop. Or to my place, Grim, or to yours."

"Not on your life," Charlie said. "I'm coming."

"It isn't safe, Charlie." The kobold's eyes blinked like hummingbird wings. "Think how sad your father would be if you were hurt."

"My father would be sad just to know that I had left the house." Charlie laughed. "He'd probably pinch me. But my father's been kidnapped, and I'm going to rescue him. This is my business, as much as it is any of yours. More. I'm going to Waterloo Station."

"Charlie—" Mr. Clockswain tried again.

"Enough!" Grim roared. "The lad says he's coming, so he comes." The troll dropped to one knee to talk to Charlie. "I'm sorry I didn't let you have a weapon earlier," he said. "I was confused and surprised and, well, uncertain what to make of you after Bob said . . . after Bob showed us you could hold your breath. But you've proved yourself."

"I don't need a sword or a gun," Charlie said. "I've got a good knife. A good knife is all a fellow needs."

Grim threw back his head and laughed.

"Fine." Henry Clockswain fussed with his jacket collar. "But stick close to me, Charlie."

"Too right," Ollie said. "Charlie'll keep you safe."

They boarded the Sky Trestle at a station a few streets away. Charlie tried not to look at the automaton token dispenser, but at least *it* couldn't notice how bloodied and bedraggled Charlie's friends were. Other passengers did, and they squeezed close to each other as Charlie's friends climbed aboard, to huddle together at the far end of the car.

This time Grim managed to keep one eye open so he could duck when they climbed onto the train. Once they were all sitting down, he shut them both again.

Charlie pressed himself to the window as the train chugged

slowly into motion. Limehouse passed beneath them, and Wapping, under sheets of coal smoke. Then Charlie was beyond the little area of his hard-earned knowledge of the streets of London, and everything was a maze.

Church bells *tolled* and brass angels sprang out of a bell tower's windows to wave their trumpets as the train rumbled by. "St. Mary-le-Bow," Bob said proudly, and jerked a thumb at herself. "Born within the sound."

The sun came up as the train rolled by a great stone cupola. In the square below, Charlie saw idling steam-carriages throw open their doors to deposit their owners, who were beginning to straggle into morning services. "St. Paul's," Ollie told him, scratching behind his ears.

"Fleet Street," Henry Clockswain pointed out. Charlie was amazed at the thickness of the crowd that began to clog the streets. Its many colors astonished him too. What he had seen of Whitechapel had been dirty and gray, but London had its scarlets and whites and purples, too. "And the Embankment."

Charlie got his first glimpse of the Thames. It was huge, a flood, a plain, a great silvery-pink sheet in the morning sun. A paved footpath wound along the edge of the river, crowded with little food stands and Egyptian monuments: obelisks and stone sphinxes and statues of Egyptian gods Charlie knew from his bap's library: Anubis and Osiris and Wepwawet, Opener of the Ways.

Ahead, Charlie saw the enormous face of Whitehall's famous clock tower. He had read about it. Everyone called the tower itself Big Ben, he knew, though technically that was just the name of the big bell inside the tower. Beyond it was a jagged, pointy-topped palace that Charlie thought must be the Houses of Parliament.

Then the Sky Trestle turned to cross the river. The tracks soared on high, delicate arches of iron and wood. Below, bridges carried other kinds of traffic over the river.

"Waterloo Station," Gnat said, pointing ahead of them.

"About time," Grim muttered.

"'Ome," said Heaven-Bound Bob.

The sky above them cracked open, and rain poured down.

Only then did Charlie realize he'd left his father's hat behind in the dairy.

Traditionally, a Cockney is any person born within earshot of the bells of the Church of St. Mary-le-Bow, though residents of a broader area may refer to themselves by the name. Cockneys employ a distinctive rhyming slang, in which a word may be replaced by the first word of a pair of semantically connected words, or the beginning of a phrase, where the second word in the pair or the final word of the phrase rhymes with the word substituted. For instance, *apples* may be substituted for *stairs*, because the phrase *apples and pears* rhymes with *stairs*, and *frog* may be substituted for *road*, because *frog and toad* rhymes with *road*.

—Smythson, *Almanack*, "London"

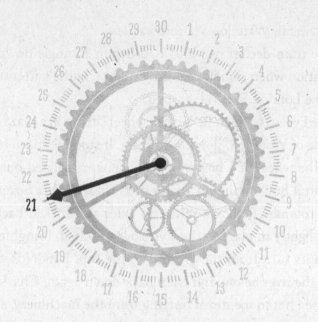

Waterloo Station was one part anthill, one part wheel hub, and one part cocklebur. It gleamed with a dull brass-and-iron glow even in the rain, towering majestically over the Thames on the river's south bank and launching arms of the Sky Trestle in all directions. Below the Sky Trestle a stream of wagons, hansoms, steam-carriages, velocipedes, riders, and pedestrians rushed in and out of the near side of the station; out the far side raced iron rails that carried trains away into the green hills of southeast England. Upon the flat roof grazed swollen zeppelins, tethered and drifting just above the broad surface. Mooring towers shot up at forty-five-degree angles all around the station like the spikes of a crown, to which gliders, montgolfiers, and flyers of other sorts were anchored.

Above all, Waterloo Station was *busy.*

The train decelerated and had begun to angle down into the station when something else caught Charlie's attention.

"The London Eye!" he gasped.

The Eye was a gigantic leisure wheel sitting in a plaza off to the side of Waterloo, slowing turning. It stood vertical, resembling the wheel of a hansom. Long spokes radiated out from its central hub, ending in a ring of brass-and-glass boxes, like metal rooms. The boxes hung on axles and rocked back and forth slightly in place as the Eye slowly rotated, bringing each box in its turn from the ground to the top, hundreds of feet above the river below, and then back down again. Charlie was surprised not to see steam puffing from the machinery, and he wondered how it worked. Maybe Bob knew.

His bap certainly would. Charlie plunged a hand into his pocket and wrapped his fingers around his bap's pipe.

Charlie had read that the Eye never stopped. If you took a ride—once rides had actually started, on the Jubilee morning—a conductor would help you board one of its boxy brass-and-glass carriages as it slowly passed at ground level. You would go once around, which might take half an hour or more, and when your carriage reached the ground again, you would get out. It did look magnificent, and great fun.

But it also looked like a giant cog, and at the sight of it Charlie fell silent.

The stampede of rain on the rooftop ceased, and the carriage went dark as their train plunged into the station. Light returned when the train rolled to a stop at a long concrete platform, illuminated by gaslights on tall poles. Charlie and his friends piled out and stopped beside a rickety wooden newsstand to stretch and shake the kinks out of their backs and necks.

"We smell like pigs," Ollie commented.

"We rescue Mr. Pondicherry, I'll stand you a bath," Grim rumbled.

"'Ey, look 'ere." Bob pointed at the headlines of the morning's newspapers, painted with black ink onto large sheets of paper and tacked to the sides of the newsstand. HEAVY SHOWERS DAY BEFORE JUBILEE, they announced, and ROYAL MAGICAL SOCIETY WARNS OF CLOUD SQUEEZING. "'Eavy showers, getting all the rain out an' making it nice for the queen tomorrow."

"Could have warned us yesterday," Ollie complained.

"Who d'you think you're fooling, lad?" Gnat shook her head. "This is England. When was the last day you had *without* a risk of heavy showers? Why do you think my folk live underground?"

"Check your weapons, gentlemen," Grim suggested. He then loaded his pistol; Bob drew her sword and swiped it through the air as she struck various martial poses; Ollie snapped his umbrella open twice and playfully stabbed at Mr. Clockswain. Charlie opened and closed his clasp knife.

"I've lost my spear," Gnat said sadly.

"I remember." Grim smiled. "But you've still got your teeth."

The pixie laughed, but it sounded forced.

The newsstand had a basket of apples for sale. Grim bought

them all and passed them out. After two minutes' munching, the cores were tossed into a rubbish bin and Charlie and his friends were moving again.

The Sky Trestle platform was part of a maze. With Gnat flitting ahead as a scout to look for trouble, Charlie and his friends limped through it. Charlie stopped counting how many platforms he'd seen at an even dozen, all tangled together with yellow-lit halls and concrete stairwells.

The walls were decorated with scenes in mosaic tile. The scenes celebrated the defeat of Napoleon Bonaparte—the station was named after that famous battle, of course—and the greatness of Britain generally. British dwarfs and kobolds worked with Isambard Kingdom Brunel on his bridges and trains; Jamaican ships sailed up the Thames heavy with sugar; alfar planted and defended England's great reborn forests; Indian elephants carried huge baskets of gems to lay at the feet of the young empress Victoria; hulders farmed England's rolling green hills.

"Not all folk are equally represented in these pictures we're seeing," Gnat complained.

"That's right." Ollie snickered. "If I was a ghoul or a shaitan, I'd be right irritated that my contribution was not being taken seriously."

"When you've slain your three mighty beasts," Grim told the pixie, "I promise you I'll commission a monument."

"Hmm," Gnat snorted, and flew on ahead. Almost immediately she zipped back into view. "Welcome to Waterloo Station proper!"

Charlie emerged from the tunnels onto a broad balcony and immediately had to step aside. Four moving staircases, shoulder to shoulder, lifted and deposited passengers on the balcony right in front of Charlie. They were tall ramps with dark wooden walls to waist height, broad bronze steps, and a long hand railing of leather. Charlie jumped out of the way to avoid getting trampled by the herd of frock coats.

"How do we get down?" he asked. "All the staircases go *up*."

The balcony ran all around an enormous waiting room. Below, people swarmed out of gates opening onto train platforms and into the city. Some of them rode the moving staircases up and toward the Sky Trestle. Others flooded out wide doors to waiting hansoms and rickshaws.

"Over there," Ollie pointed. "With the flyer passengers."

Across the big room Charlie saw another set of moving stairs. There were two of them, and they were spiral staircases, bronze and polished to a high shine. One carried people up into the ceiling, toward the mooring towers (it was mostly empty), and the other brought them down again (it was packed).

They skirted the balcony and forced themselves onto the downward staircase. It didn't look like there would be enough room for them until Grim growled and stepped close. The sight of the huge hulder, bloodied and disheveled, made two men in dark wool suits jump back and bury their faces in newspapers. Charlie and the chimney sweeps popped into the newly opened space.

As they rode the moving stairs down through the floor, Bob nodded at a hallway that opened from the balcony. Before it was out of sight, Charlie saw walls of tall, narrow metal doors. "The lockers," Bob whispered, and she winked.

Charlie looked around to make sure no one was listening to them. "Were you just planning on . . . on *launching*, tomorrow?" Ollie huddled close. "I mean, how would you do that, without getting stopped? This place is so busy."

"Right out the window," Bob nodded. "There'll be coppers all over the towers, of course, but my flyer's so small I can launch it without a tower. It don't need a runway, only the gyroscopes. Just need a small drop, really."

"What is your flyer, a pair of wings?" Charlie asked. "For just one person?"

"Two. Ollie's my copilot."

"Copilot, my eye," Ollie chortled. "I'm the pretty lady on the front of the ship. Can't have a ship without a pretty lady."

"Finger bread," Bob chuckled, and elbowed Charlie in the ribs.

"Figurehead, you mean," Charlie said.

"Yeah," Bob agreed. "That's what I thought I said."

They crossed the big room. Above the gate to each land-train platform was a signboard made up of clacketing rows of characters that spun around to show departure times and destinations.

"Alton," Ollie read the sign over platform thirteen. "Sounds like a real hole."

"You think everything outside London is an 'ole," Bob reproached him.

"Everything outside London *is* a hole," Ollie agreed. "A fellow's gotta have standards. But you can say this for Alton: at least it's in England."

They crossed through the gate and onto the platform. It was narrow, paved with small gray stones and posted with multiple warnings to MIND THE GAP and HAVE YOUR TICKET READY. A white line ran along each edge of the platform, just before a drop into the deep trench where the trains idled. The Alton-line train had not arrived yet.

The platform ended in a brick wall, featureless except for a metal door, painted red.

Henry Clockswain tried the handle. "Locked."

Grim gripped his Eldjotun by the barrel and raised its heavy handle like a hammer.

"'Old on!" Bob called. "Let me give it a try." She whipped a thin wallet from her peacoat pocket and extracted what looked to Charlie like two long steel pins. Bob inserted them into the keyhole and fiddled briefly with them.

Click.

Bob pushed the door slightly ajar and stepped aside. Grim shouldered forward to have a look.

"Goodness gracious," Henry Clockswain said, eyes blinking furiously. "Almost like a burglar."

"Burglar!" Ollie flared. "He's a top mechanick, you thick-witted midget, and don't you forget it! He's an inventor, too, not second-fiddle errand boy to the real brains of his shop!"

Bob grabbed Ollie by the front of his peacoat, trying to clamp a hand over her friend's mouth.

"You little weasel!" Mr. Clockswain barked. The kobold's

voice had a fierce edge. "I was cutting my teeth on cogs and springs while your mother was an orphan strumpet picking horse apples off the street with her bare hands and selling them for firewood at ha'penny a bushel!"

Ollie fought free of Bob's hands and wound up to shout back at the kobold. "I—"

Grim clapped a hand over Ollie's mouth. "Bob's a top mechanick," he agreed, "and you're very loud."

"Mmmph, mmmmph." Ollie thrashed about for a moment and then calmed down. Henry Clockswain rubbed both eyes with his hands and backed away.

"Right," Grim agreed. "It's a staircase going down. I'll lead the way, and then Bob, Gnat, and the kobold. I need you and Charlie to stay up here and keep an eye out."

"For enemies," Charlie suggested.

"Yes." Grim let go of Ollie, and he straightened himself up. "Or train staff, or passengers, or anybody else. Bang hard on the door three times if you need to warn us of anything."

Ollie sulked, but he didn't argue.

Grim led the way down into the darkness below Waterloo Station. Gnat followed, and then Bob and Henry Clockswain. The kobold shut the door behind them.

"Horse apples," Ollie muttered. He kicked a light-pole.

"Mr. Clockswain's not so bad," Charlie said.

"You wouldn't say that if it was your dad he called an orphan picking up horse droppings, though, would you?"

Ollie was right. Before Charlie could think of a good answer, a group of men sprang onto the platform. They came out of the Alton-line trench, dragging themselves up and rolling to their feet. They were big and brutish, and they were waving cutlasses.

Five men. Six, seven.

"Ollie!" Charlie shouted.

Eight, nine!

Ollie had just enough time to spin around and raise his umbrella to a defensive position, and Charlie had just enough time to pull his clasp knife from his pocket, before they were both swept away.

The society funds magical research, employs professors of magic at the nation's universities, and advises the Crown with respect to arcane matters. Although it does not limit itself to weather management, ensuring clear skies for important civic events, such as the Greater Cloud Sealing that guaranteed dry streets for the February 1840 wedding of Queen Victoria and Prince Albert, and the Lesser Cloud Sealing of 1859 for the funeral of Isambard Kingdom Brunel, is the most visible and broadly beneficial of the society's acts. Fellows are commonly referred to as *weather wizards*.

—Smythson, *Almanack*, "Royal Magical Society"

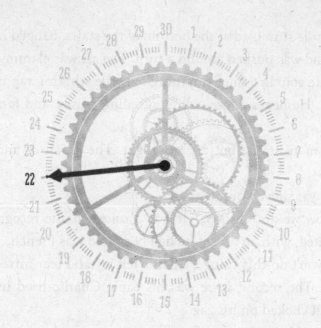

en threw a sack over Charlie's head and yanked his knife from his hand. He kicked and squirmed, but the men shoved his hands into shackles and then gagged him with a bitter, oily-tasting cloth.

"Hands off!" he heard Ollie shout. Through the sack Charlie smelled rotten eggs.

"In the bag!" someone yelled.

Charlie heard men shouting, and the scraping of boots. Then quiet.

He heard the groan of door hinges, and hands pushed at his shoulders. He stumbled down stairs, banging his head against a wall. When he fell, hands caught him. They were rough hands, and being caught felt a lot like being hit.

Charlie stumbled at the bottom of the stairs, banged into a wall, and was pushed around a turn. The air was clammy and cold. He couldn't smell anything over the stinking rag in his mouth. He heard clicks, whirs, grinding noises, and faraway booms.

Up more stairs, but a short flight. The groan of another door.

He was shoved onto a stool.

"Now we are all here." It was a voice Charlie recognized and hated, with an accent he had been told was French.

"I won't do this thing." Charlie felt joy and fear mixed together. The second voice was his bap's. Charlie tried to call out, but choked on his gag.

"Not if I threaten to kill you?"

"Kill me, I don't care. I am done with the Cog. I only want to be left alone."

"But, Dr. Singh," the Sinister Man said, "don't you see that you *are* fighting against us? The Cog invested so much in your research, and then you and the other turncoat stole our technology. Now I am giving you one last opportunity to make things right. You will finish our queen, or you will regret it."

"You can make no threat that will persuade me."

"No? Let us see if that is true."

Charlie was pushed off the stool and forced to stumble across an uneven floor. He barely managed to keep his footing. The sack was whipped off his head, and he heard his bap gasp. One of the men behind Charlie ripped the gag from his mouth.

"Bap!" Charlie shouted.

He lurched forward, but strong arms grabbed him from behind.

Charlie was in a large chamber with walls and floors of rough red brick. Like the workroom at Pondicherry's Clockwork Invention & Repair, this room was full of tools and parts, stacked on shelves and piled on tables.

Charlie's friends—Bob, Grim, Gnat, and Mr. Clockswain—sat on a row of stools against one wall. They all had shackles on their wrists, like Charlie. Their guns were gone, and they had sacks over their heads. On the floor in front of them rested a bulging, writhing sack; Charlie guessed that Ollie must be trapped inside, in snake form. Behind them stood men with cutlasses.

Charlie's bap and the Sinister Man stood next to the biggest table in the center of the room. Mr. Pondicherry was dirty and rumpled, and his ankles were shackled together with a short chain. The Sinister Man held a long-barreled pistol.

Beside them, her back perfectly straight, stood Queen Victoria. Her presence made Charlie feel like his entire family was here, and he tried to bow. He couldn't quite do it, because of the arms holding him, but he managed at least to bob his head. He thought Her Majesty would understand.

The Sinister Man laughed. "Oh, Doctor, how your toy delights me!"

"He is not a toy," Mr. Pondicherry said. "He is my son."

"Even better," the Sinister Man said. He raised his pistol and pointed it at Charlie's forehead. "Can I make a threat that persuades you *now*, Dr. Singh?"

Charlie's bap slumped on his stool.

"That isn't the queen," Charlie realized. She didn't move at all. He had heard of Madame Tussaud's wax figures, but he had also heard that they didn't look very lifelike. They *looked* like wax. This Victoria looked like flesh and blood.

"No, it isn't. That's Dr. Singh's *daughter*!" The Frenchman laughed uproariously.

The Sinister Man cocked the hammer of his big pistol. The gun looked especially huge so close to Charlie's face.

"I'll do it," Mr. Pondicherry said, and he looked down at the shackles on his feet.

"Bap!"

"Take them all away!" The Sinister Man uncocked his pistol and shoved it into his belt. "Give the good doctor a few minutes with his *son*."

Charlie's bap reached out to grab Charlie, but Charlie was whisked out of his reach by two sword-slinging men. Both the Pondicherrys, and all of Charlie's hooded friends, were hauled off through a door, down a dark brick passage, and down more stairs, and then tossed through an open doorway. Charlie landed hard, and his bap and all his friends hit the ground around him.

The door slammed shut behind them and total darkness fell.

The smell of rotten eggs, and the sound of tearing cloth.

"That ain't my dad," Ollie said.

"Course it ain't."

"Just because he's French don't mean he's my dad."

"Course not. You're a good English lad, same as me. Now get this bag off my 'ead. I can't see a thing."

"It's completely dark," Charlie told Bob. "You wouldn't see a thing anyway."

"Aye, but *I* would. Get this mess off my face and I'll have a look around."

"A butcher's," Charlie said. Nobody laughed.

Charlie heard muttering and scraping sounds. "Charlie," his bap said. "I must tell you something."

"Aye, tell him everything," Gnat agreed. "Only get this sack off my face first."

"It's about what you must do when you escape," Bap continued.

"I'll help," Ollie offered.

More scraping sounds, and shuffling, and then Gnat gasped.

"We're in a tunnel," the pixie announced. "I think an unfinished train tunnel. There are tracks."

"I can feel that," Ollie agreed. "Right in my back."

"There's a door, the one we came through. And the tunnel ends in a wall in one direction, and bars in the other. Close together; I'd not be able to squeeze between them."

"Not a very good train tunnel, then," Grim snorted.

"The Iron Cog must have barred off the end of this unfinished section," Charlie's bap guessed. In the darkness his hand found Charlie's and squeezed it. "Is there any other way out? And is there anyone watching us?"

"One of the sets of bars has a door in it. 'Tis shut with a lock. There's nobody else here but us . . . except . . ."

"What is it?" Charlie asked. His arm gave a twitch, sudden and herky-jerky. That had never happened to him before. He must be tired.

"There's folk beyond the bars. Rotten-smelling, nasty folk."

"Rats?" Ollie asked. "We can handle rats."

"They smell like dust and dead flesh," Natalie de Minimis said. "Ghouls."

Mr. Pondicherry squeezed Charlie's hand again. "I have to tell you something."

"Bob can pick that lock," Ollie said. "Or a snake could get through."

"They stole my tools," Bob complained, "so I don't think I could. An' if there's ghouls, I don't think I want to. An' you don't want to either, mate. Not alone."

"If it was the only way out?" Grim pressed.

"I think it *is* the only way out," Gnat said.

"What is it, Bap?" Charlie asked.

"Remember," Mr. Pondicherry said. "If anything happens to me, and if you can escape—"

"I'll go to Cader Idris," Charlie answered, "in Wales. I've got a good memory, Bap."

"Good," Mr. Pondicherry continued. "So you remember I told you to find Caradog Pritchard? He's an old friend of mine. He'll help you."

"Yes." Charlie's arm twitched again. He tried to ignore it, but he felt out of sorts. "Is it true, Bap?" he asked. He knew the answer, but he hoped his father would deny it. "Am I like *her*? Like that Queen Victoria?"

"No." His bap laughed. "No, Charlie, you're a good boy.

And you're nothing like her. That Queen Victoria the Iron Cog have made, it is a *thing*. It is nothing more than a thing. They've made her to obey orders, and that's all she can do. That's the plan, you see? They will replace the real queen with a fake queen, who will do everything they tell her."

"I'm a natural boy," Charlie whispered, but he didn't think that was what his father was really telling him.

"You, my boy, you are different. You *don't* obey orders. You have a good heart, and you want to do right, but you have a very hard time obeying."

"That doesn't make me a good boy," Charlie objected. "That makes me naughty. I get in trouble for that. I get pinches."

Mr. Pondicherry chuckled. "I try to keep you safe," he said, and he wrapped his arms around Charlie and gave him a hug. "But I can't really be angry with you, Charlie. I made you that way. I gave you a good heart, and I made you just a little bit disobedient. I did it so you would never make my mistake and follow orders when you shouldn't."

Charlie's legs jerked this time, kicking straight forward. He wasn't sure how to feel about what his bap was saying. So he *was* a machine. But his father didn't hug the Articulated Gyroscopes.

"I don't want a good heart," he said. "I don't want to be disobedient. I don't even want to have adventures anymore. I just want to be a real boy."

A shuffling sound. Someone was standing up.

"You *are* a real boy," Charlie's bap said, and hugged him tighter.

"A *natural* boy," Charlie insisted. "I want to be like you."

"You *are* like me, Charlie," Mr. Pondicherry said. "Handsome is as handsome does, and that makes you a very handsome boy. How many boys could have organized a rescue party like this for their father?"

"Is that a light you've got there?" Gnat said. Charlie barely noticed the question. The only real thing in the whole world was the hug that held him tight, and that hug held a tiny bit of a lie inside it.

Wrapped in his father's embrace, Charlie felt his father's pipe in his pocket, squeezed against his side. He should give it to him now.

Charlie's legs jerked.

"Oh, no!" his bap exclaimed. "Haven't you been winding Charlie?"

"Winding Charlie?" Ollie asked.

"His mainspring!"

"'Oo knew as we 'ad to be winding 'is mainspring?"

"Is that a gun?" the pixie asked. There was a sudden fluttering of wings.

A light snapped on in the darkness. Charlie's legs kicked spastically again, and the violence of the kick threw him out of his father's arms.

"Charlie!" Mr. Pondicherry wept.

"Come on, Raj," said Henry Clockswain. Charlie's vision was jerking like his body now, but he thought the voice came from behind the bright light that now shone on him. "Don't make a fuss. Let's go get the queen ready for her Jubilee."

There was a terrible moment of silence.

"You . . . Henry? You're with the Cog? Henry Clockswain, my friend?"

"Heinrich Zahnkrieger," the kobold said, and he pronounced the name with a foreign accent. His hearing was also starting to splinter into nothing. "Thank you very much for telling me how to find our other missing engineer."

Charlie's bap scrambled to his feet—

bang!

Brick dust fell onto Charlie's head, and a bullet whined away into the darkness.

"Don't make me shoot anyone," the kobold said. The door creaked open, letting in more light and men with swords. "Come along, now."

"But . . . but Charlie," Mr. Pondicherry objected.

"Really, Raj," Heinrich Zahnkrieger said, "I thought you would have realized by now that I don't care about your Charlie."

Then Charlie fell, into darkness and silence and nothing.

Despite their utter lack of reasoning faculty, ghouls are humanoid. Their greatest distinguishing features are their hairlessness, their diminutive nose (reminiscent of the nose of a gorilla or a chimpanzee), and their extraordinary proliferation of sharp teeth. Any of these characteristics immediately identifies a ghoul and warns the observer to flee and notify the authorities.

—Smythson, *Almanack*, "Ghoul"

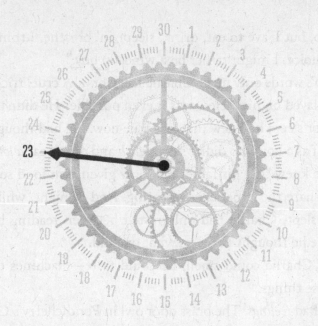

Charlie opened his eyes to darkness.

His father had been taken from him. Again.

"He's awake," he heard Gnat say.

"Charlie, you there?" It was Bob's voice. "What do you remember?"

"I'm not a real boy," Charlie said.

The darkness felt absolute. It was dark *inside* Charlie.

There was an awkward silence.

"'Ere now, that ain't right," Bob said finally. "You're a real boy, same as me." She chuckled. "Maybe even more of a real boy than I am."

Charlie didn't laugh, even though he knew Bob was telling a secret joke, just for him. "You don't have to be wound up or you stop working."

"No, but I 'ave to eat, drink, sleep, an' breathe. I think if I 'ad a choice, I might rather be a wind-up boy."

Bob's words only made Charlie feel worse. A cruel trick had been played on him. How was it even possible? He didn't have to eat or sleep; he knew that was true now. He had thought of himself as a boy who didn't sleep *much* and didn't eat *a lot,* and now he knew that his father had only given him food so they could share the experience of eating. And at night, while his father slept, Charlie had only rested between reading books because he thought that was what one did.

But Charlie could smell; he could taste—machines didn't do those things.

He had *feelings.* The brass door owl in Pondicherry's Clockwork Invention & Repair didn't have feelings, did it? Did Lucky Wu's steam presses have feelings? Did the Sky Trestle?

Still, Charlie knew he was just a thing. In his heart he'd known it since Bob and Grim had tried to tell him, outside Cavendish Hats, but he'd refused to face the fact.

Only he didn't have a heart, did he? He had gears.

Charlie sobbed. His weeping sounded harsh and metallic to his own ears.

"'Ere now."

Charlie felt a hand patting at his side, and then an arm wrapped around his shoulder. In the darkness he felt Bob hug him and kiss his cheek.

His bap, Charlie thought. Charlie might not have to eat, but his father had shared food with him anyway. His father had called Charlie his *son.*

Charlie's bap had never treated him like a thing.

And his bap needed to be rescued.

Charlie shuddered, tried to clear his thoughts. "What time is it?"

"Grim, show me the watch again." It was Gnat's voice. Scuffling sounds. "'Tis half two."

"Two thirty in the afternoon!" Charlie exclaimed. "We've lost the morning!"

"Two thirty in the morning, mate." Ollie's voice was gentle, for Ollie.

Charlie was stunned. "But that means that . . . today is the Jubilee!"

"And the progress flotilla and the garden party." Grim sighed. "And yesterday was the bar exam."

"What happened? Why have I been . . . uh, knocked out so long?"

"Easy, Charlie, you ain't missed anything," Bob told him gently. "We ain't seen nobody nor nothing since your dad and Clockswain left."

"Rotten little kobold," Ollie growled.

"Aye," the pixie agreed.

"Spent time looking for any other way out," Grim added. "There is none. And we debated whether we should . . . ah, wake you up. Might have been kinder to let you . . . sleep."

"At least Charlie ain't hungry or thirsty," Ollie grumbled.

"An' then it took a long time to figure out your mechanism, Charlie," Bob finished. "I'm sorry I couldn't do it any faster, but I 'ad to do it in the dark, with the pixie telling me where to put my fingers."

"My back rubs. That's what bap was doing when he rubbed

my back, he was winding my . . . mechanism." Charlie focused. He had to get out and save his father. "There are two doors, right?"

"One's barred, and I've already tried to knock it down," Grim said. "No good. The other is locked. Can't break it, either."

"An' I ain't got my tools," Bob finished. "Clockswain 'ad 'em taken from me, I guess, since 'e knew I could pick locks. Must 'ave been giving 'is boys directions while I 'ad a bag over my 'ead. Filthy kobold."

Ollie laughed, but he didn't sound amused. "*Now* you see it my way."

"What do you need?" Charlie remembered seeing Bob pick the lock of the maintenance door on platform thirteen. "Two long pins, right?"

"Yeah. Sounds like nothing until you ain't got it."

"And if you open the door, what then?" Grim pointed out. "We're unarmed, and on the other side of that door is a passage full of ghouls."

Charlie had an idea. "How smart are ghouls?"

"Motleys are as dim-witted a folk as Britain 'as," Bob informed him. "I reckon as they're somewhere between a stupid dog an' a really clever turnip."

"Still terribly dangerous," Grim said.

"Motley fool, ghoul," Charlie guessed. "Do they have language?"

"What, like English? Not as I ever 'eard."

"Maybe they can be tricked. Bob, do you know how to

open me up?" Charlie had an idea. In his own head it sounded crazy, but it was the only idea he had.

"What?" Bob sounded startled.

"Maybe there are pins inside me you could use to pick the locks. Could you stop me, open me, use any pins you find to pick the locks, and then restart me again?"

If he was a thing, Charlie thought, at least he could be a *useful* thing.

Bob thought about it for a few moments. "Probably. With Gnat's 'elp, yeah. But why?"

Charlie explained his idea. He whispered, just in case the ghouls *could* understand.

Afterward there was silence.

"I don't know," Grim said.

"But do you have any better ideas?" Gnat asked, and there was silence again.

Charlie laid himself carefully facedown on the ground. The rough gravel of the railroad bed dug into his face and hands. "Right. Get going, Bob."

Charlie opened his eyes to darkness again. He smelled troll stink, strong. That was good; that meant that Grim had done his part.

"Any luck?" Grim's voice called. He sounded far away.

"His eyes are open!" Gnat answered.

Charlie heard an explosive sigh of relief. "Charlie!" Bob said. "Charlie, can you 'ear me?"

"Yes," Charlie said.

"Thank 'eaven! I thought I might 'ave killed you!"

"You can't kill me. I'm a machine." Charlie sat up. "Did it work?"

"Yeah, the gate's open," Ollie said. "Grim's holding it shut right now."

Charlie heard pawing and snuffling noises. "Grim, are you all right?" he called. "Are they attacking your hands?"

Grim laughed, the sound booming loud in the prison. "Trying. If they were taller, they might succeed."

Charlie stood up slowly. "I smell right now," he said. "How about everybody else?"

"I rubbed my coat on all of you," Grim said.

"Yeah, we all smell like cows now." Ollie laughed. "It's making me hungry for steak and kidney."

"I 'ope this works," Bob added. "If it does, Ollie, I'll buy you a pie."

Ollie laughed dryly. "And if it don't, we're all food for the motleys."

"Which way to the gate?" Charlie asked. "No sense waiting."

"Turn left and walk in a straight line."

Charlie turned, stepped—

and stumbled. He fell to the ground.

"What's that?" Ollie asked.

"Something's wrong with my leg," Charlie said. "My left leg is . . . it doesn't work the same."

"The 'eck!"

Ollie muttered darkly.

Charlie climbed to his feet again. He stepped again, slower this time.

Again his left leg buckled, but this time he was ready for it and didn't fall. He took a few experimental steps. "I can walk."

"I twisted one of the pins," Bob said. "They're brass, not steel, an' not really made for sticking into locks. I'm so sorry, Charlie; I mucked it up."

Charlie kept walking, carefully. He could move all right, but it would take some getting used to the way his legs worked now. The right one functioned just like it always had, but the left one was jerky. It moved in quick lurches. As he picked up speed, he became lopsided, like a rickshaw with one enormous egg-shaped wheel and one tiny round one.

"I'm fine," he said.

"I'm sorry, Charlie," Bob repeated. "Your dad'll fix you up in no time. Or maybe I could do it, I reckon, with decent tools."

"Good." Charlie kept lurching forward.

"Come on, lads," the pixie called. "This way." Charlie heard the scuffling of his chimney-sweep friends standing up behind him, and the grinding of their boots on the gravel under the tracks. "Left, Ollie," Gnat called, directing the sweeps.

Just as Charlie had worked up enough confidence to move at something like a walking pace, he smacked into Grim Grumblesson's back.

"Be careful," Grim said. Charlie heard snuffling and scratching noises, very close. "Don't get any closer to the bars, not just yet."

"Sorry about the pin," Bob apologized again as she caught up.

"It's okay, Bob. Now we're *all* injured. It's only fair. And if my plan doesn't work, three minutes from now it won't matter anyway."

"Here are a couple of rocks." Grim pressed them into Charlie's hands. They had a comforting weight, and one of them had a sharp edge. "I wish they were a brace of pistols."

"Thanks."

"Be careful," Gnat told Charlie.

"'It 'em 'ard," Bob agreed. "You know, after they nosh on you a bit."

"If you're wrong," Grim said, "yell for help. We may be able to get you out."

"If I'm wrong," Charlie disagreed, "then I made you unlock the gate for nothing, and you're probably all doomed. So if we don't talk again, then I'm sorry, and thank you. You're all brave, and you've been very good friends to me."

"Just good client service. Ha!" Grim rumbled.

"Think nothing of it," Bob said.

"No worries, mate." Ollie's voice was as gentle as Charlie had ever heard it.

"Get on," Gnat added. "Enough of the chitchat. In five minutes we'll all be racing down that passageway and clapping you on the back."

"Right." Charlie felt good. He was happy to be surrounded by friends. He was almost happy enough to forget that his bap was a prisoner, and that Queen Victoria was hours from being replaced by an automaton, which would then turn around and massacre a group of foreign leaders to start a war. Also, he almost forgot that he himself was most likely about to be torn to shreds by ghouls.

Almost.

"What time is it?" he asked.

"Five," the pixie said. "Still in the morning."

"You ready?" Grim asked.

"Let's go."

Grim roared. The noise was shatteringly loud. At the same time, the troll swung a big rock across the bars, sending up a row of sparks and a deafening *clang-ng-ng-ng-ng!*

In the weak light of the sparks Charlie saw the faces of the ghouls. Although they were his size, and roughly his shape, they looked totally different. They were naked, with leathery skin and big white eyes. They had big ears, too, and practically no noses. Their mouths were enormous, and bristled with teeth like inside-out hedgehogs.

The ghouls staggered back from the noise and the light. Darkness fell again immediately.

"Now!" Gnat hissed.

Charlie heard the gate swing open, and then with one big hand the troll scooped him forward, throwing him among the ghouls.

He really hoped this turned out to be a good idea.

Do not go where the grave-winds blow
My bright and fearless son
And never creep where the eyeless sleep
Once the day his race has run, my boy
Once the day his race has run

In his winding sheet on velvet feet
Your death makes not a a sound
You are naught but meat to the one who eats
And your bones upon the ground, my boy
Your bones upon the ground

—Child, *Popular Ballads*, No. 17

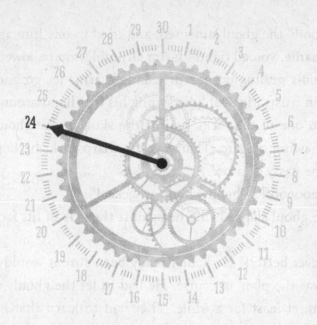

A dozen hands tugged Charlie in all directions.

He'd made a terrible mistake.

But the ghouls pulled and gibbered, and Charlie didn't come apart. If he'd been a real boy—flesh-and-blood, like Ollie or Bob—the hands would have torn him to bits. Instead he just felt stretched . . . painfully.

But the ghouls could do more to Charlie than just pull on his arms and legs.

The snuffling and whimpering in the darkness around him turned to hooting and shrill whistles and whines. A mouth bit Charlie on the shoulder, hard.

That hurt even worse.

But Charlie's skin didn't break, and he heard a crunch as the ghoul lost a tooth.

"Hoot!" the ghoul lamented, and tried to bite him again.

"Charlie, you all right?" Grim Grumblesson bellowed.

Ghouls pulling on one of Charlie's arms let go and gibbered in frustration. Charlie swung his free hand around and cracked one of the rocks against the skull of the ghoul that was gnawing on him. That was the sharp rock; he hoped it hurt the nasty creature.

"Hoooooot! Whoop-whoop-wheeeee!"

The ghoul slapped Charlie against the side of his face and let go.

"Never better!" He hadn't really been sure it would work. This was the plan, of course. He had to let the ghouls nibble on him, at least for a while. They had to learn that he was inedible—which he hoped he was. Then, with a little bit of luck, they'd leave him and all his friends alone. That was why they all had to smell the same.

Hands still pulled at him. Charlie was tempted to swing the rock some more, but he didn't want to scare the ghouls off too soon. He wanted them to try to take more bites of him.

"Come on, you lot!" he shouted. Maybe they understood English and maybe they didn't, but he could at least get their attention with noise. "Try harder!"

They bit him again. Ghouls chewed on his arms and legs, sucked at his fingers, nibbled his ears. Charlie's skin didn't break, but he felt his clothing being shredded, and all the teeth gnawing on him did hurt.

"Hoot, hoooot!" the ghouls wailed. "Whoop-whoop-whoop-wheeeee!"

"Charlie?" Gnat yelled. Charlie could barely hear the pixie's voice over the gibbering noises of the ghoul mob. "I can't see you any more for the pile of beasties. Are you still there?"

"Yes!" Charlie yelled as loud as he could, but he still didn't think Gnat could hear him.

And the gnawing had gone on long enough. Charlie jerked one arm free, and then he started swinging.

At first he clobbered the ghouls that were still trying to bite him. They howled louder and hissed at him, but he could feel the rocks in his fists colliding with skulls and chests and shoulders, and the ghouls pulled off him a bit.

He went after them.

Charlie couldn't see, so he spun around like a top, smacking anything he could hit with the stones in his hands. He stumbled over the tracks but didn't fall. He was out of control, and more than once he hit the brick walls and hurt his own fingers, but he kept going.

"Hooot! Hoo-ooo-ooooot!"

Charlie felt his blows land hard on leathery bodies. He heard feet padding and scratching away in the darkness. He kept spinning.

"They're on the run, Charlie!" Natalie de Minimis shouted.

Charlie let himself stop. He fell to the ground from sheer impetus, but he didn't feel sick from the spinning.

Of course not, he thought bitterly. He was a machine, not a real boy.

But a real boy would have been eaten by the ghouls.

He heard the crunch of footsteps around him as his friends caught up.

"Link up hands, everyone," Grim ordered. "Gnat, lead the way."

Charlie stood and tossed aside the rocks. He held Bob's hand in front of him and Grim's fingers behind, and Gnat led them deeper into the darkness at a trot.

"I 'ope you're right about the smell." Bob sounded nervous, but she didn't stumble.

"Course he's right," Ollie grunted. "They broke their teeth on Charlie and then he beat them silly. We all smell the same as Charlie. That's got to make them think twice."

"They'll have to think more than twice," Grim rumbled.

"We all smell like 'ulders," Bob said. "We're 'oping they don't think too much about it an' realize Charlie ain't an 'ulder, so we might not be 'ulders either. We're counting on 'em to be stupid."

"Yeah," Ollie agreed. "And if there's one thing I'm always willing to bet on, it's stupid. Stupid grows on trees. Stupid is more common than air, mate."

"Touché." Bob surrendered.

"I ain't French."

They walked through darkness for a long time. Eventually Gnat led them away from the gravel bed of the train tunnel and up concrete steps. Occasionally she left them to scout ahead. Charlie couldn't see the pixie, but the whir of her wings made him feel happy; it told him that her pulled back muscles must be healing well. Charlie squeezed the hands of his friends and listened for the snuffling and hooting that would mark the return of the ghouls.

But the ghouls didn't come back.

More tunnels and more darkness, and then Gnat led them through a crumbled wall into a dank, stinking passage lined with brick. Charlie's feet splashed in shallow water.

"The 'eck! Really, Gnat? The sewers are the only way out of this 'ole?"

"Shh!" Gnat urged her. "Look ahead."

There was a light.

And Charlie heard voices.

They crept forward, taking careful steps and straining with their ears. The light shone down through a grate overhead.

"And the simulacrum?" The voice belonged to the kobold, Heinrich Zahnkrieger. He sounded hard and cruel, not very much like the fussy engineer Henry Clockswain. "Her Ersatz Majesty? Have you determined how you will substitute it for the queen?"

"That was the easiest part." The Sinister Man. "The queen's carriage has been waiting for her all night in the station. It was child's play to put the simulacrum in the carriage ahead of time."

"Especially when a policeman or two is willing to look the other way." The captain.

Charlie and his friends huddled under the grate. Charlie looked up through the fist-sized, irregular gaps between the bars and tried to listen to what his enemies were saying.

"You couldn't find us a way out without these people standing over it?" Ollie whispered.

"Don't you think we should hear what they're saying?" Gnat hissed back. "Besides, all our weapons are up there."

"And for me?" Zahnkrieger asked.

"There is room in the carriage to hide you," the Frenchman answered. "You go with the queen."

"And you go with Pondicherry."

"The explosives are already in place on the Eye," the captain said. "They'll see the explosion in Greenwich. Pondicherry will be found dead on the wheel, and when the police search his shop, we'll find the manifesto for the Anti-Human League."

Zahnkrieger chuckled low. "And in the chaos after the explosion I will dispose of Victoria. The queen is dead."

"Long live the queen," the Sinister Man added. The Iron Cog's men laughed together.

"Time to go," Zahnkrieger said. Charlie imagined himself punching the little man in the face. "I will see you at the garden party."

"So much to do when you have a war to start," said the Sinister Man.

Footsteps, and the slamming of a door.

Charlie wasn't sure, but he thought he heard chittering noises in the tunnel.

Gnat poked her head up into one of the gaps in the grate. "All clear."

With one heave Grim dislodged the grate. He tossed

Charlie up first, and then Bob and Ollie. Charlie stood blinking in the light, examining himself and his new surroundings while the troll struggled to squeeze himself through the hole.

Charlie looked like a scarecrow, torn and filthy.

They found themselves in the Iron Cog's workroom, where he had seen his bap and the simulacrum. In the steady yellow gaslight coming from the wall sconces, Charlie saw shelves and parts and tools and several big metal doors, all of which were shut. There was a big worktable and several four-legged stools. In a pile on the table lay his knife, all his friends' weapons, and the boxes of inventions the Iron Cog had stolen from Charlie's father. Charlie recognized the Articulated Gyroscopes and the Close-Reading Spectacles.

Patent pending, Charlie thought, and his shoulders slumped.

"Gaaaaarrrh!" Grim Grumblesson grunted. Bricks snapped out of their mortar around the edges of the hole, and he squeezed up in a fountain of dust and mortar crumbs. The chimney sweeps were already arming themselves, and the pixie was closely examining a long steel rod with a sharpened end.

"Let's get out of here." Charlie knew what he had to do. "And then you should all go home."

Bob stared at him. "The 'eck."

"Yeah," Ollie agreed. "The heck, Charlie."

Grim frowned and Gnat flexed her steel rod.

"This isn't your fight anymore," Charlie went on. "Look, your devices are here on the table. You should take them and go. You don't need to risk getting killed."

"You reckon that's the only reason we're 'ere?" Bob asked. "For *things*?"

"Well . . ." Charlie hesitated.

"Your father's a client," Grim said. His head hung low and jutted out as he spoke. "I don't abandon clients."

"It's true: at first I just wanted the gyroscopes," said Bob. "Well, an' also you made me curious, because I guessed you might be, well, you know."

"Yeah," Ollie added. "And also I wanted to stick it to the kobold."

"I reckon we all want to stick it to the kobold now," Bob said, and she laughed. "An' we're mates, Charlie. We ain't gonna leave you."

"Not when there are mighty beasts to be slain." Gnat swooped in a circle and pantomimed stabbing a foe with her new spear.

"Besides," Grim added, "Her Majesty is in danger."

Charlie felt like crying again. He managed to keep it inside and just nod.

"Gentlemen—" Grim rumbled.

"Check your weapons," Ollie finished for him. Grim nodded and began to load his gun.

"I think I heard rats in the tunnels," Charlie said.

"Good thing we're out of the tunnels, then," Ollie shook himself like a cat shaking off water. He sighted along his umbrella at their exit from the sewers.

A big door at the far end of the room opened—

and Egil One-Arm walked in.

The troll gangster was still missing his mechanical arm. He

spotted Charlie and his friends and stopped; his face broke into a snarl.

"You!" Egil roared.

"Back for more?" Grim bellowed, snapping the cylinder of his Eldjotun into place with a resounding click.

"Tear you apart this time, you meddling cur!"

Grim Grumblesson laughed. "Not with one arm, you won't. Sleipnir's saddle, not without a weapon!" He raised the Eldjotun. "Not by yourself."

"Not by myself," One-Arm agreed, and he stepped farther into the room.

Behind him followed more thugs. One hulder, then a second and a third. And behind them came men with cutlasses.

"Run!" Gnat snapped, spinning on Charlie and the sweeps. "We'll hold them here."

"Ha!" Grim barked. "Got enough bullets for all of you."

"But . . . ," Charlie objected.

Ollie tugged on his arm. "Come on, you idiot, we've got to get your dad."

"'Ave you, then?" asked one of the cutlass-bearing men, and he drew his sword.

"An' the queen," Bob added. The two of them started dragging Charlie toward the exit.

"But . . ." He didn't want to abandon the troll. "We can't leave Grim alone!"

One of Egil's trolls reached under his greatcoat and pulled out a stubby thing like a short rifle with a big open mouth. A scattergun.

"He'll not be alone," Gnat said. "Run!"

"Last warning." Grim cocked his pistol. "Won't miss."

The other two trolls pulled back their coats. They were all carrying scatterguns.

"Got to thank you, Grumblesson," Egil laughed roughly. "You convinced me my boys needed to get serious weapons."

"Run!" Gnat pushed Charlie. Charlie and the sweeps staggered toward the door.

"You're welcome," Grim said calmly.

"Good-bye," Egil grumbled.

Charlie grabbed for the door handle just as a horde of rats swarmed out of the sewer opening.

Nevertheless, the story is told in the Lake District of a young man who fell in love with a hulder maiden. The young man was a cheesemaker, and by gifts of a variety of delightful cheeses, he won the hulder's heart. For seven years she was his wife, and they had seven children, but then in a great storm the man's business was destroyed. His dairy cattle were scattered and his shed of cheeses burned to the ground. When he awoke the next morning, his wife had also gone, and taken all their children with her.

—Smythson, *Almanack,* "Troll"

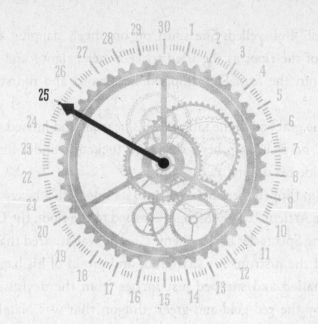

The wave of rats rolled toward Grim Grumblesson.

Charlie ducked, and the air of the room was torn to shreds by flying metal.

Grim took a hit from one of the scatterguns and staggered back. As the men with cutlasses started a ragged charge, he fired on them.

Ollie jerked the door open. He, Bob, and Charlie started to scoot through it, but Bob hesitated.

Gnat swooped low at the leaders of the rat horde, slicing at pointy snouts and big ears. "What are you doing here, you devils?"

The only answer she got was shrieks.

The men fell back, and Grim grabbed the corner of the table.

"No!" Bob yelled. She spun on one heel, slapping at the stone of the floor as she tried to keep her balance and lurch back into the fray. She dropped her sword and didn't stop for it.

Ollie grabbed at the tail of Bob's peacoat and missed. Muttering, he picked up her sword and tucked it under his arm alongside his umbrella.

Grim flipped the table over onto its side with a heavy thud.

The Articulated Gyroscopes crashed to the floor, the Close-Reading Spectacles beside them. Charlie was amazed that neither of the instruments shattered, and proud of his bap. The rats snarled and snapped just inches from the devices, held back by the red-gold-and-green dragon that was Natalie de Minimis in combat. But for every rat that fell, two followed it.

"Bob!" Ollie shouted.

Grim spun around to kneel behind the table.

Bang!

Another scattergun blast hit the troll in the shoulder. He swayed, snarled, and fired back. His clothes hung on him in tatters.

BANG!

One of Egil's trolls crashed to the floor.

Bob dropped to her belly and slid. Charlie scrambled after her on all fours. Somewhere in the dive he lost his grip on the knife, which disappeared into the chaos.

"Go!" Grim roared.

"Come on!" Ollie hollered.

Bob grabbed both devices, one in each hand.

One of Egil's men bore down on her, sword raised over his head. Bob turned to scoot away, but she wasn't moving fast enough—

Gnat swarmed in, and the swordsman batted the pixie aside with an elbow—

Grim pointed the Eldjotun and pulled the trigger—

click!

The policeman swung his cutlass and Charlie tackled him.

He got his shoulder squarely into the man's belly, and he felt the breath whoosh out of his target's body. The sword clattered to the stone, and then the swordsman. He lay still, groaning.

Bullets whizzed overhead.

"Come on!" Ollie shouted again.

Charlie picked up the fallen cutlass, grabbed Bob by the back of her belt, and pulled them both toward the door. He lurched, but it was a very fast lurch.

Bang!

A blow struck Charlie in the back and knocked him and Bob both through the door and to the ground. His whole body stung and he lay still.

"Charlie . . . Charlie, you all right?" Ollie shook him. "How do you feel?"

"'E got shot!" Bob snapped. "'Ow would *you* feel?"

"I'm fine." Charlie sat up. He hurt, but he could move. He picked up the cutlass and peeked back into the firefight. Grim had reloaded and was raising his gigantic gun again. Natalie de Minimis flitted over the heads of their attackers, stabbing at their faces to injure and distract them. A twisting carpet of rats spread in Grim Grumblesson's direction.

"Run!" the pixie shouted one more time, and finally they did.

They pelted down a passage and through a room and down another hall, past pipes and grates and jets of steam.

"Where are we going?" Charlie asked.

"Up!" Bob rattled up a concrete staircase.

"What about Grim?"

"We 'ave . . . to think . . . about the queen!" Bob was short of breath. "An' . . . Franz-Joseph . . . an' the others!"

"He'll die! He and Gnat both!"

"Their . . . choice . . . Charlie," Ollie reminded him in grunts. "No . . . other . . . way."

The three of them burst through the maintenance door onto platform thirteen and ran right into a pack of trolls.

Ingrid stood at their front, a heavy club in one hand and a hard glare on her face. Now that she wasn't standing behind a desk, Charlie saw that she had a cow's tail, just like Grim's, and it lashed the floor behind her. So the *Almanack* wasn't always wrong.

Following Ingrid were half a dozen hulders, male and female. They were all armed, and they all scowled.

"Oh no," Charlie said.

But then Ingrid smiled at him.

"This is the hue and cry," she said. "Where's Grim?"

Charlie stepped out of the way and pointed down the stairs. "He needs your help!"

The trolls charged past him and down into the darkness.

"Thank you!" Ingrid called as she disappeared.

"Didn't expect that." Ollie scratched himself.

Platform thirteen was dotted with only a tiny smattering of Alton-line passengers. Their backs were turned, so they didn't see Ollie holding his umbrella and Bob's sword, or Charlie with his cutlass. Maybe they had even missed the hue and cry.

At the end of the platform stood policemen in blue hats and short capes. They wore cutlasses at their belts, and they were carefully checking each passenger's ticket before admitting him onto the main concourse.

"The 'eck," Bob muttered.

The three of them hid behind a billboard of schedules to spy out the terrain. "They could just be security for the progress flotilla," Charlie thought out loud. "Innocent policemen. Or they might be the Iron Cog's men."

"That's right," Ollie agreed. "But even if they ain't with the Cog, they won't be happy about us not having tickets."

"An' 'aving swords instead."

"We've got to stop the explosion and save my bap. If there's no explosion, there's no distraction, and the plan fails. And if we don't stop the explosion, my bap dies."

"Agreed," Bob said. "We stop the explosion. So 'ow do we get past those blokes an' get to the London Eye?"

Charlie smiled at the aeronaut. "I can't believe that you of all people are asking me that, *Heaven-Bound* Bob. The explosives will be somewhere up in the Eye, off the ground. We'll need to scout it out—"

"From the air!" Bob finished the sentence and patted the belt of gyroscopes over her shoulder. "An' the coppers?"

Charlie peeked around the billboard. There was a last trickle of exiting traffic. "Follow me, but not too close. I'll meet you up at the lockers. Go fast, and be ready to launch."

Ollie chuckled. "Fast and ready is the only way we know, Charlie."

Charlie held the cutlass behind him and walked down the platform. He let himself lurch along after a man in a greatcoat and stovepipe hat who was dragging a steamer trunk on a little wheeled cart. He looked over his shoulder and saw Bob and Ollie drifting behind him.

When the man was a few steps from the gate and the two police constables, Charlie picked up his pace. He rushed in front of the man, step-lurch, step-lurch, step-lurch, and he watched the surprise on the constables' faces.

They went for their swords.

Charlie burst into a sprint, throwing himself forward. His pace was still ragged and irregular—

but Charlie discovered that he could run very, very fast.

Just to be sure he had their attention, he attacked the coppers. He knocked one with his shoulder, sending him tumbling against the short rail of the gate and falling to the ground. With his cutlass he chopped at the other constable's tall blue hat. The lopped-off crown fell to the tiles.

"'Ey, you!" the decrowned man yelled through his bushy mustache. "Stop!"

Charlie sprinted. The concourse was busy, but the travelers were not all frock-coated businessmen. The crowd included children now, and women with parasols, and then men who wore lighter, less serious-looking coats. They must be here for the Jubilee, Charlie realized.

Charlie was fast enough to dodge around them all and still keep his pace at a sprint.

"Stop that child!" the policeman yelled. "Stop 'im!"

Charlie looked to make sure they were both following him. Up the moving stairs he ran. At the top another constable loomed, grabbing for Charlie with both his arms.

At Charlie's speed, the copper seemed to be moving in slow motion.

Charlie ducked—

arms groped over his head and missed—

and he grabbed the constable's ankle and pulled his foot out from under him.

The man hit the ground, and Charlie kept running.

Charlie glanced down over the railing as he loped. Bobbies streamed from all corners. Some of those men, he knew, were in the service of the Iron Cog. They were criminals and traitors. But others must be innocent men, even good men. They were men who were doing their job, trying to protect both the day's festival travelers and the queen.

Charlie couldn't tell the difference. So he tried not to hurt any of them.

Unnoticed by the bobbies, Bob and Ollie were cutting across traffic. They were almost to the spiral staircases. Charlie wondered how long it would take Bob to assemble the flyer and be ready to go. He needed to buy her some time.

He ducked down a passage toward the Sky Trestle platforms.

"Stop it!" he heard someone holler behind him. "Stop that thing!"

Charlie clattered down onto a platform and stopped. Behind, booted feet thumped. Ahead, at the end of the platform, another staircase descended. Out of it rushed another mob of men in short blue capes.

"Got him!" yelled the copper at the front of the crowd.

To Charlie's left was the trench through which ran the Sky Trestle tracks. On the other side, across a gap of ten or twelve feet, was another platform. At the far end of the platform a train rumbled into view.

"Get it!"

Charlie waited. Boots pounded the concrete; the train rumbled closer. A gaslight shone bright in the center of its face, over a wide grill that looked like gnashing teeth.

"There's the lad!"

Charlie waited. Closer.

"Now!"

Policemen jumped for Charlie from in front of him and from behind. At the last possible moment, he turned sideways, took two steps, and threw himself across the trench and over the tracks—

the train whooshed by, inches behind him—

and Charlie tumbled to the ground on the opposite platform. He managed neither to cut himself nor lose his grip on the cutlass. He wasn't ready to drop the sword just yet; he might still need it.

Charlie's jump had only gained him a few moments. When

the train doors opened, the policemen would come charging after him. He turned and sprinted back up the stairs.

There were other bobbies blocking his ascent, but in ones and twos, not in a crowd. Charlie ducked around some of them, waved his cutlass to keep others at bay, and kept running.

He was very fast. His body hummed with energy. He felt alive.

Charlie pelted out of the stairs and whipped along the balcony in the direction of the lockers. Travelers stared at him, jerking parasols and newspapers out of his way.

"Bob! Ollie!" he yelled, slowing to a lope as he reached the spiral staircases.

"'Ere, Charlie!"

He lurched down a short hallway under a sign that read WAITING ROOM. They were in a high-ceilinged chamber full of leather-cushioned benches. In the corner a drinking spigot gurgled over a brass basin. The far wall was entirely made of glass.

Bob was wearing wings.

They looked like bat's wings, but they weren't strapped onto her back. She stood in a harness of leather straps beneath them. The wings were made of fabric, stretched over a spindly metal frame. The Pondicherry Articulated Gyroscopes ranged across the tops of both wings, joining in the center. Bob held cords in her fists that attached to the gyroscopes themselves. She grinned to see Charlie, and brought her elbows down. The wings flapped.

In front of Bob dangled a second harness, and Ollie stood next to it.

"Why aren't you strapped in?" Charlie asked.

"Because, you idiot, the flyer don't fit three people. Looks like *you* get to be the pretty lady on the front."

"Where did it go?" Charlie heard shouting from the balcony.

"'Urry up!" Bob hissed.

Charlie stepped into the shadow of the wings, and Ollie snapped buckles around his waist and shoulders and under his legs. "But what about you, Ollie?" he asked.

"There he is!" "What's that?" "Get them!" "The queen!"

Bamf! Ollie the boy was gone, and Ollie the Snake slithered up Charlie's leg and coiled around his neck. Charlie threw aside his cutlass.

Feet pounded on the floor behind them.

"Run with me!" Bob shouted. She and Charlie sprinted together toward the windows.

Demonology, or the summoning and binding of beings not native to this plane of existence, is not a British pursuit, but is practiced by Russians and other peoples of the steppes. The pretender Bonaparte learned this to his sorrow when the Romanovs' summoners, in their last-ditch defense of Moscow, routed his Grande Armée. The sheer scale of that act, as well as the nature of some of the particular beings unleashed, permanently changed the order of things.

—Smythson, *Almanack,* "Demonology"

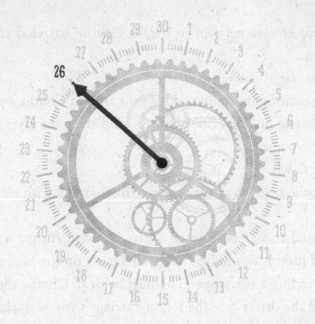

C rash!

   Glass shards rained around him, and Charlie launched into space.

London lay beneath him. He was at least a hundred feet in the air. The whole city stretched in all directions, a dense, sunlit warren around the Thames.

There was nothing between him and the ground.

"Whooooooooaa!" he shouted.

They fell.

Bob tilted the flyer's nose downward, and for a second Charlie rushed face-first toward the cobbled street below. Startled travelers coming in and out of Waterloo Station scattered. A cabbie threw his reins aside and jumped out of his hansom. Horses neighed in fright; Charlie barreled straight at them.

"Aaaaaagh!" he yelled.

Ollie the Snake tightened his grip around Charlie's neck.

"'Aaaang oooon!" Bob shouted, and then the flyer's nose began to come up.

But slowly.

Charlie held on to the straps of his harness with clenched fists.

A gold-and-green-painted steam-carriage rushed straight toward him. It was idling, its driver sitting on the high seat in front reading a newspaper. He must be deaf, Charlie thought. Behind the driver rose the steam-carriage's smokestack, puffing gently in the bright morning.

The flyer hurtled at the steam-carriage.

Bob pulled the nose up a little higher. "'Oooold ooon!" she howled again.

Charlie raised his knees up to his chest—*dong!*

Charlie's left foot just grazed the top of the smokestack. It smarted. The driver dropped his paper and tumbled out of his seat, and then Charlie lost him from view as the flyer pulled up, away from the ground and into the bright blue sky.

"Can't beat the Royal Magical Society for weather wizards, innit?" Bob yelled as they climbed. She was cheerful, as if they hadn't just almost died. "I reckon it's all the practice they get, what with our bad weather an' all. To 'ear Ollie talk about it, you'd think it was just talent. Like the French an' the loups-garou, or the Eye-talian illusionists, or the Russian demolitionists."

Ollie the Snake hissed.

"Demonologists!" Charlie said.

"That's what I said, ain't it!" Bob agreed. "Only it ain't fair to talk about what Ollie thinks when 'e can't talk back!" She flapped the wings gleefully, and the flyer climbed.

The sky above the station was thick with airships: globe-shaped montgolfiers full of hot air; elongated zeppelins; cylindrical balloons, both vertical and horizontal; craft with propellers, wings, sails; and things Charlie could barely focus on, much less describe, at the speed at which they were rocketing upward.

The airships circled around the mooring towers, except for a lone bulblike montgolfier that floated away from the rest. It tugged at a long anchor rope above Waterloo Bridge, red and gold. One of the men in its basket made a sign with signal flags, probably to direct the flotilla's traffic. Charlie saw other airships that were blue and brass, and he wondered if they were police vessels.

The flyer looped up and around Waterloo Station. They dove under some Sky Trestle tracks and sailed above others, and Charlie felt like the eyes of the entire world were on him.

"'Ere we go!" The London Eye rolled into view. A crowd wound around its base in a long line, but that wasn't what caught Charlie's gaze.

Halfway up one side and rising, there were people on one of the carriages.

"There!" Charlie pointed. "That must be my father!"

Bang!

It was far away and almost disappeared in the wind, but Charlie definitely heard a pistol shot.

He looked over his shoulder at the station. The red-and-gold traffic montgolfier now had a shimmering cloud of confetti streaming beneath it. The airships around the mooring tower nearest to the bridge began to unwind their circle and roll slowly out above the river, toward Whitehall and Buckingham Palace.

"The progress flotilla!" Charlie shouted into the wind. It was as glorious as he'd imagined it would be: a parade of airships that would accompany the queen. Bob was missing the flotilla, which was where she had planned to launch her public career as an aeronaut.

Also, if the flotilla was starting, the queen's carriage must be leaving the station.

Time was short.

The flyer zoomed down toward the Eye, homing in on the occupied carriage. Bob must have heard Charlie point out his bap. Charlie squinted, and he could make out four men in the compartment. The Sinister Man stood apart, pointing a pistol at the floor. Two other men held Charlie's bap.

"Fly close to the windows!" he called to Bob. He pointed, and he started unbuckling himself from the straps.

Ollie tightened his grip around Charlie's neck.

The flyer zoomed closer. Charlie opened the last buckle and hung by the strength of his arms. Ollie tightened his grip even more. If Charlie were a breathing boy, he'd have choked to death.

The flyer zoomed closer still. It looked to Charlie like Bob was aiming to slide just over the rooftop.

The Sinister Man raised his pistol and pointed it at Charlie's bap.

"Pondicherry's of Whitechapel!" Charlie yelled. He jumped.

For a long second he flew through the air.

Crash!

Charlie smashed through the glass of the carriage feetfirst. He bowled into the Sinister Man and knocked him backward, over a wooden bench and to the floor. The Sinister Man's pistol went off, shattering another window.

The carriage lurched to one side, and Charlie rolled with it. He and the Sinister Man were tangled up in arms and legs.

Ollie uncoiled from around his neck and slithered at the two men holding Charlie's bap. Charlie grabbed for the Sinister Man's gun.

Bang!

The Sinister Man's bullet hit Charlie in the chest and threw him backward. He slammed onto the floor.

"That hurt," he croaked.

Bang! Bang!

The henchmen fired at Ollie. The snake slithered into the corner of the carriage and curled up, still.

The carriage swung wildly. Charlie struggled to sit up, but the Sinister Man rose first. He wrapped one arm around a railing and pointed his long black pistol at Charlie.

"No!" Charlie's bap shouted, struggling against the henchmen. His face was bruised and his hair was a mess; his eyes were full of sadness, defiance, and fear.

"You are an irritating piece of junk," the Sinister Man snarled. "Good-bye."

Bamf!

The smell of rotten eggs filled the carriage, and Ollie stood up in the corner. He was bleeding. He held a wobbling pistol—Charlie didn't know where it had come from—pointed at the Sinister Man.

The Sinister Man spun—

bang!

Ollie shot him. The Sinister Man staggered back, bleeding from one arm.

"You ain't my dad." Ollie fell to one knee.

Bang!

Ollie's second shot went wild, and then he collapsed.

The Sinister Man raised his pistol again.

Suddenly Charlie's bap broke free, and he rushed across the carriage. He stepped on one of the benches in the middle of the compartment and launched himself through the air, grabbing for the Sinister Man and his gun.

The Sinister Man shifted his aim.

Bang! Bang!

"No!" Charlie shouted.

Mr. Pondicherry crashed into the Sinister Man, and they fell together.

They rolled across the swinging floor, punching.

"Stop this!" the Sinister Man shouted.

"Leave my son alone!"

They bounced toward a window. Mr. Pondicherry punched

the Sinister Man in the throat and in the face, and in return he got the butt of the pistol hammered onto his forehead. Just as he got his thumbs into the Sinister Man's nostrils and was pushing his head back—

bang!

One of the Sinister Man's henchmen got off a shot, and hit.

Mr. Pondicherry fell back, letting go of his enemy. As he slipped, the floor rolled away under him, and he tumbled, bleeding, toward a gaping window.

"No!" Charlie cried again. He threw himself after his bap, sliding across the floor and grabbing with both hands—and missed.

His bap tumbled through the open window. Charlie got one last look at his father's face, surprised and frightened, and then he was gone.

The wind sounded like a hurricane in Charlie's ears.

He had failed.

"Enough of this!" The Sinister Man stumbled across the carriage and fumbled with something near the door.

Charlie stared at the open window. The gulf beyond it seemed infinite and cold. When the carriage again reached the extremity of its arc, Charlie saw a ragged dot below in a circle of bare pavement surrounded by a crowd.

That was his bap.

Dead.

Pffft!

Charlie heard and smelled the match being struck, and finally he looked away from his father. The Sinister Man held a bundle of cords in one hand, and they were all burning, sparkling. He threw the cords out the window and spat on the floor.

"Come on!" shouted one of his thugs. They had the carriage door open, and Charlie saw beyond it a blue-and-brass zeppelin.

It looked like one long balloon, like a floating blue whale. The gondola hanging underneath it had a very wide door and was full of policemen.

Three looped lines stretched from the gondola's open door into the carriage. The two henchmen stepped into the loops and pulled the ropes up under their shoulders before jumping out of the carriage and disappearing.

The Sinister Man stepped into the third loop and pointed his pistol at Charlie.

Click.

"Sacre bleu!" he shouted. Then he jumped out of the swinging carriage and disappeared.

Charlie lay on the floor.

He wanted to weep for his bap, broken on the ground below.

He wanted to weep for Ollie, crumpled in the corner.

But he couldn't.

Ollie wasn't dead, and the queen was still in danger, so Charlie forced himself to go on. He crawled across the floor to the carriage railing and gripped it tightly. The next time the carriage rolled so that the window faced downward, cold fear seized him.

The cords the Sinister Man had lit were fuses. There were dozens of them, winding away to clusters of Extradynamit packed around the hub of the leisure wheel. The fuses were all out of Charlie's reach, and they were sparkling.

The Eye was going to explode.

And then the Iron Cog would move against the queen.

London certainly cannot be matched in Britain for the size of its buildings and its amusements.

—Smythson, *Almanack*, "London"

The carriage shook, and Charlie flinched.

There had been no explosion, though. Still, Charlie was going to die. He was hundreds of feet off the ground. There was no way down, and no way to stop the explosions.

He should at least check on his friend.

Charlie crawled across the carriage floor, avoiding the splashes of blood. Ollie lay in the corner, his pistol beside him. He bled from his side and from one leg.

He was breathing.

Ollie was going to die in the explosion too.

Thump!

The noise came from the roof. What new mischief did it signal? It didn't really matter.

"Ollie," Charlie whispered, and then stopped. If they were going to die, maybe it was more merciful to let Ollie stay unconscious.

Thump!

"It ain't my fault, Bob," Ollie muttered. His eyes were still shut. "Everybody's got a dad. Not everybody can have a *good* dad."

"It's not your fault, Ollie," he reassured his friend.

"What?" Ollie opened his eyes.

Thump!

"There's something on the roof," Charlie said. Now that Ollie's eyes were open, Charlie felt like he had to act. Charlie was responsible.

As long as they were alive, wasn't there some hope?

"You ain't leaving me here."

"You can't follow me where I'm going."

"Yeah, I can." Ollie muttered under his breath—

bamf!

Ollie the Snake looked bruised, but he slowly wound his way up Charlie's leg and back and settled in around his neck. He hissed in Charlie's ear, and Charlie nodded.

"Yes, you can." He climbed out the window.

The ground spun beneath him, the cloud of airships above. All around, the spokes of the Eye inched forward without mercy. Charlie couldn't see the police zeppelin, and he deliberately didn't look at his bap's body.

He just climbed.

One hand and foot over the other, up the outside of the

carriage. Charlie's lurching leg was tricky; when he moved it, it slammed into place in a hard blow. Charlie clanged and rasped his way up the brass like a monkey with one wooden leg.

He heard distant yelling, but he couldn't make out the words.

Thump!

Charlie pulled himself up to the lip of the roof and laughed in relief. Ollie hissed and slithered around Charlie's shoulders in a snaky dance.

It was Bob.

She was turned away from Charlie and couldn't see him. Her arms were still looped into the wings of the flyer, which she held very still. She was crouching to keep out of the way of the wheel's spokes as the carriage rolled under her feet. She had one boot jammed under a long bar that ran across the carriage top, and she raised the other to stomp again.

Thump!

"Come on, Charlie!" Bob hollered into the wind. "Get up 'ere; I can't 'old on forever!"

Charlie shot a glance in the direction of the Extradynamit. The fuses had burned very short.

"Bob, we're here!" He pulled himself up.

Bob craned her head around and saw them. "Lads!"

Charlie skittered across the carriage top on his belly. It lurched and swooped under him, and he clung to the same rod that anchored Bob. "No time!" He stood up into a crouch, pressed against Bob. "We have to take off!"

"Right," Bob agreed. "Buckle up!"

She hadn't seen the explosives. Charlie stood to his full height and grabbed the flyer's harness straps. "No time!" He dragged Bob and the flyer forward off the top of the carriage.

"The 'eck!" Bob yelped.

They fell.

Charlie held tight with both hands and stared at the pavement.

They plummeted toward a crowd. Bob flapped the flyer's wings.

The ground rushed closer. The flyer's nose began to pull up.

Charlie saw faces. Expressions of fear and surprise.

"Run!" he yelled.

Bob flapped her wings and the flyer pulled level, barely over the heads of the scattering crowd.

"Run!" Charlie yelled again. "The Eye is going to—"

KABOOOOOOOM!

A hot wind pushed at their backs and threw the flyer forward. The crowd screamed.

KABOOM! KABOOM!

"The 'eck!" Bob yelled, flapping her arms and twisting her body with each new blast of burning air. Ollie hissed. The flyer whipped around like a bit of newspaper blasted down the Gullet in a heavy storm.

Charlie risked a look back. Fire had swallowed the hub of Mr. Ferris's leisure wheel. It really looked like the city's eye now, a big flaming eye staring evil and hatred right across the river at the Houses of Parliament and Buckingham Palace.

A final explosion rocked the center of the Eye.

KABOOM!

Spokes and carriages shook—

tipped—

tumbled off the tower that held them—

and crashed to the ground.

The leisure wheel landed upright. Glass and bits of torn metal flew in all directions. The remaining crowd scattered.

And the London Eye rolled.

In Charlie's direction.

It hit a broad, gentle slope of pavement that dropped toward the river. The wheel began to pick up speed.

"Go, Bob!"

"I'm trying!" She flapped her wings.

Charlie looked away from the giant flaming eye. To the right rose Waterloo Station. Before them the progress flotilla stretched out over Waterloo Bridge. The airships flew in multiple tiers, and together they blocked out the sun, casting a long ribbon of shadow across the bridge, past Big Ben, and on toward Buckingham Palace.

On the bridge pranced a parade line of cavalry. They were almost to the far side of the river. In the middle of all the high-stepping horses, Charlie saw a puffing steam-carriage. It was red and gold, like the traffic montgolfier. It was far away, but if he squinted, Charlie thought he could just make out the royal coat of arms on its door.

The queen, he thought. The queen is in danger.

"Bob!" he yelled. "The queen!"

"I'm busy!" Bob flapped her arms frantically and the wings flapped with her. She was slowing down. Her left arm seemed not to work much at all. They gained altitude, but not very fast.

Maybe not fast enough to avoid getting squashed.

Charlie twisted to look again at the wheel. It was getting closer. The compartments crunched and shattered as they rolled under the Eye, and as they rolled around its top some of them were flung off as missiles. Charlie winced as he saw carriages impact: in the river with a distant splash, on the concourse with a crunch, or splattering with a loud *ka-changgg!* against the tracks of the Sky Trestle.

As Charlie looked, a carriage crested the top of the London Eye and broke free. It shot straight at them.

"Faster, Bob!" he yelled.

"I can't!"

The compartment hurtled past them. Charlie heard the crash over his shoulder as it struck something, but he didn't take his eye off the big wheel.

The London Eye crunched down the slope, still gaining on them.

Charlie watched Bob awkwardly pull down at the wings again. She winced with pain, and he realized the problem.

Bob was still hurt. She had been shot, and here she was trying to get them out of the Eye's path by flapping her injured arm.

Charlie swung himself right against Bob.

"'Ey now, what're you doing?"

Charlie twisted himself around and backed against Bob. All three of them were very close: Bob pressed against Charlie's back and Ollie slithering about on their shoulders.

"Stop it!" Bob flapped furiously. "Ouch!"

Charlie grabbed Bob by one wrist harness.

He heard the gigantic crunch of the wheel behind them.

He grabbed Bob's other wrist.

CRRRRRUNCH!

Charlie pulled with both arms. He flapped Bob's wings for her.

He flapped as hard and as fast as he could. The flyer shot up into the air—

and the London Eye rolled just inches beneath their feet, flattened a hand railing at the edge of the pavement, and plunged into the Thames.

Water surged up onto the shore. A huge wave threw itself over the bridge, taking cavalrymen and their horses with it. Even the queen's steam-carriage, just touching the far side of the river near the clock tower, was splashed.

Charlie let go of Bob's arms and scooted back into his place. "The queen's carriage!" He pointed.

"I see it, Charlie!" Bob turned the flyer over the river, cutting toward the carriage. "An' thanks!"

Ollie hissed. The snake had transferred to Bob's shoulders now.

Below them the leisure wheel tipped onto its side. It threw a second wave up onto the shore, and then the black waters of the Thames swallowed it.

Charlie thought about his father, lying dead on the pavement. He would never see his bap again.

But it didn't matter what he felt right now; he had to save the queen.

The progress flotilla splintered. The wave had snapped the anchor rope of the traffic montgolfier, and it now drifted; without guidance, each airship went its own way. The neat lines and spinning circles drifted apart into confused clouds.

Charlie looked for the police zeppelin with the Sinister Man aboard, but couldn't see it.

The cavalrymen who hadn't been washed away turned and rushed back across the river toward Waterloo Station. Charlie's mouth fell open—how could they just abandon the queen?

But of course, he realized, they almost certainly thought she had told them to do it. The simulacrum had probably ordered them to rescue the other horsemen, or respond to the explosions, and they were obeying.

The steam-carriage chugged on alone.

"Get as low over the queen's carriage as you can!" Charlie shouted.

Bob nodded and swooped down. Charlie saw the red-and-gold trim, the big gold-colored wheels, the crimson top hat of the queen's coachman, and the broad roof of the carriage.

"Thanks, Bob!" he yelled. "Be safe!"

Charlie jumped.

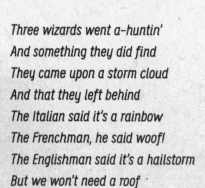

Three wizards went a-huntin'
And something they did find
They came upon a storm cloud
And that they left behind
The Italian said it's a rainbow
The Frenchman, he said woof!
The Englishman said it's a hailstorm
But we won't need a roof

Three wizards went a-huntin'
And something they did find
They came upon a hurricane
And that they left behind
The Russian said it's a devil, da
The Dutchman said let's fish!
The Englishman said it's a monsoon, boys
But we'll stay dry as you wish

—Child, *Popular Ballads*, No. 64

Charlie slammed down onto the roof of the steam-carriage. He tumbled forward over the flat carriage top. The coach-man, a man with bushy eyebrows dressed in long gloves, a tall top hat, goggles, and a driving coat, turned to see what the commotion was.

Charlie bumped past him, grabbing for anything he could.

The coachman tried to catch Charlie with one hand, but Charlie ignored him and seized the long-axled steering wheel; in his fingers it spun sideways, and the carriage lurched to the left—

people in front of the carriage scattered out of the way—

CRASH!

The carriage slammed into the wall of the big clock tower.

Charlie and the coachman flew off the carriage and into the street. Charlie's side smarted, but he rolled to his feet.

The street itself was empty. Crowds filled the sidewalks and peered from all the windows. Fifty thousand eyes had come to see the queen's progress from Waterloo Station to Buckingham Palace on her Jubilee, and fifty thousand eyes now stared at Charlie.

He gulped.

"Get him!" the coachman croaked.

Bobbies in blue capes and hats rushed Charlie. The cutlasses slapping in their belts reminded Charlie what he was there for.

"Your Majesty—" He jerked open the door of the steam-carriage.

The carriage was empty. Across its red-carpeted floor and past its leather-upholstered seats he could see that the carriage's other door was open. Beyond it stood the wall of the clock tower and an open door into the building.

Charlie saw the last swish of a skirt disappearing into Big Ben.

"Stop!" the nearest policeman shouted.

Charlie hopped up into the carriage, lurched through it at top speed, and then leaped across the intervening space and into the clock tower.

Behind him men collided with each other trying to catch him.

Charlie's whole body hummed. He was alive. He was *powerful*.

Behind the door were a small room and a hallway with

more doors. A stairway climbed up toward the top of the tower and its famous bell, Big Ben. Charlie was reaching for the first doorknob when he heard footsteps above him.

Looking up the square stairwell, he could see an elbow in a red-and-gold dress, turning as the person whose elbow it was raced up the steps.

Charlie raced after her. It had to be the simulacrum, the fake queen. Who else could it be? And the kobold and the real Victoria must be with her, because they weren't in the carriage. But why would Henry Clockswain—*Heinrich Zahnkrieger*—run up the inside of the tower? He'd be trapped.

"There he is!" "Up the stairs, lads!"

The policemen were inside the tower. Charlie ran.

Charlie wanted to stop the Iron Cog, and he wanted revenge for his father's death. But also, in a way that Charlie couldn't quite explain even to himself, he felt like the queen was family.

The queen was his mum.

Charlie had to be careful, especially on the turns. He could lurch really fast with his bad leg, but the combination of speed and his limp made him knock against the whitewashed walls, and if he wasn't careful, it might throw him over the banister.

Above him, he saw two queens. He was gaining.

One Victoria ran. She carried the other Victoria in her arms and sprang full tilt up the stairs. She had the kobold on her shoulders, too.

The two Victorias looked identical, down to matching dresses.

The stairwell had no windows. Charlie climbed up, hopping

on his bad leg through a white tunnel with a black iron railing in the center of it. He steadily pulled away from the puffing policemen below him, and gained on the ersatz Victoria.

Careful not to accidentally throw himself over, Charlie ventured a glance down.

The ground was a long way away.

And there were a lot of blue capes swarming up the stairs.

"There it is!" "What is it?" Charlie heard from the policemen, with much puffing.

Ahead of him, Victoria disappeared.

Charlie raced around the last flight of steps and saw a door, slamming shut.

He leaped—

and Charlie crashed into the door just before it could close, bowling it open with his body. He rolled like a ball through the doorway and into the room beyond.

Bang!

Someone shot at him. Charlie kept doing somersaults, as fast as he could. They weren't quite straight, with his bad leg, but they were very fast.

Bang! Bang!

Charlie's vision was confused because he was in motion. He saw gears of all sizes, swinging pendulums, walls of glowing white glass, and an enormous bell.

This was the belfry.

Charlie broke out of his roll and scrambled, diving behind a cluster of gear shafts. He had survived one gunshot already, but he was pretty sure enough shots would kill him.

Also, they hurt.

Bang! BONG!

The shooter had hit the bell. The sound of the bell was *much* louder than the gunshot.

Charlie pressed himself up against his shelter.

The shots had stopped.

He peeped up from behind the gears. Queen Victoria sat on a stool, hands tied and mouth gagged. The kobold Zahnkrieger jammed a second stool under the doorknob, and then turned to yank two brass rods out of the clock's machinery. Another Victoria stood to the side of the door, head slumped and arms at her side.

"Gehorche mir!" the kobold shouted at the simulacrum. Charlie didn't know what the words meant, but the ersatz Victoria heard them and snapped to attention. "Get him!" Zahnkrieger pointed at Charlie.

The fake queen charged.

Charlie scrambled back, wishing he hadn't left his cutlass behind at Waterloo Station.

He saw now that the four glowing glass walls were the four faces of the giant clock. And the bell, that was Big Ben itself.

The kobold shoved the rods underneath the door, fixing it shut, then turned his attention back to Charlie.

The real queen sat very still, her back straight, glowering at the kobold. Even her harsh glare made Charlie feel warm inside. It made him feel like he wanted to sit down and have tea.

Fake Victoria lunged for Charlie. He ducked under her arms. She wheeled and jumped at him again.

Charlie's heart sank. The simulacrum was every bit as fast as he was.

Maybe faster.

He jumped. He meant to spring straight up, but as he leaped, his bad leg shot out sideways, so he flew up and into the air diagonally.

The ersatz queen jumped after him, clawing at him, but her spring was straight up, and she missed. She knocked her shoulder into the high ceiling.

BONG!

Charlie struck the bell and bounced up its curving surface. It trembled powerfully from the collision, but he managed to scramble up to the hinge where Big Ben hung from a horizontal axle just below the ceiling.

The fake queen grabbed at the axle on her way down and caught it with both hands. She glared at Charlie with the same expression the real queen had. Her fierce stare and her puffy silk dress dangling from under the big axle made Charlie laugh.

Seeing the two queens in the same room, it was easy for Charlie to tell which was real and which was fake. There was something missing from the fake queen.

"Enough of this!" Zahnkrieger barked.

Charlie flattened himself against Big Ben.

Bang! BONG!

Charlie scooted around, trying to keep the bell between him and the little man.

The ersatz queen shuffled closer, hand over hand along the bell's axle.

"Charlie," Zahnkrieger laughed. "You can't win!"

The fake Victoria reached out to grab Charlie, and he kicked her hand away. She reached up to move closer along the axle and stopped.

The axle was greased close to the bell, Charlie realized. She couldn't crawl along it any farther.

"Clock off!" Charlie shouted.

She swiped again at Charlie, and again he kicked her hand away.

"The funny thing, Charlie," the kobold said, "is that you get to be the hero. We've made your father take the fall as a villain, you know. His body will be found with papers in his pockets identifying him as a member of the Anti-Human League. When the league takes credit for the explosion, people will think he was the bomber. Poor, mad inventor, working away in his little slum shop and plotting to kill the queen."

"You're mad!" Charlie shot back, trying to think of a plan. If he could free the queen and get her into the stairwell, then maybe he could hold off the fake Victoria and the kobold long enough for her to escape.

"He will be a guilty man behind a failed plot. When the police break through that door, they will find a shattered clock face, the queen unharmed, and a brave little automaton that saved her from her kidnappers."

"No one will think I'm a brave little automaton when your fake queen murders all her important guests at the garden party."

"You underestimate the patriotic feeling of your countrymen, Charlie. They will believe that their queen was attacked, and that the Emperor Franz-Joseph and King Umberto and the others died because they were the assassins! The Germans and the Austrians and the Italians will feel differently, of course—we'll see to it that they do—and that's how one starts a war."

Fake Victoria grabbed for Charlie again. She missed, and lost her grip on the axle. She fell to the floor with a thud.

"Her Majesty will never cooperate with your evil schemes!" If he could distract the kobold, maybe Charlie would have enough time to untie the real queen and open the door. He'd have to be quick.

Heinrich Zahnkrieger laughed dryly. "Quite." Fake Victoria glared up at Charlie. Zahnkrieger snapped his fingers at her to get her attention. "The window!"

She turned and punched a hole through the clock face behind her, smashing it wide with her elbow to reveal a ledge on the other side. A stiff breeze whipped in and around the belfry.

Charlie saw his chance. He jumped through the air, landing a little off-balance next to the real queen. He grabbed the rope tied around her wrists and fumbled with the knots.

"Your Majesty." He couldn't think of anything else to say.

Zahnkrieger shouted a word Charlie didn't understand, and Charlie's hands stopped working.

Charlie stared down at his frozen fingers. His legs worked . . . why had his hands seized up?

He stared up in horror as the kobold advanced, raising his pistol. "You're a redcap!"

Zahnkrieger chuckled. "Yes," he admitted. "A brownie. A

wizard of chaos and entropy. I make things fall apart and stop working. It's what we're good at, you know, we kobolds. We're good at making machines because we know so well how to break them."

Charlie lunged at the kobold.

Bang!

He took the bullet in the chest and hit the floor hard.

"Come with me, my dear," the kobold said to the queen.

Hulder magic is blood magic. A benevolent troll witch is an effective healer, but a malevolent troll sorcerer can effect terrible curses. Naturally, the Home Office and the Royal Magical Society tightly control and license hulder magical practitioners.

—Smythson, *Almanack*, "Troll"

Charlie hurt.

"*Gehorche mir,*" Heinrich Zahnkrieger said again. Then Charlie heard whispers.

The fake queen stomped across the belfry and loomed stonily over Charlie. She lay down beside him, arranging herself with one hand to her side and the other to her forehead, as if she had swooned. The kobold dragged the real Queen Victoria to her feet and pulled her toward the shattered clock face.

Charlie struggled to move. His arms from the elbows down didn't work, but he managed to lurch into a sitting position. The fake Victoria slapped him back to the floor with one hand.

"It is still functional!" she called.

"Destroy it!" Zahnkrieger called back.

"You can't do this," Charlie muttered, but there was no compassion or regret in the eyes of the simulacrum Victoria. She didn't care.

She *couldn't* care.

She really *was* different from Charlie.

Zahnkrieger dragged the real Victoria out the shattered window and onto the ledge.

The ersatz queen reached for Charlie's throat—

bam-bam-bam-bam-bam!

Hammering at the door. "This is the police!"

The fake queen looked to the door, and away from Charlie.

Charlie threw himself out of her reach, rolling across the room.

She grabbed for him and missed.

Charlie staggered to his feet and moved as fast as he could toward the window.

What did he think he was going to do? His arms didn't work, so he couldn't wrestle Heinrich Zahnkrieger.

Maybe he could hit the kobold with his head.

As he tried to cross the belfry, the fake queen grabbed his ankle and tripped him.

Charlie hit the floor and bounced. His bounce tore him out of the simulacrum's grip, and he tumbled against the wall. He landed upside down on his shoulders, his own legs flopping over him like an umbrella. Ouch.

"You can't do this!" he shouted.

The ersatz queen stalked rapidly toward him.

Bam-bam-bam-bam-bam! "Open up!"

The kobold was waving at someone outside the tower.

Fake Victoria kicked at Charlie. Charlie saw the foot coming, but he was slowing down. He threw himself sideways, collapsing in a heap and narrowly avoiding the boot aimed at his chest. Instead, the ersatz Victoria kicked a crater in the wall. White plaster rained around Charlie.

Charlie was slow and broken. His leg didn't work very well, and his arms didn't work at all.

"Stop," he whispered.

A shadow drifted over the broken window, and then blue and brass. It was the police zeppelin, and its crew threw lines to Heinrich Zahnkrieger.

Charlie thought about his bap. The Iron Cog and its servants had kidnapped his bap and then killed him. The Sinister Man, the bad policemen with their captain, and the traitor kobold.

And now they were attacking his queen.

The fake queen kicked again.

This time Charlie was faster. He rolled and sprang out of the way. The simulacrum pounded another hole in the wall.

The kobold was standing on the ledge outside the glass and throwing a loop around the real queen. At the same time, the Sinister Man swung on another line from the zeppelin and landed by Heinrich Zahnkrieger. He pulled a large sack from his belt and jerked it down over Queen Victoria's head.

Charlie was outnumbered. He was broken. He couldn't defeat all of them alone, despite his last burst of energy. He was beaten.

Unless . . .

"*Gehorche mir!*" he shouted to the fake Victoria. He hoped his father had been right, that the simulacrum had been built simply to obey orders. And he hoped that he was right in guessing the code words she had to hear before she would accept an order. And he hoped she would obey an order from *him*.

She stopped, cocked her head, and listened.

"Save the queen!" Charlie shouted, and pointed with his head at the real Victoria.

The simulacrum sprinted into action. Charlie rolled to his feet and tottered after her.

The real queen struggled on the ledge. The Sinister Man waved to his men in the police zeppelin, and they pulled on the rope, to drag Victoria off the ledge and haul her away.

The rope pulled taut—

and the simulacrum grabbed the queen.

"What?" Zahnkrieger stared.

"Fix it!" the Sinister Man yelled to the kobold.

The simulacrum yanked on the rope. The real queen stumbled back through the window and into the belfry. The men holding the other end of the rope screamed and fell forward. One tumbled out of the zeppelin's gondola and only caught himself by one hand.

Queen Victoria fell to the floor, and the loose rope fell over her.

Bam-bam-bam-bam-bam!

"*Gehorche mir!*" Charlie shouted. "Open the door!" If the kobold wanted to keep the policemen on the stairs out of the belfry, that meant they weren't the Iron Cog's men.

"No!" The Sinister Man tackled the simulacrum. She thrust him off with a single push of her arm and rushed to the door.

Charlie followed her.

The Sinister Man lurched to his feet and chased Charlie.

Heinrich Zahnkrieger the redcap shouted something, and the fake queen fell to the floor. She didn't stop completely; her legs were stiff, but she dragged herself on her forearms.

Charlie raced just behind her.

The Sinister Man came third.

The real queen, with her wiggling, managed to roll out of the bag.

Zahnkrieger shouted again, and the fake queen's arms stopped moving too. Her head spun and jerked and pounded against the floor, like she was trying to drag herself to the door by her teeth, but she didn't move any farther.

Charlie vaulted over her.

"Wait!" the Sinister Man shouted.

Charlie slammed against the door. He kicked away the stool and the rods under the door and then staggered back.

Police flooded into the room, a wave of blue and brass and shining cutlasses. The Sinister Man grabbed Charlie and dragged him back toward the window.

"Stay back!" He clapped a pistol to the side of Charlie's head.

Charlie's vision jerked a little.

Then his legs twitched, together, once.

How was this possible? Had Bob not wound him up all the way the night before? Or maybe, he realized, running around really fast and jumping far and otherwise exerting himself had made his mainspring wind down sooner. Maybe this was one of the reasons his bap hadn't ever let him wander far from the shop.

Oops.

The policemen advanced cautiously. They pulled Queen Victoria into their midst and took the gag from her mouth. Meanwhile the Sinister Man backed slowly away toward the open clock face.

"You're under arrest," the lead policeman said, pointing his sword at the Sinister Man. He was tall and heavy and had a mustache like a paintbrush. "Give it up now and don't make trouble."

"He's not one of ours," Zahnkrieger muttered.

"I'll kill the boy, Sergeant!" the Sinister Man shouted.

"Don't let him hurt the child!" the queen called as two coppers helped her up. Her voice was clear and calm, and when he heard it, Charlie loved her. "The boy is a hero."

Charlie didn't feel like a hero. He felt slow and broken. His legs jerked. His arms still weren't working. The gun at his head terrified him, and reminded him of his bap, shot and falling out of the leisure wheel.

Still, Charlie had saved the queen.

"Lines!" the kobold shouted.

The Sinister Man dragged Charlie back toward the shattered glass.

"Let him go," Sergeant Brush Mustache said.

"Oh, yes?" the Sinister Man asked. He pulled Charlie through the clock face and onto the ledge. "From the window I should let him go?"

Charlie looked around. The ground was very far below. The police zeppelin blocked out most of the sky, but a shadow flitted across Charlie as something flew overhead.

He could feel his body slowing to a stop, and he wasn't frightened. He had saved the queen, so he didn't care what happened to him now. It wasn't like he could go home and be with his bap again.

But then he wondered what the Iron Cog might do with him. Apparently, the same thing that made him function was what his bap had put into the fake queen. Maybe the Iron Cog would take Charlie apart to see what made him work; maybe they *did* want to reverse-engineer him.

Then they would build another simulacrum. A better one.

He had to get away.

Or at least he had to destroy himself, so completely that the Iron Cog couldn't use whatever was left. "They won't drop me," he said.

"Shut up!" The Sinister Man cuffed Charlie on the top of his head. It hurt.

"You can't escape," Sergeant Brush Mustache predicted.

The Sinister Man only sniffed in answer.

Heinrich Zahnkrieger threw a rope around Charlie's chest. Charlie saw the shadow again, and he looked up—at least his head could still move. Above the zeppelin swooped something that looked like a bird, only larger. Something with flapping wings and two people aboard.

Bob's flyer.

"Sergeant, it's one of ours," said one of the policemen, pointing to the zeppelin. Bobbies gently urged Victoria to come away and back down the stairs, but she swatted them into submission.

"There will be an inquiry," the sergeant said grimly. "Nothing worse than a bad copper. For now, protect the queen."

Heinrich Zahnkrieger and the Sinister Man both put loops around themselves. "I will go first," the kobold said. He jumped, and the men in the zeppelin quickly hauled him up and into the zeppelin's gondola.

One of the men, Charlie saw, was the captain with the pouchy eyes. "Over here!" the captain bellowed. "I'll take this one personally!"

Gripping a handle on the gondola wall, the captain leaned toward Charlie. He grinned with his mouth wide open, like he was going to bite.

At that moment, an umbrella fell from the sky. It was closed, and it fell straight like a lawn dart, striking the captain in the head.

Ollie.

"Ooof!"

The captain staggered back inside the craft and fell to the floor.

Bob's sword hit next, and plunged into the cylinder of the zeppelin itself.

The zeppelin men cursed and looked up. The zeppelin drifted, and started to sink.

"There!" The Sinister Man raised his gun to the sky.

Charlie jumped, straight toward the gondola. He knocked the Sinister Man over the edge with his shoulder as he went.

Bang!

The Sinister Man's shot went wide, shattering more glass in the clock face.

Charlie's vision jerked so hard he could barely aim, and his bad leg sprang sideways as he jumped, but the gondola's door was a big target, and he made it through. He landed hard, on his face, on the unconscious captain.

Some of the zeppelin's crew rushed around, trying to drag the Sinister Man up by his rope. The others were too stunned to grab Charlie. Only Heinrich Zahnkrieger reacted to his sudden entrance.

"You . . ." The kobold raised his pistol.

Charlie kicked. He could barely see to aim, but he felt his foot ram into the little man's belly. The redcap Heinrich Zahnkrieger went silent.

Charlie stood and staggered for the gondola's door. The zeppelin was drifting away from the clock tower, and policemen were watching him from the shattered face of Big Ben. Good policemen, it seemed. The queen was safe.

Charlie stepped out into space.

Good-bye, Bap, he thought.

He fell—

and someone grabbed him.

Charlie's whole body was twitching, except for his frozen arms. For a despairing second he thought he had been captured.

Then he realized that the arms around his shoulders belonged to Ollie.

"Blimey, you're heavy."

"Get into the straps, Charlie!" Bob yelled. "Ollie's got to change; we're too 'eavy!" She made a long sound that was half grunt and half scream.

The flyer raced down, struggling under the combined weight of the three of them. Charlie knew that Bob must be in pain. He wanted to help. He wanted at least to buckle himself in so Ollie could change into his snake shape and the flyer could bear all their weight, but he couldn't. He couldn't do anything but twitch, and he felt himself about to lose consciousness.

"You'll have to land, Bob!" Ollie shouted.

"Immersionary landing it is!" Bob turned the flyer toward a strip of green. It shuddered and jumped in Charlie's vision.

"*Emergency*, Bob!"

"Yeah, I thought that's what I said!"

The green was coming closer, and fast. Charlie passed out.

It is my hope in presenting this modest work to a new generation of readers that I may somewhere, in some young mind, plant seeds of knowledge. Knowledge does not, as an iron-clad rule, lead to wisdom, but it is an iron-clad rule that without knowledge, there can be no wisdom. And without wisdom, there can be no character.

—Smythson, *Almanack*, "Introduction"

Charlie limped through the steam outside Lucky Wu's Earth Dragon Laundry. He was battered and his leg still jerked, but his arms both functioned again.

It was late afternoon. He had returned to consciousness in Grim Grumblesson's office, lying on the floor with all his friends leaning over him. Gnat and Grim had been reinforced by Ingrid at the head of the hue and cry, but the battle against Egil One-Arm and his men had only ended when they had all felt earth tremors caused by the London Eye exploding.

"The cowards ran away, the lot of them," Ingrid said. She had a fierce gleam in her eye, and Charlie thought he didn't want to ever see her at the head of the hue and cry coming after *him*.

"Or their job was done, and they didn't care anymore," Grim suggested.

Before Charlie was even awake, Grim had had some kind of hulder witch in to treat Bob and Ollie and Gnat. Whatever she'd done had not only patched up their wounds, but left them refreshed and lively. Grim didn't need the witch's help; he was healing nicely on his own.

And no witch could patch Charlie up.

Grim had bought new clothes for Charlie to replace everything but his coat, and then paid for a couple of hansom cabs (pulled by yokes of large flightless birds) to take them to Irongrate Lane. The cabbie bubbled with rumors about the destruction of the London Eye. Grim stopped to buy a newspaper. Ingrid never left the lawspeaker's side, and she never laid down her club.

Charlie emerged from the steam and saw his father's shop. Mickey, Skip, and Bruiser were peering into the window of Pondicherry's Clockwork Invention & Repair. Mickey bent to the ground, picked up a loose cobblestone in one hand, and saw Charlie.

"Hey, it's the fungus!" Spittle flew around his big teeth.

"And look, he's limping!" Skip sneered, his lip flapping low. "What happened, Charlie, you get home late and catch a spanking or sumfing?"

"Ha-ha, a spanking!"

Charlie sighed.

"What now, Mickey?" he said. "Breaking windows?"

"Where you been, fungus?" Mickey shot back. "You and your dad both, you take a holiday or something?"

"Yeah," Skip snickered. "Too bad you ain't got a mum. She could have come along."

"Clock off." Charlie walked straight for the door, fishing the key from its string around his neck. He did have a mum, sort of. He'd saved her that morning from the Iron Cog.

Not everything good in his life had been taken, after all.

"You hear me?" Mickey demanded. "I was talking to you."

"Yes," Charlie agreed, "but you weren't saying anything."

Mickey hefted the rock. "Do I have to hurt you again?"

Charlie thought of the treacherous Elisabel, of Scabies and his rats, of Cavendish Hats, of Egil One-Arm, of the ghouls beneath Waterloo Station, and of his fight inside Big Ben. He laughed out loud. "You can't." He unlocked the door.

"Get him, Broo," Mickey ordered.

Charlie turned to face Bruiser. "Don't do it. Just stop and leave me alone, or you'll be sorry."

Bruiser grabbed him by his shirt.

Charlie brushed Bruiser's hands off easily. A look of stupid astonishment filled the boy's face. Charlie pushed Bruiser into the dirt.

"Ha-ha . . . what?"

Skip stumbled backward, but Mickey raised his rock over his head. "That was lucky."

Charlie shook his head. "Try it. *Please.*"

Whack!

Mickey hit him with the rock. The cobblestone struck Charlie on the side of the head and bounced off. It hurt, but not very much. Not as much as getting shot, or eaten by ghouls.

Charlie turned to face Mickey, and he grinned. Mickey shifted from foot to foot and rubbed his hands together.

"The thing is," Charlie said to Mickey, speaking slowly and very carefully, "I'm not like you."

He grabbed Mickey's belt with both hands and lifted the other boy into the air. Skip's shuffling steps now turned into full-blown flight, and Bruiser covered his eyes. Mickey slapped at Charlie's face and shoulders. Charlie shook it off.

"Put me down!"

Charlie shrugged. "If you like." Unfortunately, the work of the Royal Magical Society's weather wizards had dried up all the Gullet's mud, or he would have sunk Mickey in the biggest puddle he could find.

Instead he just tossed him aside.

"Ooomph!"

Charlie's friends strode out of the steam. Grim Grumblesson came first, cleaned up and impressive in a yellow frock coat and black top hat. He carried a heavy ax that looked small in his hand. At his side marched Ingrid, with her club. Buzzing at Grim's cowlike ear flew Gnat, who still held her spear, though she again wore breeches and a tricorn hat. Behind them trailed Bob and Ollie, carrying between them a collapsible canvas crate that held the flyer.

Mickey stared.

"Trouble, Charlie?" Ingrid hoisted her club onto her shoulder. She towered over every other person in the alley except Grim, who just lurked behind her and growled.

"I don't think so. Do we have trouble here, Mickey?"

Mickey backed away slowly. Skip was already out of sight, and Bruiser stumbled to his feet to follow. "No trouble," Mickey agreed. "No trouble at all."

He turned and pelted away down the Gullet as fast as he could go.

The inside of the shop was a bigger mess than Charlie remembered. There was plaster everywhere. He nodded a quick greeting to Queen Victoria on the wall, and she seemed to wink in reply.

Charlie and Bob moved methodically through the workroom, looking at every cog, wheel, and piston one by one, until Bob opened a small, unmarked wooden crate that she found high on a shelf and called out, "'ere it is!"

Charlie joined her, and together they looked at neat rows of very fine-toothed cogs, rods, and other brass components.

"How do you know this is it?" Charlie asked.

The others had lugged the flyer up the stairs and were making loud chopping and crashing noises in the attic.

"Because, my fine china," Bob replied, "I 'ave felt around inside your guts, an' they felt just like this."

"China?"

"China plate, mate," Bob explained.

Charlie took the box; it was light. He also took the small stack of cash his father kept on hand and tucked it into his pocket. Bob filled the pockets of her peacoat with small pliers, spanners, and other tools. They were turning to climb the stairs when Charlie heard a voice.

"You mold-encrusted ball of monkey dung!"

It was Wu. He stood in the reception room with his arms crossed over his bright green waistcoat, next to a basket of clean and folded clothes.

Bob looked the laundry owner up and down, then looked at Charlie. "You got this, mate?"

Charlie nodded. Bob went upstairs.

"Go away," Charlie said to Wu. "I'm busy right now." He didn't talk to his own feet this time, and he didn't mumble.

Wu spat on the floor. "You think I care that you and your father live like wild donkeys?" He snapped his head as he gestured around at the mess, so it looked like his long, black, dancing braid was pointing too. "I don't care. I don't care if you sleep with pigs and eat their filth! You are not civilized people, and I gave up all my expectations long ago!"

"So did I." Charlie wanted to say more, but he held back and turned to go up the stairs.

Wu followed. "My shirt presses are not calibrated!" He jabbed at the air between him and Charlie with long fingers, stabbing it to death. "You gave me baskets of clothing so dirty I think it must have been worn by water buffalo! I cleaned it all; I pressed it! Now, when will your stinking lazy father fix my shirt presses?"

Charlie almost punched Wu.

Almost, but he didn't. Wu didn't matter anymore either. He wasn't a threat to Charlie. Charlie would happily have suffered Wu's abuse forever if it would have brought back his father.

"Never," Charlie said softly.

"*What?*" Lucky Wu shrieked.

Charlie pulled the key from around his neck and tossed it to Wu. "My father's dead, Mr. Wu," he told the laundry owner. "He was on the London Eye when it exploded."

Wu waved the key excitedly. "Who will fix my presses?"

Charlie shrugged and started up the stairs. "I don't know. The shop is all yours. Maybe you can figure out how to fix the presses yourself. Just leave me alone."

"You scrofulous hamster!" Wu hollered. "You insolent hippopotamus fart! You *bad boy*!"

"You've got me wrong," Charlie said. "I'm none of those things."

Then he was up the stairs and in the attic. Wu didn't follow.

It was only when he was at the top of the stairs that, purely by accident, Charlie put his hand in his coat pocket and felt his bap's little round-bowled pipe. When he did, it nearly broke his heart.

The pipe was in two pieces, the stem neatly snapped off from the bowl.

Charlie took out the two halves and held them in his hand. They looked weak and lonely, detached from each other. The pipe was useless, and Charlie told himself he should throw it away.

But he didn't.

Instead he put the snapped pipe back in his pocket and looked around to see what his friends had done to his bap's attic.

Grim and Ingrid had smashed a hole through the ceiling where it sloped low, and late afternoon sun poured in. Through the new opening, Charlie saw the flyer. It was fully assembled, and Bob was buckling the straps on her harness. Gnat flew slow circles around the aeronaut.

"I've got a question," Bob said to the pixie as Charlie joined them. "I can't 'elp but notice you're dressed as a lad."

Gnat laughed. "Nay, not quite." She took off her tricorn and waved it about. "This is clothing for being out among big folk. Our men wear it, aye, but so do we women. It hides from outsiders who the baroness might be, you see. 'Tis what I wore on my tithe."

"You're still on your tithe, then?" Charlie asked.

"In a manner of speaking, aye. And also, I only had the one dress at Grim's place. I kept it for two years, looking forward to wearing it on my return to Underthames. And after all we've been through in the last few days, it just has a few too many holes in it now." The pixie turned to Bob. "'Twon't bother you that I dress in this fashion, will it?"

"Dress 'ow you like," Bob said, focusing very closely on the last of her buckles.

"Guess this is good-bye," Grim said to Charlie. "Will you ever come back?"

"I don't know," Charlie confessed. "My bap told me to go see a man in Wales. He was my father's friend, and I have to go warn him that the Iron Cog knows how to find him." He didn't mention his secret hope that Caradog Pritchard, whoever the man really was, might be able to help Charlie.

"I'm looking forward to meeting 'im myself," Bob added.

Charlie nodded. "The Iron Cog may already be on its way."

"And then?" Ingrid asked.

Charlie shrugged. He looked at the attic around him. Its shelves were knocked over and its books scattered about the floor. Ollie was browsing through the library by turning volumes over with his toe and glancing at the covers. "I kind of wish I could bring some books. A little Walter Scott, maybe, or Dickens."

"What do you need to read adventure stories for now?" Grim chuckled. "You're an adventurer yourself, Charlie."

"You could take the *Almanack*," Ingrid suggested, fishing a copy out of the chaos.

"I'll look for a copy of the first edition." Charlie smiled. "If you and Grim don't mind."

Grim nodded. "Yes, well, who's to say we were right to pressure poor Smythson? Hiding uncomfortable facts didn't make them go away."

Ingrid only smiled.

"I'll be back, for one," Gnat said, "when I've slain my three great beasts."

"There are beasts in London you could slay," Grim said.

"Aye," Gnat agreed, "but nothing heroic enough. Just rats and ghouls and hulders and the like. Little things."

Grim laughed out loud, and then bent over to gently kiss Gnat on the back of her hand. "Far as I'm concerned," he declared, "you're the Baroness of Underthames already."

Charlie hugged Grim, sort of enjoying the cow smell.

He hugged Ingrid, too; she smelled much nicer, and her tail swished back and forth as they embraced.

"You'll have to be your own *in loco parentis* now," Grim told him. The big hulder looked a little sad.

"You were a great dad for a while," Charlie said. "Just when I needed one."

Grim smiled at him gently. "The only dad you ever needed was your own bap. You're a very special boy, Charlie Pondicherry."

Charlie looked at his feet and shrugged. He knew he'd done some unusual things, even amazing things, but nothing he'd done had saved his bap. And Grim's comment reminded him of something else. "I think my father's real name was Singh."

"Will you change your name, then?" Gnat asked.

Charlie shook his head. "My father named me Charlie Pondicherry, and he called me his son. That's who I want to be."

They climbed out onto the rooftop together. Other roofs surrounded them, some above and some below, stretching out to the horizon in every direction. Vapor curled up from the Gullet in front of Lucky Wu's Earth Dragon Laundry.

Charlie strapped himself into the front of the flyer.

"Don't drop me." Ollie gave himself a good long scratch under both arms. *Bamf!* He turned himself into a snake and nestled his coiled, scaly body around Charlie's neck, smelling faintly of rotten eggs.

"Fly all the way to Wales without stopping?" Grim asked.

"We've the sunshine for it," Gnat piped cheerfully. "I don't want to get rained on, you know."

"An' Charlie can spell me off if 'e 'as to," Bob added. She flapped her wings once. "But my arm's feeling peachy now. I reckon we'll make it in a day or two."

"God speed you," Grim rumbled. Charlie thought he saw a tear in the troll's eye.

"And you, Grim Grumblesson," he returned. "And Ingrid."

"Right," Bob said. "'Ere we go!"

They ran down the roof, and she launched the flyer into Wu's cloud of steam. With a single flap of Bob's arms they rose above the vapor and then turned, still rising, over Irongrate Lane. Below, steam-carriages and hansoms and riding animals of all sorts continued on their paths, unaware of the flying machine above them.

The buildings fell away as they climbed. Charlie saw the river first, and then all of London was at his feet, gnarled and dirty and crawling with millions of people. The farther they rose, the prettier the city became. He saw Brunel's Sky Trestle like a web ensnaring all of London. He saw Waterloo Station, the stump of the London Eye still smoldering. He saw the clock tower with its shattered panes like a broken eye. He saw Buckingham Palace, and he hoped the real queen and her important guests were enjoying her Jubilee garden party.

Would he ever see the queen again? She had called him a hero, but Charlie didn't feel like a hero. He didn't *want* to be a hero—not anymore.

He wanted to be a boy. Just a normal, flesh-and-blood boy,

his father's true son. He didn't know if that was even possible, but he hoped the man Caradog Pritchard might be able to help. But Pritchard could do nothing unless Charlie first saved him from the murderous agents of the Iron Cog.

Bob turned the flyer to follow the sun west, to Wales and the future.